this is not a vampire story

ALSO BY SIMON DOYLE

Snow Boys
The Sound of You

this is not a vampire story
simon doyle

3 5 7 9 10 8 6 4

Copyright © Simon Doyle, 2025

The right of Simon Doyle to be identified as the author of this Work has been asserted by him in accordance with the Copyright, Designs and Patents Act 1988

All rights reserved

First published in 2025 by
SD Press
Unit 1A Heatherview Business Park, Athlone Road SSC8117
Longford, Co Longford N39KD82, Ireland

ISBN 978 1 7397276 7 3

This publication may not be used, reproduced, stored or transmitted in any way, in whole or in part, without the express written permission of the author. Nor may it be otherwise circulated in any form of binding or cover other than that in which it has been published and without a similar condition imposed on subsequent users or purchasers

All characters in this publication are fictitious and any similarity to real persons, alive or dead, is coincidental

Cover design by SD Press

A CIP catalogue record of this book
is available from the British Library and the
Library of Trinity College Dublin

Typeset in Caslon Pro by SD Press

For everyone whose heart was made to stop

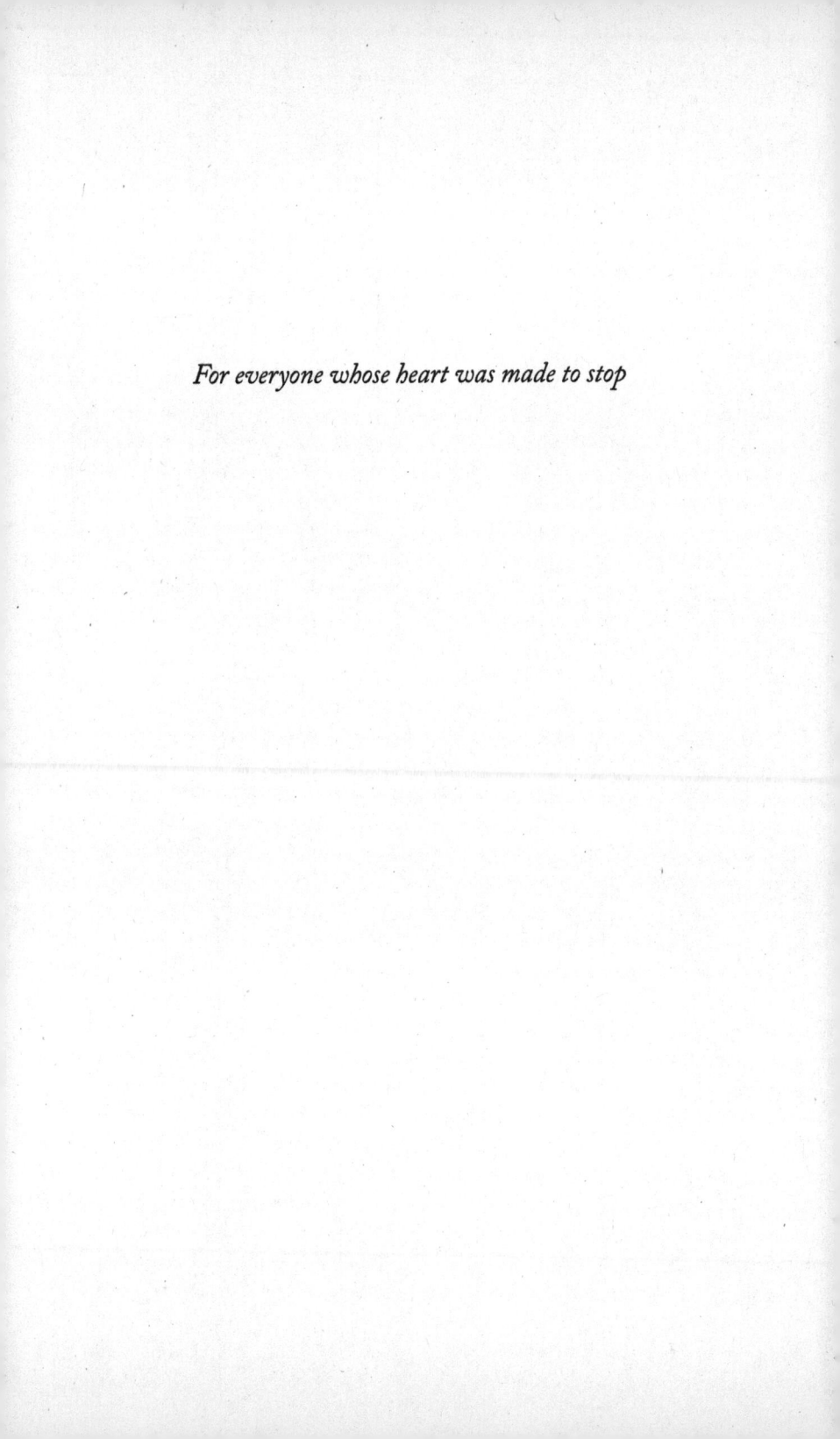

chapter 1

the present

When I was seventeen, I'd slept in a cave for fifteen years. I was seventeen for a very long time.

And I missed that cave.

I had walked from Jaipur to New Delhi, and from there to Kathmandu, sleeping in deep trenches along the side of the dusty road when the sun was up and scorching the desiccated earth. It hadn't rained since I arrived and my lips were dry and chapped. I was glad I had nobody to talk to because when I opened my mouth, they would crack and sting.

If I passed somebody at night, when the moon was high and the sound of crickets and katydids droned across the quiet landscape, I'd keep my head low and offer them a humble greeting. "Namaste," they'd say. And they'd marvel at the white teenager with a T-shirt over his head. "Very nice eyes," they'd tell me. People don't remember my face, it's my eyes that capture them.

I suppose that's a good thing.

In Kathmandu, a farmer let me ride in the back of his tempo van among crates of underweight chickens and a single goat that stared at me as if he was reading my mind. I'd eaten goats before. And I think he knew that.

The farmer dropped me as close to the Tibetan border as he could and pumped his sharp horn as he drove away. He gave me a chicken as a gift—"for luck," he'd said—and as we watched him turn down the dusty road in the blue darkness of early morning, I called the chicken Georgie, and said, "Shall we go?"

Georgie clucked her agreement and we crossed the border among the morbidly barren Himalayan foothills, under a navy sky dotted with more stars than I'd ever seen. In the east, the horizon was turning grey.

I zigzagged from the foothills into the mountains, Georgie trapped under one arm, using my free hand for support when the cliffs got too steep to walk on. I had a lifetime of pain to hide, and when I found a cave whose mouth was open against the northern wind, I ventured inside, slowly, a torch flashing in front of me. I stomped my feet and cawed like a bird. Were there leopards in the Himalayas? Or jackals? I wasn't sure.

But the cave was empty, so I unpacked my travel case, a thin sleeping bag and a handful of soil from home that I'd carried with me for years. I pressed my fingers into that soil, tasting a grain of it to remind myself why I was there, five thousand metres above sea level, surrounded by a thick wind in the thin air and a blanket of snow beyond the cave's entrance.

I tied a piece of twine around Georgie's leg and trapped

the other end under a rock so she couldn't escape, though I knew she wanted to. Everybody leaves me. They always do.

I sat on the sleeping bag and folded my hands in my lap, and I spoke to Georgie, partly in English, partly in Vietnamese, which I'd been learning recently, and Georgie wobbled her head like she was objecting to my story.

When I grew tired of her incessant clucking, I said, "Sorry, Georgie." I caught the twine, pulled her to me, and stroked her small head. She turned away from me like she knew what was coming.

Her eyes were as orange as her feathers. She fussed in my arms until I held her tighter and soothed her with gentle noises. And then I ate her.

When I was done, I wrapped what was left of her in an age-worn Nirvana T-shirt and built a small cairn over her remains, just outside the entrance of my cave where I could see it.

I crossed my legs on the sleeping bag, stared out at the distant peaks, and watched as the sunlight shifted across the earth, falling inside the cave's opening but never outstaying its welcome. Day became night became day.

I stopped counting after two hundred and thirty-seven days. Or was it two hundred and thirty-eight?

During my third winter, a fierce wind knocked over Georgie's cairn and I imagined I heard her clucking in the days while I watched the driving snow.

"Are you back?" I asked. But the noise of her stopped.

And I was alone.

When I came down from the mountains, I was a new man. And I was seventeen.

I walked back to Kathmandu, bought a plane ticket to Dublin via London, and from there I walked through the late summer nights towards County Clare and the coastal village I once called home. As I walked alongside the empty football field, up Comer Street, past the old apple orchard whose walls were crumbling, I didn't feel tired. I was renewed. Fifteen years in a cave might drive a man to insanity. Or it might make an insane man sane. You decide.

I gathered up the money I'd been saving over the years and made a few calls. And two months later, I stood outside Lakeshore Manor Nursing Home under a waning moon that was hidden somewhere behind the building.

Death was in the air. I smelled him.

I rang the bell, and when the door opened, Mrs Conway filled the frame like death's advisor. I mumbled my name and she folded her arms, her silhouette swelling as though she could block out more than just the light.

"You're late," she said, her tone as cold as the frigid air.

I smiled. She wouldn't have wanted me there any earlier.

She leaned forward, her face emerging from shadow—narrow eyes sunk deep into puffy cheeks, a broad nose casting a shadow over thin, stern lips. "How old are you?"

When I'd sent her my application, I'd fudged my date of birth. "I'm twenty," I lied.

"You look fourteen." Mrs Conway's voice was dark with suspicion.

"Good genes," I said. "Trust me, when I'm a hundred, they'll still be asking for my ID."

She grunted, the sound like wet gravel underfoot, and stepped aside as warm orange light spilled out past her swollen ankles.

When I didn't move from the steps, I heard the impatience in her voice. "You're letting the heat out. Come in."

I stepped over the threshold onto the pale blue tiles. An overhead heater pushed fingers of warm air through my hair and a hum of electricity buzzed inside the walls. The reception desk—unmanned at this time of night—had a thin computer monitor with the nursing home's logo sliding around the screen. I was sure the computer was as old as some of the residents.

Mrs Conway walked ahead of me without a word. In her office, she closed the door and sat behind her desk with a sigh, like the exhalation of a dying soul. I couldn't tell how old she was. In her fifties, no doubt. Maybe sixty. She adjusted her thick glasses and the swivel chair groaned beneath her.

She opened a drawer, pulled out a roll of stickers, and wrote my name on one, tearing it from the roll with careless fingers. "It's only temporary, until we get you a name badge," she said, then added, "You don't look like a Victor."

"What does a Victor look like?" I asked, peeling the sticker from its backing and patting it to my shirt like I was at a speed-dating event.

We'd had a series of phone interviews where she'd quizzed me on the aspects of a night porter's role and the experience I'd claimed to have. I'd nursed people through death before, but never in a formal setting. Not in a care home. "It's not much more than minimum wage," she'd told me, and I'd laughed and said the money was fine.

"It's a lonely job," she'd said. "You could go the whole night without seeing a soul."

"I thrive in my own company," I'd told her. Because people suck—but I didn't add that part. Fifteen years in a cave has you second guessing your words before you speak.

Now, she pushed a sheet of paper across her desk. "This is a list of duties that you should check off every night. When I leave in"—she checked her watch, a dainty thing that looked out of place on her thick, freckled wrist—"twenty minutes, I will hand you a set of keys for the front and back door, but you should only use them in an emergency, do I make myself clear?"

What did she think I was going to do, throw a party? "Yes, ma'am," I said.

She clasped her hands together on the desk and studied my thin face. "Are you sure you're twenty?"

I smiled. Again. "You flatter me, Mrs Conway. Trust me, some days I feel like I'm ninety-two."

Her nod told me she felt the same. "Gloria is the duty nurse tonight. She'll look after you for the first few shifts; make sure you're settling in. Most of the residents are already in bed, but there are some wily ones that will try to sneak out before the doors are locked. There's a spare dressing gown on each floor—Mr Buckley is fond of gallivanting around in the buff after dark and that's not a sight for the faint of heart. And if they ask you for food, don't feed them."

"Like the Mogwai," I said.

"Excuse me?"

"Gremlins. Do not feed them after midnight. And whatever you do, don't get them wet."

She narrowed her eyes.

"I watch a lot of old movies," I told her.

"Please don't get my residents wet," she said.

"I'll try my best."

She wasn't amused. "Do you believe in ghosts, Victor?" she asked.

"No," I said. I didn't hesitate. But I looked at her. I could smell the garlic potatoes she'd had for dinner and my stomach churned. Garlic makes me sick. She'd tried to mask it with a cheap perfume but it wasn't up to the job.

She said, "I need you to be a ghost. Can you do that for me?"

"Do I need some clanking chains and a white sheet? Wouldn't that shorten the lifespan of the residents?" My smile was lost on her.

"Ghosts are never seen, Victor. If a porter can get through the night without being seen, he has done a good job. Do you understand?"

I tapped the side of my nose. "I excel at not being seen. You won't even know I'm here."

Mrs Conway led me upstairs and introduced me to Gloria Pinto, the duty nurse. She barely looked up from her clipboard long enough to register my presence, but I noticed she had a nice neck. A long, slender one. If you were into that sort of thing.

Mrs Conway didn't have a neck. Her head sat between her shoulders, meaning that her shiny earrings had nowhere to dangle.

When she handed me a set of heavy keys, she shrugged herself into a thick wool coat and left. Outside, she tapped on the glass panel of the front door and pointed at the lock.

I locked it.

When she had left and I heard her car cutting into the night, I looked around the empty foyer. A clock ticked somewhere deep in the bowels of the manor. Somebody was crying themselves to sleep and a radio was on in the empty kitchen.

A fluorescent light blinked twice, like it was too weak to stay awake.

Behind me, Gloria said, "Tidy up the entry hall and run through the tasks on your list. I'll be in the office if you need anything." She looked at me. "Please don't need anything."

She strode through the foyer, disappearing into the back office where the medications were kept, and then, with her arms full, she walked past me with a fine dust of silence behind her. I waved as she went and then sat back in the creaking chair at the reception desk.

The crying had stopped and the distant radio played a soothing ballad. It was ten p.m. and the rest of the night was mine.

I liked this time of night the best. An hour or two after dark, with the sun below the horizon and the moon still weak, and an early autumn breeze pushing languid leaves around outside. I hadn't lied to Mrs Conway—I'd learned to enjoy my own company. I'd needed to. Georgie could have told you that.

"I used to talk to myself," I told the empty foyer. "But not any more."

I checked my list of tasks and the phone rang once before I went upstairs, but when I answered it, there was nobody there. Maybe it was Death, checking up on me.

I slipped up to the next floor and when I stood in the corridor surrounded by heavy wooden doors, I closed my eyes and inhaled.

Death was close. I could smell him. When I sniffed the air, I knew he was two days out. Maybe three.

I spread my arms and touched the bedroom doors as I moved down the corridor until I felt death's energy sizzling in the air like a current of dark fear. I stopped. The label on the door said AGNES O'SHEA. I eased it open. As the light spilled inside, the old woman's white hair shone against her pillow. There was barely a rise and fall in her narrow chest.

I stood by her bed. Her hands were small and I could see the veins at her wrists, blue and latticed. Her eyelids fluttered. There was an ache on her face that made her frown even in her sleep.

But she wasn't why I was here.

Death was coming. And for Agnes, perhaps it would be a relief. I took one of her hands and felt her pain, drawing it into me. I closed my eyes and let it flood my body. Pain was transformative; it strengthened me.

And a smile curled at the corner of her lips as her features softened.

"Rest easy," I whispered. "Death knows you. But when he takes you, I'll be here. I won't let you go alone."

"Stephen?" she mumbled in her sleep.

I drew the blanket over her hand, still reeling from her dizzying pain in my limbs. I could feel it, flushing through my body where blood used to run.

In the corridor, I inspected the remaining doors and then went up another flight. I read the names. Alexander Martins, Terry Grimes, Daniel and Joseph Maguire. And opposite their room was the name I'd been looking for. The reason I'd left the desperate comfort of my Himalayan cave.

I approached his door, but the lift at the end of the hall pinged and Gloria stepped out. "Vincent?" she asked.

"Victor," I reminded her.

"Victor. Have you watered the plants in the common room yet?"

I moved away from the door and said, "I'm just doing my security checks. It's next on my list."

She nodded and disappeared into the east wing.

I listened to the sound of her soft shoes on the tiled floor and I sniffed the air to see where Death was. At the bedroom door, I opened it, just a crack, enough to let the light in.

The old man was asleep in his bed, one hand on his chest, the collar of his pyjama shirt cocked at one side, a half empty jug of water on the nightstand next to a framed photo. His quiet snoring was melodic. I'd heard those snores before, and I smiled.

I went inside and closed the door. The shape of him lit the darkened room like a flame that I was drawn to. I lifted the heavy chair from the far wall and moved it beside the bed, easing it down gently. When I sat, I closed my eyes before looking at him. The man in the bed was my heart. I'd be dead without him.

I opened my eyes. His nose was bigger now, longer, and his jowls were sunken. But I could never mistake him.

I reached out. I wanted to feel his pain, but I stopped myself from touching him, my fingers hovering over his age-blemished hand. My body trembled and I made a fist, then shook my hand loose.

His eyebrows were long, flecked with white. And although

his lips were thinner now, paler, they were unmistakable.
I leaned over him.
And I kissed his forehead.
"Hello, James," I whispered. "Did you miss me?"
He didn't wake, but as my lips touched the wrinkled skin of his broad brow, I felt some of his pain. Just enough to spark a tear of longing behind my tired eyes.
I wiped the tears with a finger and touched the wetness of it. It was slick against my skin.
I smiled. It had been a long time since I'd cried.
And James had been the cause of it then, too.

chapter 2

1949

I didn't know Dad was dead for three days.

I woke up in a room that wasn't mine, surrounded by beds that were filled with sick children. I was seventeen, but they still put me in the children's ward. The ten-year-old boy in the bed beside mine had a bandage covering half of his face. He said, "You're awake."

I tried to sit up but couldn't. Mum came through the double doors at the end of the ward and ran to my side. "Victor," she said. "I was so worried."

I didn't ask what happened. I remembered as soon as I'd opened my eyes. "Dad," I said. "Where's Dad?"

Mum stroked my hair and said, "Just rest, sweetheart. You're going to be okay."

There was a pain in my arm. I looked down. My left hand was wrapped in so much dressing that it was twice the normal size. A dark stain ran like a smudge along the edge of the bandage and my fingers throbbed.

Mum kissed my cheek and I let my head fall back against the cool pillow. When I closed my eyes, I remembered the clatter of scaffolding, the dry splintering of wood, and Dad screaming.

A nurse in a white uniform and headscarf took my blood pressure, and she wrote something on a chart that she hooked over the end of the bed. I fell asleep again and when I woke, Mum was slouched in the chair beside me, her chin tucked into her chest, a string of rosary beads looped around her fingers where she'd been praying before she nodded off.

The weak electric lights around the room turned the walls yellow but failed to light the ends of the two rows of beds, and dark things lurked in the centre of the room.

"Mum?" I said, and my throat was dry. The pain in my bandaged hand was getting worse.

She didn't wake up.

The boy beside me, with half of his head wrapped like a mummy, was sitting up in bed, writing a letter beneath a wall light.

"What are you writing?" I asked him. My throat didn't want to let the words out in the warm darkness.

He swung his legs out of bed to face me, sitting his notepad aside. "A letter to my pops. He went to England to get a better job. We were supposed to follow but"—he pointed to his face—"I got burned and lost an eyeball." He looked at Mum and then said, "Where's *your* pops?"

I shrugged. "Probably the men's ward where I should be."

"If you're an adult, why are you in with the boys and girls?"

he asked, picking his notepad up again and turning away from me.

I didn't know.

In the morning, Mum wasn't there. They gave me porridge and a cup of tea for breakfast and I had to eat it with one hand. I couldn't move the left one, not even to grip the bowl. By lunchtime, Mum still hadn't appeared, and the boy in the bed beside me had been taken down for surgery. He never came back.

A nurse came through the ward ringing a handbell, and Mum was out of breath as she came in.

"Visitors must leave in ten minutes," the nurse said.

Mum was wearing her Sunday coat that extended to her knees and although her hair was tied back in its usual fashion, a strand had come undone at her temple.

"How's Dad?" I asked.

She patted my hand. The good one.

"Was anybody else hurt?" I'd been working on the construction crew alongside my dad since I was fifteen. I'd left school at fourteen like most boys—except the brainy ones—and Dad had put in a good word for me with his boss. I was a hard worker, great with my hands. But the pain in my left arm made me wonder if I'd ever build another wall.

There were accidents, minor ones that resulted in broken fingers or stubbed toes. And once in a while you'd hear about a man who fell from a great height and broke his neck, or somebody falling foul of a cement mixer. But not our crew. We were good at what we did. We had each other's backs.

Usually.

But this time was different.

"Mum," I said.

She smiled, and I could see the pain in her eyes. She must have thought I'd be useless now, unable to work if my hand was crushed. I wanted to take the bandage off and have a look but I didn't dare.

She was about to say something when the nurse came back and ushered everyone out. The wall lights were dimmed and we were given bread and butter for supper. Food supplies hadn't been the same since before the Emergency and even though the war had been over for a few years, rationing was still common. The Emergency was what the rest of the world called the Second World War. Éamon de Valera decided Ireland would maintain a policy of neutrality during the conflict and even though the blackouts were terrifying for adults, to us children, the darkness was fun. I was thirteen when the war ended. We listened on the wireless to the celebrations held across the water in England. Dad had turned the radio off afterwards and said, "The fighting might be over, but the hardships are only beginning."

He wasn't wrong.

That night, in the darkened hospital, I unravelled the bandage to inspect my hand. It was swollen and purple, and from the elbow down, I couldn't move it. Nobody told me anything, but I knew I'd never have the use of it again.

And on the third day, Mum came to me and cried. She still wore her Sunday clothes. She told me Dad was gone. He'd been two levels above me on the scaffolding where we were repairing a school roof. But the structure gave way. He shouted my name before he screamed, telling me to jump. I did. I landed on my arm and rolled backwards on it before a pole crushed my hand. Dad saved my life.

I couldn't see.

There was dust everywhere and a white-hot pain in my arm. People were shouting. I heard footsteps, and then I passed out.

Mum leaned into me on the hospital bed and cried until she yawned. She fell asleep with her head on my chest. She was pressing against my injured arm but I didn't move her. I deserved the pain. Dad was gone and I wasn't. My injury would be a constant reminder.

Six weeks later, we had packed as many of our things into Dad's green Ford Anglia as we could. Mum, who knew how to drive but seldom did, got behind the wheel of the car and drove us to the coast. We were going to live with Mrs Morgan, who I was instructed to call Aunt Cara.

The construction crew had a collection to help with Dad's funeral costs, but without his income, we couldn't afford to keep the house. Mum took a new job as a cleaner in a school and one day soon, when I had adjusted to life with one hand, I would need to find suitable employment to help with the bills.

The swelling had gone down but it remained discoloured, a darker shade than my right hand. My fingers were disfigured and so I wore a glove to hide the ugliness of it. If the temperature was cool enough to wear a jacket, I would ease the hand into my pocket so that it didn't swing at my side like the broken mast of a windmill.

Mum choked the engine on a cold start and grinded the gears when we were going uphill, but we made it to the coast in one piece. I was glad, because if I had to get out and push,

I don't think I could have done it.

Aunt Cara—I'd never met her before, and I wasn't convinced she was a real aunt—met us on her doorstep. She was a tall woman who wore a black dress with a high neck and she kept her hands clasped at her waist. She nodded when Mum thanked her for letting us stay, and Aunt Cara said, "You must be Victor. Bring the bags, please, boy. Your mother and I must talk."

Mum said, "He only has the use of one arm."

"Do your bags not have handles? One hand is the sole requirement for a handle, dear. Come now, I will show you where the tea things are."

I spent almost an hour emptying the car, one bag at a time. Our rooms were on the top floor, under the sloping roof, and when I couldn't sleep at night, I listened to the incessant tick of the grandfather clock in the hallway outside. It chimed every fifteen minutes, marking the slow passage of night. I hated the nights. In bed, my arm ached and my fingers itched. At times, I would prop it on a pillow for comfort. Other times, I wanted to cut it off at the elbow and be done with it, bury it in the yard where Aunt Cara's Irish terrier would dig it up and carry it into the parlour to terrify the old woman.

Mum, when she wasn't working at the school, was cleaning Cara's house or preparing dinner. The old woman sat in her parlour at a bureau, writing letters to God knew who. I could see her from the garden where I'd mastered the art of turning soil with one hand. I did what I could to keep out of her way. She never smiled. "Children should neither be seen nor heard," she said.

I didn't tell her I was no longer a child, even if, as a cripple,

I was a useless adult.

When I was pruning her geraniums one Saturday afternoon, with my shrivelled hand tucked into my blazer pocket, I turned to reach for the watering can and saw that she was standing over me, a silent threat. I didn't know how long she'd been there.

"Can you drive?" she asked. Her hands were still clasped at her waist.

I pointed to my injury to remind her. "My hand is dead."

"That's not what I asked, child. Can you drive or not?"

I stood up, dusting my knees off.

She sat in the back seat of Dad's Ford and I steered the car with one hand towards the village square, driving the whole way in first gear because I was too afraid to let go of the wheel to shift the stick. Black smoke burned along the empty road behind us.

While she ran her errands, I stood on the pavement, leaning against the side of the car. I smoked a cigarette—a luxury I couldn't afford often, usually stealing them from Aunt Cara when she wasn't looking—and I watched a group of young men coming out of a corner shop.

As they walked by me, the tall one, an attractive lad around my age, with hair that was combed high and the radiant skin of an outdoorsman, gave me a nod and said, "Could you spare us a smoke?"

I had one left, a cheap brand that the old lady was fond of, but I gave it to him because his eyes were bright and his smile was soft.

My gloved hand slipped out of my blazer pocket and I turned, leaning against the car to hide its uselessness. If he noticed, he didn't say anything.

He put the cigarette between his lips and I flicked my lighter for him. "What's your name?" he said.

"Victor."

He stuck his hand out and I was never so grateful that men shake hands with the right and not the left. He said, "I'm James."

"I'm Michael," the youngest boy said. He was probably fifteen. His red hair was thick and messy and his shirt was a size too big. I hadn't even noticed him; I was staring at James' square jawline and high cheekbones.

The other two—brothers—were called Danny and Giuseppe.

"That's not his real name," James said. "He's called Joe."

I didn't ask why they called him Giuseppe.

The guys carried on down the road, leaving James to smoke his cigarette in front of me. He pointed at the car. "Is that yours?"

I shrugged. I had no need to impress him, but I wanted to.

"Are you new here?"

"Just moved into Comer Street," I said.

"What happened to your arm?" he asked.

I blushed, tucked the hand back into my pocket. "Scaffolding accident."

"Sounds painful."

I shrugged again like it was no big deal.

He kicked the car tire. "What year is she?"

I couldn't remember. Dad had bought it second hand. "Thirty-eight," I guessed, and James nodded his approval.

Down the street, his friends called to him. They were

staring through the window of a hairdresser's shop and somebody hammered on the glass from the inside. The boys jeered and ran off.

James said, "I'd better go. We'll be on the beach later. If you're around."

And I watched him walk away, his hands in his trouser pockets, the end of his cigarette trapped between his lips before he flipped it into the gutter. He gave me a wave and crossed the road.

I didn't know anything about him.

But I knew I wanted to.

"James," I said to myself, sounding his name out.

And Aunt Cara startled me from the end of the car when she said, "You'd better not be talking to yourself or they'll throw you in the looney bin with the rest of the cripples and murderers."

If I had the use of both hands, I'd have strangled her there and then.

chapter 3

the present

I stood in Agnes O'Shea's room with the lights off and her hand in mine. Her pain surged through me and the darkness it created made my skin prickle. It was my third night at Lakeshore Manor and Death was near.

Agnes cracked her eyes open, translucent lids peeling apart. She looked at me in the dark of her room, a thin sliver of light crumbling through the slit of the door that was ajar. I'd been listening out for Nurse Gloria, making sure she wasn't nearby.

Agnes' voice was dusty and quiet. "Stephen?"

I patted her hand and her skin was like paper.

"You're an angel," she told me.

I was not. Angels don't feed from your pain.

The shadows in the corner of the room moved and Agnes looked. "Stephen?" she asked again.

But Death wasn't called Stephen. He came in the silence between whispers and slipped into bed with her. I didn't see him but I felt him. I held her hand tighter, taking what I could from the ravages of her old age. Death wrapped her in his arms and she sighed. Her mouth went slack.

I put her hand on the bed and slipped the blanket over it. I leaned down and kissed her cheek as if I'd known her pain all my life. "Go to Stephen," I said. Her agony was gone. I closed her eyes.

And I left the room, easing the door closed behind me. Gloria would find her in the morning with a smile on her face.

Death didn't linger. I felt him leave as quietly as he came, though he would be no stranger to Lakeshore Manor.

I went to the boiler room and adjusted the thermostat for the first floor. The cooler Agnes' body was, the longer her smile would hold.

And then as Agnes' pain still fizzled in my veins, long after she was gone, I mopped a spill in the kitchen that hadn't been cleaned properly by the kitchen staff. I needed something to occupy my mind while I avoided life. I slid the stove away from the wall with ease, pushing the mop behind it where it hadn't been cleaned in some time, and I carried the laundry bags down to the back door where they'd be collected in the morning. I couldn't settle my brain. How do you meditate when you can't even breathe?

I walked through the common room, gathering up pieces of a chess board that had been thrown on the floor by an irate resident for reasons only the day-staff would understand, and I sat in a chair by the card table that I knew James would normally sit in. I could smell him in the fabric, the familiar scent of his skin. I could smell each of the residents in the common areas. I turned Agnes' chair upside down, cleaning out the folds where the base met the chairback, making sure it was spotless for its next guest.

I didn't go to James' room tonight. Last night, my second shift at Lakeshore Manor, he had woken while I stood over him. I stepped back into the shadows and closed my eyes. The flecks of gold in my otherwise blue irises shone when I was in his presence. They always had.

He said, "Who's there?"

I didn't speak. I wanted to say, "It's me," but my voice wouldn't work.

He turned onto his side and I was out of his room before he could turn back.

Now, Mr Buckley charged down the corridor behind me, surprisingly fast for one so old. He was butt naked, except for a pair of bedroom slippers, his skin sagging and blotched with age. And although he was thirty feet ahead of me, I was at his side in a second, taking his arm.

"Your hands are cold," he said.

"And you'll catch your death, Mr Buckley. Not to mention scaring the life out of Nurse Gloria if she sees you in your birthday suit. Come on. Back to bed."

"I need snacks," Mr Buckley said and I remembered Mrs Conway telling me not to feed the residents.

"You need pyjamas," I said. "Preferably stapled to your skin."

When I put him back in his room, I was too chicken to open James' bedroom door. So I sat in his chair in the common room and held a pen that I sensed he'd been using. I wondered what words he'd written with it. Were they kind words? I hoped so.

Later, bored beyond reason, I dismantled the reception-desk keyboard and emptied a century's worth of crumbs from its innards. I'd laid the keys out in careful rows so as not to get confused, and then I pushed each one back into place. I looked up Agnes O'Shea's admission file and saw that her next of kin, her son, was called Stephen. I wondered if that was who she'd been calling out to, or if her son had been named after his father, like I'd been named after mine.

I stood by the front door, staring through the glass, and I watched the moon track across the sky. It was a waxing crescent, haloed in blue gold, like my eyes. In the garden, near the fountain that wasn't turned on, a fox watched me watching it. I bared my teeth and it disappeared through the hedgerow.

I had already completed my list of tasks for the night, and Gloria was in the office. I made a cup of tea for no reason and watched it grow cold. I can't stand the taste of it these days. I haven't for a long time.

With Agnes O'Shea's pain dissipating from my limbs, I wandered the corridors, listening to the snores and breathing of the elderly residents. When I stood outside James' room again, I pressed my hand against the door. I didn't go in.

But I heard him say, "Who's there?"

I stepped away from the door.

I knew he was shuffling out of bed. "Who's out there?"

I whipped down the corridor and into the stairwell before his bedroom door opened. His movements were slow, weighted with age, and I watched from the dark stairs until he turned and went back into his room.

I didn't go back upstairs again that night, and at dawn, I clocked out and went home. My coat was long and heavy, my hat full brimmed. If I stuck to the shadows, I could get home without incident, even if I *was* dogged by James' presence. I didn't know what I was thinking. Why would I orchestrate this? He would recognise me. I knew he would.

I slipped into the old Morgan residence on Comer Street. I'd bought it from a young couple who were moving to the city. I had made them move. It's easy to plant a seed—anyone can do it; you don't need special tricks. They were happy to sell because they said the old place was haunted and I figured if anyone would stick around a tiny village on the west coast of Ireland after death, it'd be dear old Aunt Cara. She'd have nowhere else to go because God wouldn't take her and the devil wouldn't want her.

I slept in her old bedroom on the first floor overlooking the garden that had been paved over in the years since I'd been away. Her prize geraniums had long since withered and been removed. I could still smell her in the walls, those cheap cigarettes and cloying perfumes. But if she haunted the place, she never revealed herself to me. Ghosts, if they were real, were just leftover memories, nothing more than smells and sounds.

I'd boarded up the windows in this room and I slept heavily. And when my alarm woke me, the sun had already gone down. The weather app on my phone gave me each day's sunrise and sunset times. I don't know how I coped before smartphones were invented.

There was still a warmth in the air as September was

reluctant to let go of summer's heat, but I saw the turning of the leaves, green tinged with the sadness of red. The nights were getting longer as the world shrugged on its autumn thickness.

The dark evenings meant that I could get to work earlier, and I stood on the lawn outside the weathered manor, watching the activity through the common room window. A staff member had a guitar and was singing some inane song whose words I couldn't make out despite my keen hearing.

I saw the brothers—Daniel and Joseph, their door tag had read—as they argued with each other over a card game. I didn't see James. I was too intent on looking for him that I didn't spot where he was.

In the shadows by the front door, he said, "You, boy."

I closed my eyes, but it was too late. I couldn't hide from him now.

I tried to cling to the darkness of the garden, walking around the edge of the fountain. "Yes, sir?"

He wore a dressing gown over a pair of striped pyjamas, and he leaned against his walking frame. His face, shrouded in the dark shadows of the manor, came forward and the light caught his sharp eyes. He said, "I need a bridge partner. Have you ever played?"

I couldn't look at him, preferring to study his bedroom slippers that were worn and fraying around the sides. "Where's your usual partner?" I asked, hoping my voice sounded casual.

"She's dead," he said flatly. "What's your name, son?"

I casually covered the sticker on my shirt. Mrs Conway hadn't given me a name badge yet. As I coughed, I tore the sticker off. "Stephen," I said. It was the first name that came to me.

"Well, come on, then," James said. He turned and shuffled back inside.

I followed him. I couldn't not. Where James went, Victor followed. It's what I did. And as he walked ahead of me, I studied the back of his head. His hair was white but as thick as the day we met. My fingers had been in that hair before. Many times.

In the common room, I trained my gaze on the tiled floor. James inched towards the card table where the brothers had stopped arguing, and when he let go of his walker to sit, he leaned unnaturally to the left, as if he'd lost his balance.

I was quick to his side, easing him upright, and when my hand connected with his arm, he stood up straight. He looked at me with something like recognition in his eyes.

And I lowered my head again.

"I'm all right," he said, but he let me help him into the chair. He steadied his hands on the green felt of the card table and pointed to the empty seat opposite him.

"Where's Agnes?" one of the brothers said. "We always play with Agnes."

"She's gone," James said.

"Gone where?"

"Where all good people go eventually," James said.

The brother looked up. They were so alike that I couldn't tell which was which. He said, "Is she coming back?"

And then I noticed the scar on the back of his hand, the same scar that had been there since I met him. I never knew how he got it. He never talked about it.

"Don't be silly, Danny," James said. "Nobody ever comes

back." He shuffled the cards as we made our bids, and when he won the first round, I knew his mind was as sharp as ever. I kept my face down and my cards up.

"Who's he?" Danny asked, nodding towards me.

James said, "He's my new bridge partner."

"He doesn't make a very good Agnes. What's his name?"

"Ask him," James said.

"What's your name?" Danny asked.

"Stephen."

"I'm James," the old man opposite me said.

"And I'm Danny. This one is Giuseppe."

"That's not his real name," James said. "He's called Joe."

I smiled. I never asked before, but this time I said, "Why do they call you Giuseppe?"

Giuseppe shrugged. And when he laughed, I wasn't playing bridge with a group of old men, but with three of the closest friends I'd ever had. I looked around the table and James—a young James—was turning cards over while Danny threw popcorn at Giuseppe and Giuseppe pulled a funny face like he always did.

And then Mrs Conway said, "Leave the staff alone, gentlemen, please. Some of us have work to do."

Before I stood up, Giuseppe put his hand on top of mine. He leaned in, his eyes hooded, and whispered, "Does it get lonely?"

I looked at him. He wasn't young any more. The bags under his eyes sagged like they were full of secrets.

He said, "It must get lonely."

"What does?" I asked.

But he shrugged. His eyes turned cloudy. "There's a

longevity to loneliness," he said.

I nodded. I knew there was.

And James said, "Same time tomorrow night, kid. Don't be late."

I walked away from the card table and when I looked back, the old men were reshuffling the cards as if I hadn't been there a minute before.

I heard James' laughter. And I smiled.

The boys were back.

chapter 4

1949

Mum was tired. She was always tired. When I had driven Aunt Cara back from town, Mum was on her knees in the hallway, scrubbing the floor with a brush. The green apron she wore was sparked with soapy water from her bucket and as we came through the front door, she wiped an arm across her forehead and pushed the bucket out of Cara's way.

The old woman hung her coat on a hook and slid her headscarf off before clomping upstairs.

"Dinner will be at six," Mum called after her.

"Very good," Aunt Cara said.

When we were alone, I watched Mum scrubbing the floor for a minute and then said, "May I go exploring?"

"There is too much to do."

"I won't go far," I said. "I wanted to check out the beach." James had said they'd be there, but he hadn't said when.

"You'll track sand over my clean floors," Mum said.

"I'll be extra careful."

Mum dipped the brush in the bucket of water and spread the suds across the floor. "We've been here for two weeks, Victor. Let's not upset Aunt Cara so soon, okay?"

I crouched in front of her. "You should take the day off, too. Treat yourself to a rest."

She laughed, humourless and annoyed. "Victor," she said.

I put my hand on hers and took the scrubbing brush. "I'll finish up here. You can get started on dinner."

Mum sat back on her haunches and dried her hands on her apron. "You're a good boy," she said.

"I'm not a boy."

She gripped my shoulder as she rose to her feet. "And you're not a man. You should stay a boy forever. Refuse to grow up, Victor. Children have it easy. Growing up should be a last resort."

"I'll drop a penny in the wishing well," I told her.

I pushed the bucket along and scrubbed the floor, then went back over it with a cloth. I twisted the wet rag around the outdoor tap to wring it out because I wasn't able to grip it with both hands and I watched the water bleed into the drain.

We sat with Aunt Cara at the table while Mum served fish pie. Living so close to the coast meant fish was in ready supply.

"Tell me about your day, dear," Cara said as Mum sat. Her interest was obligatory and as Mum talked, I didn't think the old woman was listening. "Elbows off the table," she said to me, interrupting Mum's words.

I cut the pie with the edge of my fork and let my other

hand rest in my lap instead of on the table.

I helped to clear the dinner dishes when we'd finished and Aunt Cara asked to be served a sherry in the parlour. The book she had borrowed from the library looked boring and wordy. I'd tried to read the first page yesterday and it was impossible to understand.

When I offered to help Mum with the dishes, she shooed me out of the kitchen and said, "Get out of here before I change my mind. But make sure you don't bring sand home with you or Aunt Cara will kick us both out. And be back before dark."

I kissed her cheek. "You're the best."

I ran to the beach, my worn shoes thumping against the pavement as I followed the sound of seagulls. When I got there, the sun was dazzling the ocean and the narrow strip of sand was busy with school children and young families. On the dunes, I kicked my shoes aside and peeled off my calf-length socks, pushing them into a ball. And despite rolling my trousers up to my shins, I knew I'd have to shake them out before going home. A slight wind meant that the sand was papering me from head to toe.

I recognised James' thick mop of hair even from here. He kicked a brown leather football across the beach with Danny and—what was he called? Giuseppe? Michael, the younger one, cheered them on from the sidelines as James skirted around one of the brothers and kicked the ball between two shirts that were laid out as goalposts.

He was wearing a pair of high-waisted navy swimming trunks with a white belt that looped through the waistband and the skin of his torso was toned and sun-browned.

When he saw me, he waved, tackled Michael to the ground, and then ran to greet me. "New boy," he said.

"Victor," I reminded him, in case he'd forgotten.

He smiled. A strand of sand-coated hair had slipped out of its pomade hold over his forehead and curled above one eye. I refused to look at his broad chest that tapered to a narrow waist, and his thick thighs that were sprinkled with fine hairs. "You didn't bring swimming trunks?" he asked.

"Next time," I said.

Danny—or Giuseppe; I wasn't sure which—kicked the ball to us and James flicked it with a foot before bouncing it on his knee. The brothers weren't twins, but they looked alike enough that I'd bet their own mother was often confused. James kicked the ball back to them.

"Where have you moved from?" he asked as we walked towards the others.

"The city."

Michael tried to kick the ball but he missed when one of the brothers pushed him out of the way. When he landed on his rear in the sand, he said, "Why would you move from the city to this pokey place?"

I shrugged. I didn't want to answer that.

I was aware of my limp arm hanging at my side, the black leather glove conspicuous among all the swimming trunks and naked torsos of early summer. I sat on the sand in a fluid movement, hoisting my arm into my lap where I let the hand fall between my thighs and out of view.

I was grateful when James slumped down beside me and the others followed suit. He stretched out on his side, propped up on an elbow, and his legs were long.

Seagulls danced across the shore's edge and an ice cream trolley wheeled across the wooden walkway behind us.

"What do you do?" Giuseppe asked. I figured out the difference between them from their teasing of each other.

That was another question I didn't want to answer. But I said, "I worked on a construction crew in the city."

"I work for the local dairy," James said, "delivering milk. I get up at four-thirty and I'm exhausted by eight."

The brothers worked in a fishery they said in unison. And, as though it had been rehearsed, added together, "But we don't always talk at the same time."

"What do you do?" I asked Michael.

"I'm a flue hygiene specialist," he said with pride.

Danny punched his shoulder and laughed and when I gave James a quizzical look, he said, "He means he's a chimney sweep."

We laughed.

Danny pulled Michael into a headlock and said, "He uses big words but he's not brainy enough to stay in school."

Slipping out of Danny's hold, I could see the blush on Michael's cheeks as he said, "My parents needed the money. No point sitting in a schoolroom when there's money to be made."

Michael and the brothers dashed off with the football and I felt uncomfortable sitting beside James. He'd leaned forward with his upper arms on his knees and I could count the rivets of his spine. I was overdressed.

I squinted and shielded my eyes as I stared across the beach with a jumble of words in my mouth and none of them coming loose. When I attempted to speak, my throat seized. I watched him in my periphery, too scared to look at him openly, but I was already counting the dark freckles on his arm.

James filtered some sand through his fingers before saying, "You don't work in construction any more, do you?"

I shook my head.

He said, "You should work with me on the milk float. It's an early start, but it's easy work. And it keeps you fit."

"I don't know," I said, tightening my legs around my dead arm to hide it.

"I'll ask the boss," he said with a bright look on his face.

I smiled. I watched the sand fall through his fingers onto his toes that were long and slender.

James stood up, dusting sand from the seat of his trunks, and I let my eyes trail from his ankles to the backs of his knees before I forced my attention onto the ocean. The tide was coming in just as the blood was rising in my veins.

To fill the silence, I said, "Do you like working for the dairy?"

We walked along the edge of the water as the others ran ahead with the football, passing it between them. The ice cream vendor was coming back down the walkway, but I didn't have a penny to my name. Doing chores for Aunt Cara was meant to help cover our board. As a cripple, Cara had said a few days after we arrived, she didn't think I'd ever get a job.

James picked up a shell, scooping the sand out of it and wiping it on his trunks until it was spotless. Then he cupped it in his hands, made a silent wish, and tossed the seashell into the ocean. He said, "It's a job. But it's not what I want to do for the rest of my life."

"What do you want to do?" I asked.

"I'm going to move to Dublin. Become the big-wig CEO of a proper company."

"What kind of company?"

He shrugged. "Agriculture, probably. That's where the future is. What about you?"

"I don't know. But it'll be something big. 'You're destined for great things.' That's what my dad used to say."

"Used to?" he asked.

"Yeah," I said. I didn't need to elaborate.

Michael whipped back between us with the ball, dribbling it around James' back before James flicked a foot out and took possession. Smaller than the others, Michael tried to grip James' waist and retake the ball but James was too quick for him.

Their laughter was genuine, even when James clicked his fingers and the brothers picked Michael up by the armpits, dragged him to the waves, and threw him into the ocean. Michael stood up like a sea monster, water flailing, and he screamed. The water was freezing.

I laughed, but quickly shut my mouth when Danny and Giuseppe stepped in front of me. "Funny, is it?" Danny asked. He reached for my arm.

"Woah," James said, coming between us. "No dunking the new boy. Not when he's fully dressed."

Danny chewed his mouth into a scowl and the brothers stepped away from me. But I didn't want preferential treatment. James was just being nice because of my dead hand. So I ran into the water, turned to face the lads, and said, "So long, boys. It was nice knowing you."

I fell back, just as a wave swelled around me, and I was engulfed by the salty water. I coughed and spluttered until the brothers dragged me onto the beach.

And I pushed my hair out of my face. I looked up and said, "Jesus H. Christ, it's freezing."

James stood over me with his arms folded. The others laughed, but he nodded. I saw the pride in his features. And I smiled the whole way home.

I went around the back, hoping to avoid Mum and Aunt Cara, but Mum was unpegging laundry from the line. She took one look at my sodden clothes and frowned.

I said, "You told me not to bring sand home, but you didn't say anything about the ocean." I was shivering.

And Mum couldn't contain her laughter, which was nice, because I hadn't seen her smile since before the accident.

She stood watch outside the parlour while I darted up the stairs at the back of the house to change, and when I came down, she was cleaning the trail of ocean water from the floor. I heard the radio in the parlour, tuned to a news broadcast, and I could smell Cara's sherry. I think she needed a sherry-coma just to sleep at night.

"I might have a job," I told Mum. "It's not definite, but I'm a shoe in."

She hugged me. "What about your mickey?" she asked. She'd taken to calling my disfigured hand my "mickey" instead of calling it what it was—a life sentence.

"Let me worry about that," I said.

But I knew she'd do enough worrying for the both of us.

chapter 5

the present

Giuseppe stared at me.

I combed a hand through my hair, trying to pull it over my face, but it wasn't as long as it used to be. Styles change. We all change. Well—most of us.

"Are you finished with this?" I asked, lifting the plastic beaker of water that was almost empty. When I was around them, I didn't feel seventeen. I felt ancient. The table beside his armchair in the common room was a clutter of large-print detective novels and out-of-date magazines.

"Giuseppe?"

He didn't answer. He just stared at me with an intense awareness. Or confusion. It was hard to tell. He wore a shirt and tie, but the shirttail had worked itself free from his trousers and the tie was done up wrong, too short at the thick end, too long at the skinny side. I wasn't sure who dressed him, or if he'd done it himself, but they must have been blindfolded. It was odd, seeing a man in a suit and wearing bedroom slippers.

"Giuseppe," I said.

He blinked.

"Are you done with this?"

"No," Giuseppe said. There were whiskers under his nose that had been missed by a nurse's razor.

I couldn't shake his words from the other night when he asked me if it gets lonely. He hadn't clarified what he meant, but he'd been looking at me with those same eyes at the time, alert and cloudy all at once. Like he knew me.

I crouched in front of him. "Giuseppe?"

His eyes were hooded now. I draped a fleece blanket over his legs. And as he edged closer to sleep, I touched the back of his hand. "Do you know me, Giuseppe?" I whispered.

He smiled and his words came soft and dreamlike. "I never forget a face."

"Who am I?" I asked.

But he fell asleep.

I'd sat with them the following night at the card table and James won two-thirds of the hands. I didn't know he was so good at it. And the night after that, Nurse Gloria stuck close to my side, making sure I worked through my tasks for the evening before the residents were escorted to their beds and the front door was locked. "Best not to get the old men wound up so close to bedtime," she'd said.

On my security rounds, I checked the window locks and made sure the internal fire doors weren't propped open with boxes or fire extinguishers, and I sensed Mr Buckley was on the prowl again. I went upstairs.

I saw him escaping into the stairwell, mooning his way through the door, and I darted down to the floor below to head him off. As he came into the corridor in nothing but socks and slippers, I greeted him with a towelling robe.

"I thought you were upstairs," he said.

"And I thought we'd talked about this, Mr Buckley."

"I need snacks," he said.

"You're in the ladies wing," I told him. I knew what kind of snack he was looking for. "Turn about," I said. "Let's get you back to your room."

Mr Buckley limped up the stairs, clinging to the banister and feigning joint pain. "It's my knees," he said. "You go ahead and I'll be right up behind you."

"I saw you take those stairs two at a time on the way down. You're not pulling the wool over my eyes." I heard the blood in his veins. It was thick and moving languidly.

"Where's Gloria? She never manhandles me."

"Never you mind," I said as I marched him down the corridor on the top floor. We walked by Albert McInnis' room, another of the residents who never had visitors and hardly left his bed. I knew Death wouldn't be far away for him.

Further down the corridor, James' door was propped open. He was sitting on the edge of his bed in a pair of polyester pyjamas. I heard the catch in his throat as he squeezed the life out of a handkerchief in his fist. "Are you all right?" I asked.

Mr Buckley said, "It's like a prison around here."

James shook his head, then nodded.

"You," I said to Buckley, "into your room, please. And stay there this time." I closed the door behind him and then returned to James. At his doorway, I said, "Everything okay?"

"I'm fine," James wheezed.

"You don't look fine."

"Just hand me that glass of water," he said, pointing.

I said, "Do you need the nurse?"

He shook his head and coughed. "For God's sake, boy, just give me some water."

I rushed to his side, pressing the glass into his hands. He drank and gasped.

"Is it dead?" I asked.

"What?"

I indicated his fist. His knuckles were white as he throttled the life out of his knotted handkerchief.

"I can't unlock my fingers," he said, holding the hand up for me to see.

"May I?" I held his fist between my hands and his pain choked me. It surged into my palms with an icy tingle, darkening my veins and making my fingers pulse. I said, "Open your fist."

"I can't."

"Yes, you can. Open it."

James straightened his thumb, pointer and middle finger. The other two were still curled around the handkerchief.

"Arthritis?" I asked. He nodded. I removed the fabric from his hand and cupped his curled fingers. "I'm just going to ease them open, okay? Can I do that?"

When I looked up, he was staring at me the way Giuseppe had earlier.

I returned my gaze to his hand and closed my eyes. There was a curdling in my veins as his pain entered me. And it made me dizzy.

James flexed his fingers. "How did you do that?"

"Reiki," I lied.

He shook his hand to loosen it. "So you're into all that new age bullshit."

"I'm into anything that helps," I said. I stood up. We were sitting far too close. I poured him a fresh glass of water and said, "Were you short of breath?"

"I'm in an old folks' home, kid. I'm short of everything."

"You're old? I hadn't noticed."

"And you're not too old for a kick up the backside," he said.

I backed out of his room. "But are you young enough to catch me?"

He laughed. And the seventeen-year-old James I once knew was lighting up his face. Old age is just wrinkles and bad posture. Keep those two things at bay and you could be young forever.

"You remind me of somebody," he said.

My smile dropped. "Just one of those faces," I said.

James eased himself up from the bed and gripped his walker. The handkerchief fell to the floor.

"You should be in bed," I said.

He notched across the room, the rubber stoppers of the walking frame loud in the quiet.

"Come here," he said.

I tapped my wrist like I was wearing a watch. "Got a long night ahead of me. You get some rest, okay? You'll feel better in the morning."

"Who is it?" James said.

"Who's what?"

"Who you remind me of."

I shook my head. But then, I don't know what changed—his face? My bravery?—I faced him in his doorway. I puffed my chest up and said, "Who do I remind you of, James?"

The old man looked at me. I knew the flecks of gold in my eyes were bright.

"A long time," he said.

"What's that?"

He shook his head. "Time."

And I nodded. "It's not time," I said. "You should go back to bed now."

James blinked. There was a slight tremor in his neck, making his head shake just enough that I noticed it.

I said, "Are you going to be all right?"

"A long time," he said again. He turned the walking frame and shuffled across the thin carpet tiles to his bed.

I breathed.

James slid into bed and I closed his door. I stood outside his room for a minute, listening to the sounds within. His breathing was slow and deep. He'd be fine.

But would I?

Mr Buckley opened his bedroom door and I scowled at him. "Not again," I said. "Don't test me."

"Whippersnapper," he said before closing his door again.

I went downstairs. The staff room was empty, like it always was at this time of night, and I cleaned the disgusting microwave just to keep my mind on ordinary things. I'd do another security sweep in an hour, and I could watch the cameras from here, inside and out, and I contemplated the silence. The corridor outside James' room glowed on the monitor. It was empty. I wanted to go to him but I knew I couldn't.

Silence wasn't something I heard often. There was always something, the background hum of electricity, the distant roar of traffic. But I was getting better at filtering out the sounds I didn't need. I could concentrate on the emptiness behind the drone of the fridge and the hiss of the boiler at the far end of the corridor. And in that blindness, there was peace. But also sadness.

Gloria came into the staff room. I'd been distracted, but when I recognised the squeak of her plimsoles, I picked up a cloth and wiped the countertop so that it didn't look as though I was doing nothing. In the rooms above, the rush of sixteen heartbeats filled my head—Anges O'Shea's room had yet to be filled, though we were expecting somebody's arrival tomorrow.

"I need a drink," she said, slumping into a chair. "I've just had to take Mrs Robertson's teeth out of her mouth by force because she insists on grinding them."

"I could have helped with that," I said.

She glared. "You're not a nurse."

I didn't argue with her. Gloria owned a high horse and she sat on it often.

"Have you finished your tasks?"

I picked up my clipboard. "I was just about to do another security sweep and then empty the bins."

She rubbed the back of her alabaster neck. From the other side of the table, I saw her carotid artery winking at me.

I hightailed it out of there before she had the chance to say another word.

By the time I got home, the sun was pushing above the

houses and the shadows I lurked through at the edges of the streets were getting narrower.

I received two emails from Lakeshore Manor. The first said, *Dear Mr Ashley, you are reminded that your next monthly payment of €2,375 is now due in respect of the residential stay of MR JAMES O'CARROLL. If you have set up a direct debit, the above amount will be taken from your account on or around the FIFTEENTH day of the month.*

The second email said, *Dear Mr Jones, you are reminded that your next monthly payment of €4,750 is now due in respect of the residential stay of MR DANIEL GRAINGER and MR JOSEPH GRAINGER.*

Nursing homes weren't cheap. I had other emails—12,867 unread messages—which I was useless at reminding myself to check, but I'd marked anything from Lakeshore Manor as high priority. When you have the same AOL email address since forever, you amass a lot of junk newsletters. We had email back in the day. Back in *my* day. Listen to me, sounding like an old man and looking like a kid.

I'd been paying their nursing home bills since I came back from the Himalayas. It was the least I could do.

I slipped into bed, hungry but tired. I don't dream, and part of me is glad that I don't, though some dark corner of my brain, a faraway itch, wished that I'd be plagued in my sleep by the nightmares I'd suffered in my wakefulness. Sometimes, all we want to do is bury ourselves in misery. We—humankind—are nothing if not depressing.

The sheets were cool and the room was dark.

Sleep came easier than it had for a long time.

chapter 6

1949

I heard the dull clip of a horse's hooves before I saw James' milk float morphing out of the morning gloom. Fog clung to me like a stubborn ghost, silent and persistent. It was five a.m. and somewhere above the low-lying clouds that dusted the streets, a weak sun was trying to break free of the night's shackles.

James called the draught horse to woah and pulled back the reins as the cart rolled to a stop beside me. He grinned. "Wasn't sure you'd come back."

I'd started working with him yesterday morning, running alongside the float, lifting bottles of milk from the back and sitting them at doorsteps, picking up the empties and dropping them into crates with one hand. James kept the horse walking at a steady pace but by the time we were done and I'd hopped onto the back of the float, my feet were killing me.

On the way to the dairy at the end of our round, James sang *Baby Face* by Art Mooney, and as we rode over the humpbacked bridge by the river, I was singing along.

I could hardly walk when I'd hopped off the back of the float and watched James brush down the horse. When I got home, I eased my shoes off and soaked my feet in a bucket of soapy water for an hour.

"Of course I came back," I said now, jumping onto the back of the float in the space he'd created for me among the crates.

Before we set off, he tossed me a thermos of sugary tea, and then a second, smaller tin.

I turned it over. Vaseline. "What's this for?"

"Rub it on your heels," he said. "Your feet won't hurt so bad at the end of the day."

I laughed, pulling at my shoelaces. "Why didn't you tell me this yesterday?"

James said, "You had to survive Day One. It's a rite of passage."

We covered the outlying houses first, the ones that were set back off the road, nestled among expansive fields and far enough apart that I could jump on the back instead of walking from one to the next. At one house, I picked up the empty bottles and there was a note rolled into the neck of one. In the early morning gloom, it was difficult to make out the drunken, handwritten words, but James took one glance at it and said, "She only wants two bottles today because Big John's gone to the city and won't be back till Friday."

I guess you get used to other people's handwriting after a while.

Some of the notes we got were matter of fact. *One extra bottle* or *None today*. But there was the occasional gem. *Dear James, I see you every morning from my window. If you love me, turn this bottle upside down and leave it here. PS, don't tell my mum. PPS, who's the new boy? He's also cute.*

I searched the upstairs windows for a face, but they were dark and murky.

I said, "Do you want me to turn the bottle upside down?"

"Do I heck," James said. He was spitting wasps.

"Who is it?" I asked.

James whipped the reins and the horse turned back down the lane. "Sally Byrne. She's only fourteen." I had to run after him to keep up, and he grumbled about her for the next twenty minutes. "As if I'd ever want to be with somebody like that," he said.

"What's wrong with her?"

"I'd sooner kiss the feet of a homeless man."

"Would that be with or without Vaseline?" I asked. He didn't see the funny side.

Later, before we rode into the main streets of the village where I'd spend the rest of the morning running from one house to the next, James pulled the float to a stop on the hill that commanded a view over the bay where the fishing boats were already out and the streetlights were still lit. The fog had lifted but its damp remnants coated the village in a wash of grey hues.

I climbed onto the driver's bench as James unwrapped the waxed paper of his sandwich and I pulled the crushed wrapper of mine from the inside pocket of my jacket. The sweet tea was still warm.

James said, "What've you got?"

"Corned beef. What's in yours?"

"Ham."

He tore his thick sandwich in two with his fingers and traded it for half of mine, and we ate in silence, listening to the morning birds and the thrum of distant farm machinery that choked the northern horizon. The ocean below us was calm.

James said, "Do you see that dark channel over there?" He was pointing left of the beach, among the trees of the coastal forest. There was a scar in the earth were the trees refused to grow. "An American bomber made a crash landing there about five years ago. Right through the trees. We all saw it. Thick, black smoke stuttering behind it. It took two days to put the fires out."

"Were they killed?" I asked.

"Not a scratch on them," he said. "The whole crew survived. Everyone called it a miracle."

We didn't have anything like that in the city during the war. My parents went about their business as normal and kids went to school and did their chores. Nighttime blackouts became a part of life, but we didn't see any of the action. We'd hear the distant burr of warplanes occasionally, but it didn't matter how much you squinted into the night, you'd never see them.

James flattened his wax paper against his thigh and folded it, pushing it back into his pocket. "I saw a U-boat once. Right out near the horizon. And there were always shipwrecks washing up on shore."

"Always?" I asked.

"Well. Twice."

I looked at the lane behind us and said, "I wasn't teasing you about Sally Byrne, you know."

"I know." He didn't pick up the reins. He was staring across the dark Atlantic Ocean.

"Do you," I said, then cleared my throat, "have a girlfriend?"

"Nah." His answer was quick. He looked at me. "Do you?"

His eyes studied my face. I shook my head and pulled my mickey up from the bench and into my lap where it taunted me like an upturned spider. I wanted to say, "I'm not really into girls," but those were words that could have had me thrown in jail. The thoughts that had dogged me for years, ever since I met Brian Walsh at school and he made my stomach turn upside down when I saw him, were illegal thoughts. And when I'd thought them under the bedcovers, I wondered if the authorities knew I was thinking them.

Instead, I said, "I guess nobody wants a cripple like me." My dead hand was itching this morning, more than it normally did.

"Hey," James said. "Stop being so negative. You're a good-looking fella. And you only need one hand for most things."

I laughed. I didn't know what things he was referring to, but one thing was running through my head and it made me blush.

James said, "Except for jumping rope. You can't jump rope with one hand."

"I'd better not go entering any skipping tournaments, then."

"Probably wise," he said, picking up the reins. "And you

can forget about playing the piano."

"I can still play Chopsticks."

"Smart aleck."

By the end of the week, my feet weren't hurting and I thought I saw some definition in my calves when I flexed them in front of the mirror in my bedroom. I used to like my body. Working in construction meant that I was always hauling something heavy or hitting something hard with a hammer. I'd developed a farmer's tan, brown arms that turned white where my T-shirt sleeves were, a bronzed face and neck, and my chest had been filling out above a flat stomach.

But since the accident, the brown tone of my skin had faded while I languished in my bedroom, unwilling to do more than I had to in order to keep Aunt Cara off my back, and the muscles on my arms and chest had softened.

This past week, walking the hills of our village, put a definite zip back in my step. I had to carry my mickey with me everywhere, a blight that stalked my days as much as my nights, but James didn't make fun of it, and the others had gotten used to it.

On Saturday, we spent the afternoon sitting on a wall at the top of the beach, sharing a bottle of beer and talking about nothing of importance. I'd taken a spot on the wall beside James, my new confidante, and Michael sat on the sand in front of us, waiting for the bottle to be passed to him. It wasn't unheard of for seventeen-year-olds to be served in a pub, but Michael was fifteen and needed to keep his head down and away from the street that ran parallel to the beach.

"Your dad's coming this way," Giuseppe said, and Michael passed the bottle over, trying to look casual. And Giuseppe laughed. "Fooled you."

He was a year older than Michael and one year younger than Danny and us. I'd never had a brother. I'm not sure why my parents stopped after me. Maybe I was perfect and they decided I didn't need an inferior sibling.

That was probably it.

Tom McShane, the dairy farmer, paid me five shillings at the end of the week, and I gave half of it to Mum, who stored it in a mason jar in her bedroom. She didn't say it, but I knew she wanted to find a place of our own one day. And now that I was working instead of handling household chores for Cara, she'd started charging us rent.

But it felt nice having some coins in my pocket.

A week later, we took up our seats on the wall above the beach, and Michael walked on his hands across the warm sand while some of the local girls applauded him. Danny and Giuseppe had an arm-wrestling contest for the right to ask one of the girls to the dance that night, and James rolled his eyes at me as if everyone else were children and only I was able to share his amusement at how petty they were being.

Sally Byrne didn't leave him any more notes when he didn't turn the milk bottle upside down, and when we saw her walking across the beach with her friends, James hopped over the wall and hid behind me until she'd passed. I felt his hand on my back while he crouched there, and I liked it.

"Is she gone?" he asked.

"Not yet," I said, and he stayed there a minute longer, with his fingers on my shirt. There was an electric charge in my spine.

When I told him it was safe, he sat on the wall beside

me and I said, "You shouldn't have to hide like a child just because you don't want to go out with her."

James draped his arm around my neck and grinned. "You'll always be my protection, won't you?"

"From little girls?" I asked.

"From everything," he said, and he wrestled me off the wall and onto the sand.

I rolled over him, my mickey tumbling behind me, but I had a good grip on his shirt and hauled him into the rushes that pocked the sand dune. He tried to grip my head in a lock but I slipped away from his reach and twisted my legs around his.

But James had two hands and I had one. He pinned my shoulders down in the sand and pressed his body on top of mine. "One!" he said, calling out a wrestler's count. "Two!"

I struggled, laughing, but I couldn't shake him.

His knees were either side of my torso and his hands held me down, his face above me.

"Three!"

I stopped struggling. I knew when I was beat.

And James grinned.

I watched his face.

The others had been chanting at our wrestling match, smashing our names into the air, but when James pinned me, they returned their attention to the girls across the sand.

I felt my stomach rise against his thighs when I breathed. And I watched his Adam's apple swell in his throat.

I couldn't speak.

James said, "You've got sand in your hair," and his fingers brushed it off, a gentle touch that I felt with a thick intensity.

Quietly, I said, "Oh, shoot," as if it mattered.

And he laughed. He rolled off me, lying at my side for a minute, staring at me, and then he helped me up. We sat beside each other on the wall, breathing hard. He looked at me, a smile tugging at the corners of his thin lips.

My words were a whisper when I said, "If you need protection, I'm all yours."

James nodded, and he held his hand out to seal the deal.

And I couldn't keep the blush from my cheeks.

chapter 7

the present

An autumn storm sparked across the sky like a snake and my skin felt as though it was on fire. The thunder that broiled in the evening clouds set the hairs on my arms on end and in the darkness that followed the flashes of lighting, I was blind. I stood under a shop awning until I could see again, and then dashed from one street corner to the next. The crackle of lightning always ignited anxiety in me, the thunder rupturing my stomach as well as the sky.

I hated lightning storms.

I could stand in the rain forever without a care—and let's face it, Ireland wasn't short of rainy days—but one distant growl of thunder and I'd be on edge for days.

I kept my hood up, drawn forward over my face, and by the time I got to work, I was drenched. Rain does not discriminate; it washes everything clean.

Some of the residents stood by the windows, watching the storm, and the staff were trying to distract them. James was there, leaning against his walking frame and staring at the dark clouds. When the sky came alive with lightning, I saw him looking at me as I stood by the fountain in the garden, a teenager in an oversized coat. In the weeks that I'd been here, the fountain was never turned on, the upturned vase in the stone woman's hands was dry. Except for now when the rain dripped from it as it dripped from me.

I waved at James, but he'd turned away from the window.

And I wanted to stand there, under the storm, beating it at its own game. If only the pounding in my chest wasn't forcing me inside to the warmth and the safety of old age. In the doorway, I stood under the overhead heater, brushing rainwater out of my thick hair, and I flinched when the sky brightened again, revealing the outline of the village outside whose buildings cut into the night like sharp incisors.

I turned my back to the storm and cowered in the staff room until it had rolled on, shaking the rain off my coat and drying my face and neck with paper towels.

"That's a night to raise the dead," Nurse Gloria said. She gripped a mug of tea like it was a lifeline. "Shiva is dancing." When I gave her a questioning look, she said, "He's dancing in fury at his wife's death until she is reborn."

I didn't know what she meant. An itch travelled up my left arm from the hand to the elbow. "It's a good job nothing can come back from death, then, isn't it?" I curled my fingers to block the tingle and put my hands in my pockets. The windows in the staff room were frosted, but they glowed when the sky fed us her lightning. I recoiled.

She said, "Don't fear the storm, kid. The worst it can do is destroy you."

"What's worse than being destroyed?" I asked.

As she left the room, still clinging to her mug, she said, "Being alive when the dead rise."

"Don't I know it," I said. But she was already gone.

In the common room, the staff were nearing the end of their bingo night, rolling numbered balls out of a spinning cage, but few of the residents were paying attention. At the card table, James, Danny and Giuseppe were playing rummy, the storm forgotten like yesterday's feeble dreams. And even from the doorway, I could hear the wheeze in James' chest when he breathed. Danny and Giuseppe were slouched in their wingback chairs, but James leaned an elbow on one of the arms of his seat so that his back was upright, and I sensed the pain he was in as he forced his spine straight.

When I stood by the table, I tapped the back of his hand, drawing in just a touch of his discomfort, and said, "Who's winning?"

"The matchstick king," Danny said, indicating James' loot. The thunder was distant now, soft and rumbling across the heavens.

I joined them at the table when they'd finished their round and we played a few hands of bridge. James was on fire as always, and when Danny started to snore, we knew that was the end of the game.

"It's a good thing most folk around here are already deaf," James said, "or he'd wake them all."

"What?" Giuseppe asked, cupping his ear and feigning deafness.

I woke Danny gently, easing him from the highbacked seat and into the wheelchair he was using more often than not in recent days. I pushed him to the lift that took forever to come to the ground floor and longer to rattle to the top of the building. James and Giuseppe gripped their walkers as we inched down the hallway and when I'd helped Danny into his pyjamas, Giuseppe had fallen asleep on his own bed.

I liked that they shared a room, just as they'd shared their lives.

James, standing in the doorway, said, "You look as tired as those two."

"I am." The storm had left me distracted. I roused Giuseppe long enough to get him undressed and when I closed their door, matching James' slow gait across the hall and into his room, I said, "Sorry."

"What for?" he asked.

But I couldn't say what I was sorry for. Nothing and everything.

James said, "Come with me." He had backed out of his room while I turned down his blankets.

"Where are you going?" I called.

"You'll see."

At the end of the corridor, he shouldered open the stairwell door and used his walking frame to hold it open for me. But instead of hobbling downstairs, he went up, dragging the walker behind him as he clung to the banister. The roof access door was locked—it was always locked—but James smiled at me.

I said, "I'm not unlocking that, James. You should be in bed."

"Shut up," he told me. He reached to the top of the doorframe and searched along it until he found a key. He opened the door.

"Where did you get that?" I asked as he pocketed the key.

"There are ways and means," James said. "You're not going to snitch on me, are you?"

"I should."

"You're better than that."

"How do you know?" I asked.

"I know you," he said. "And you have that look about you."

"What look?"

"Mischievous," James told me as he eased through the door.

I followed him outside onto the flat roof of the building and watched the night sky for signs of the storm, but it was long gone, and I heard the trickle of rainwater in the gulleys below.

James stood by the wall that ringed the edge of the roof, covered in ivy and spiders, and when I came to his side, he said, "I used to hate storms."

I wanted to say I knew that, but I kept quiet.

He said, "My wife loved them."

"You were married?" I'd seen the framed photograph in his room, a younger James with a blonde woman, smiling at the camera, but now that he'd said it out loud, I thought that it shocked me, despite already knowing. He nodded and I said, "What was her name?"

"Sylvie. She'd go outside in a sundress and stand under the storm, holding her arms out to the thunder. She said it was invigorating. I said she was insane." He tapped his walker against the wall where some of the bricks were loose. "I can't stoop," he said. "Lift those bricks away, will you?"

"If you're hiding cigarettes, I'm going to have to confiscate them," I said, pulling the dark bricks out of the wall. Behind them were three beer cans, unopened and cooled from the dampness of their hiding place.

"We can share one," James said. "Danny and Giuseppe won't mind. You're old enough to drink, aren't you, Stephen?"

I'd almost forgotten that I'd lied about my name. The metal badge that Mrs Conway gave me two weeks after I started working at Lakeshore Manor was small enough that his eyesight couldn't make out the letters. I made no attempt to hide it.

I said, "Where did you get hold of these?"

"That's none of your business," he said. He asked me to open the can; his fingers were twisted again.

And I did. I cracked the ring pull and said, "You'll get me fired." There was a glimmer in his eyes that I recognised, and I turned from him before he saw the same thing in mine. "Tell me about her," I said.

He guzzled from the can and smacked his lips like it was the nicest thing he'd tasted in years. He wiped the rim with a sleeve of his dressing gown and handed it to me. He said, "Not much to tell. She was good to me. Better than I was to her. I never deserved her."

"How did you meet?"

"Danny set us up on a blind date. Everyone else was already married, with big houses and picket fences. The works."

"Why weren't you?" I asked. My voice was low. I didn't really want to know the answer. I sipped from the can. Alcohol makes me sick, but it doesn't get me drunk. It lies in my stomach like a cancer.

James shrugged. He was leaning deeper into his walking frame and I knew he needed to sit down. But he took the can back from me and drank before saying, "I wasn't the marrying type." When there were only dregs left, he gave the beer to me and I pretended to drink from it. The night had gone quiet.

"You never had kids?" It was a question I already knew the answer to.

He shook his head. "We weren't so fortunate. Or unfortunate." His head was trembling again and he coughed.

I said, "Let's get you back to your room before Nurse Gloria kills us both."

James stared across the world at the streetlights and the distant traffic. He sighed. "Don't ever end up in a place like this," he said, and I'm certain he wasn't talking about a nursing home for the elderly.

He meant loneliness.

"You could fall," he said, looking at the grass below.

"Step away from the wall, James."

He nodded. "People tell you to take a leap of faith, but falling is easier."

"James."

"I know," he grumbled. "I'm not stupid." He turned. His walker was heavy. "I might be old, but I'm not stupid."

I coaxed him down to his room and as I helped him sit on the edge of his bed, I said, "Give me the key, please, James. For the door."

He wheezed and looked at me, something foggy and dark in his eyes. "I know you, don't I?"

"Yes, James. We were just talking, remember?"

James nodded. "Talking," he said with sleep curling around his features. He eased back on the bed and picked up the photograph of him and Sylvie. He pressed the cool glass and her smiling face against his forehead.

I said, "Do you need anything, James? James?"

He looked at me and I hated the wrinkles that folded over his eyes. His smile was gone. "Falling is easier," he said. And he fell asleep.

I took the frame out of his hands and looked at it. She was attractive, with long hair and smiling eyes. They were frozen in their forties, forever young, but there was little in the background to identify where they were. They could have been in a house in Limerick or Dublin, or a penthouse in Los Angeles. It made no difference.

I was glad he had her. He needed somebody. Everyone needs somebody.

I had popped the velvet kickstand back to put the frame on his bedside cabinet when I noticed a second photograph inside, its corner sticking through the edge of the backing.

James was asleep. And I shouldn't have, but I peeled back the tabs and took the hidden photo from its confines. It had been folded in half, a black and white image that was scratched and damaged with age. Just like James.

Five teenage boys—men, we would have called ourselves back then—were sitting on a wall, the ocean at their backs, a pale strand of beach between them. James was in the middle, with the brothers, Danny and Giuseppe, on his right. On the far left, Michael was pulling a funny face. And sitting beside James, close enough for him to wrap his arm around my shoulders, was me. James was leaning his head against mine, with his eyes tilted my way and his tongue poking out in fun.

And the smile on my face was enormous. It always was in those days.

James stirred on the bed, grumbling something in his sleep. I tucked the photo back where it belonged and pressed the velvet stand into place. And before he opened his eyes, I was out of his room and had closed the door.

James was right. Falling is easier.

chapter 8

1949

"Back a bit," James said. "Bit more. Bit more."

I backed up. "Hurry," I said. The sack in my arms was heavy and slipping, and the pain in my mickey was unbearable.

"There," he said. "Set her down."

I dropped the sack, fine white pebbles spilling over my shoes, and I cradled my weak arm.

"You all right?" James asked.

"Peachy," I said, but I wasn't.

And James knew it. He lowered his voice. "Seriously, Victor. If you need a break, we can stop."

I shook my head. Aunt Cara stood in the doorway, looking down on us like a jailor. James and the others had volunteered to help me dig up the old pavement between the front steps and the property line—because they knew I couldn't do it alone. And because Cara would never have paid anybody else to do it. When I wasn't working on the milk float, she had me mending things or running errands in the village. And if I looked tired, she'd have me running up the stairs and back, time and again, to fetch things she didn't need.

This afternoon, she stood at the top of the steps with a teacup and saucer, watching us like the thieves we must be. I swear she'd count the pebbles when we were done.

I wasn't convinced that we had enough sacks of the fine white pebbles she'd chosen, but I wasn't going to call her out on her calculations when we'd gone into the garden centre the week before to place the order. I helped the others stack them in the corner of the garden so we could dig up the cracked and broken paving stones.

We took turns with the sledgehammer and, even though I could only use one hand, I gave it a good swing and split one of the stones clean in two. Danny and Giuseppe worked its edges with a pickaxe while Michael ran around behind us with a yard brush and singing out-of-key songs. When he wasn't sweeping, he was balancing the broom handle in the palm of his hand, the brush end high overhead as he struggled to keep it aloft.

I smacked another stone, a jolt reverberating up my arm, and it glanced off the stone and cut a dent into the grass.

I didn't hear it, but I sensed the tut in Aunt Cara's throat.

She didn't offer us glasses of lemonade or water, and we worked through the glare of a scorching July afternoon. We had stripped our light jackets off and James had removed his shirt, a thin trail of sweat darkening the low neck of his undershirt. The skin at his throat glistened.

I carried some of the larger broken pieces of paving stone

to the wheelbarrow, one at a time, my gloved hand hanging at my waist.

Michael tripped over some chippings and smacked his forehead on the grass. When we rolled him over, he was smiling. "I meant to do that."

"How many fingers am I holding up?" Danny asked.

"Seventeen," Michael said as we helped him up.

"He'll live," Danny confirmed.

Giuseppe hefted the wheelbarrow up the wooden ramp to the skip that Cara had hired, and when all the paving stones had been removed, we stood back and admired our handiwork. The damp and compacted soil under the paving stones was rich with earthworms and woodlice.

Cara, who hadn't left the front steps the whole time, picked up her empty teacup from the table on the porch and said, "Make sure you rake the pebbles out evenly."

James gave me a knowing look. Cara was telling us we didn't deserve a break until we were done. He instructed the others to roll out one sack of pebbles at a time and then he said, "Do you mind if I use the lavatory, ma'am?"

I could tell she wanted to say no. Instead, she said, "Shoes off before you go inside. Straight in and straight out, mind."

"I'll show you where it is," I told him.

We went around the back and kicked our muddied shoes off at the door. Inside, swallowed in the cool shadows, James wiped an arm across his sweat-greased forehead and whispered, "She's a fun one, isn't she?"

"Told you."

"I thought you were exaggerating." He looked around the large kitchen. Mum had cleaned it this morning before going to work and the lacquered wooden countertops sparkled. The range door was open and its dark, sooty innards looked as though it hadn't been lit in weeks. He eyed the sink.

"Through there," I said, pointing down the hall. "There'll be a fresh glass of water when you're back."

I used a tall glass tumbler and ran the water tap until it was clear, keeping a finger under the stream so that I knew when it was running cold. The water pipes clanked and I hoped Cara wouldn't come and tell me off. I drank a glass, then refilled it for James.

When he came back from the lavatory, he smiled as I handed it to him, conscious that the imprint of my lip was on the side of it, and he pressed the sweating glass to his forehead to cool himself. I soaked a cloth and wrung it out, dabbing my neck with it, but the water bled into my shirt.

"Give it here," James said. He used both hands to remove as much of the water as he could, then he pressed the compress against the side of my neck. I reached up to take it from him, but he held it in place, his fingers under mine. "You've caught the sun," he said.

I'd also caught butterflies.

The damp coolness of the cloth was soothing against my skin and I rolled my shoulders, stretching my neck to give him further access. He moved the cloth to the hollow at the base of my throat.

"Better?" he asked.

I nodded. I couldn't speak.

James smiled. Then he removed the cloth, dampened it again at the tap, and pushed it into my hand. "Do me," he said. He turned so I could press it against the back of his neck where I wanted my lips to be. Facing away from me, James said, "That's nice."

"Is it?" The words caught in my throat and I forced them out. They were quiet, uncomfortable words.

I moved the cloth, cooling his sun-reddened shoulders.

James issued a noise that made me want to step away from him and fall into his arms at the same time. He said, "We should get back to work."

"Yeah," I said. But we didn't move.

He faced me. I let my hand fall away from him, my fingers locked around the damp cloth, rivulets of water curling down my thumb.

And then he stepped away from me when Michael stood in the doorway. "I've got to spend a penny," he said.

"Shoes off," James told him.

As Michael dashed past us, he said, "You're leaking."

I looked down. The damp cloth was dripping on the floor. And we laughed.

James went outside while I cleaned up the spill, and Danny and Giuseppe had raked out two sacks of pebbles when I joined them, one at each end of the path to mark the perimeter.

From the open window of the house, we heard the newscaster from Cara's radio in the parlour. *"Another spate of killings,"* he said, and we stopped to listen. Something had been killing sheep, its path of destruction coming up the coast from Castletown, past Waterville and Dingle. It was getting closer.

"It's a wild dog," Michael said.

"Wild dogs don't kill sheep," Danny said.

"Of course they do. What else is it going to be?"

"A bear?" Giuseppe suggested.

Michael leaned against the rake. "Firstly," he said, "there haven't been wild bears in Ireland since before Jesus was in nappies, and secondly, even if there was, why would a bear single out sheep as the only thing it wanted to eat?"

"Because they're damn tasty," Danny said, and we laughed.

By the time we were finished, we were sweating again and no one—except for me—had his undershirt on. I was too self-conscious around them to strip off entirely. Aunt Cara refused to pay us until we were properly dressed, and she inspected our work, crunching along the pebbles as if she was going to complain about the noise.

But she gave us two shillings and said the work was passable. It was as close to a compliment as she'd ever give.

We walked down to Brashell Road, the main street that ran across the top of the beach, and James, who looked the oldest of us, took some money and went into the pub. He bought five stumpy bottles of beer and we sat on the beach wall to drink them.

The sun was in front of us, squatting over the ocean, and we shielded our eyes while we watched the early evening surfers on their longboards.

Danny and Giuseppe wanted to go to the dance hall with our new-found cash, but Michael was too young to get in and James said he was too tired after a day's labour. Michael danced with himself on the sand. He turned his back to us, wrapping his arms around his waist, and made smooching noises.

Giuseppe whipped Michael's trousers down, revealing his

ill-fitting underwear, but Michael was far from embarrassed as he pulled his trousers back up. "Don't touch what you can't afford," he said. And when a couple of girls giggled nearby, he bowed to them and added, "You girls can touch me any time you like."

"He's drunk on half a bottle of beer," Danny laughed.

I admired Michael's way with the girls. Not that I wanted to mimic him or entertain the idea of talking formally with what boys called the fairer sex. I glanced at James, who was laughing along with the brothers.

When he saw me looking at him, he winked.

Michael and Giuseppe sauntered over to the group of girls and I was pleased to note Sally Byrne wasn't among them. They were drinking lemonade from bottles with straws in them.

James said, "Why aren't you going over to impress them too, Danny?"

Danny shrugged, leaning against the low wall. "I have my eye on Danielle McClean. She was at the dance hall last week. You know—the one with the ponytail and the gorgeous eyes."

"Daniel and Danielle?" James laughed. "Double Ds. That's a bit close to the bone, isn't it?"

"Not yet," Danny winked.

James checked how much money we had left and said, "I'm going to get another round in. Come and give me a hand, Victor."

"Good one," Danny said. "'Give me a hand.'"

I'd gotten used to them teasing me about my mickey. It didn't happen often, but when it did, I was able to laugh it off. I said, "I could still beat you in a one-handed fist fight." I punched his shoulder hard enough to give him a dead arm for a few seconds and James slapped me on the back.

We left him at the beach wall and James held his arm in front of me like a barrier when we were about to cross the road. A tractor rolled by, followed by a car that was weaving around the road, trying to get ahead of the tractor. "Maniac!" James shouted as it sped away.

At the other side of the road, he held the door of the pub open and said, "You coming?"

I'd been in pubs before, with my dad and the guys from the construction crew. Dad had let me drink a pint if I promised not to tell Mum. Licensing laws weren't as strict in the countryside as they were in the cities, but it was still weird going in without my dad.

It was dingy inside, with overhead lights that were dimmed so that beer goggles were more effective, and the tables were filled with old men and attractive women who laughed at their jokes in return for free drinks.

We squeezed into a small spot at the bar and I felt James' arm pressed against mine. He smiled at me and nodded to the barman. "Five beers," he said, counting out our pennies.

There was an old man in the corner playing a fiddle and a woman beside him with a bodhrán, striking the goatskin drum with her tipper in time with the man's tune. James bobbed his head and tapped his foot.

He said, "We can go to the dance if you want. I'll get my second wind after another beer."

I shrugged. "I'm all right, thanks. Unless you want to go."

"Not if you don't," he said. "There aren't any girls you want to dance with?"

"With one hand and two left feet?" I laughed. James frowned and I said, "I mean, no, there aren't any girls I want to dance with."

He looked around furtively before saying, "Why not?"

His arm was just there, leaning into me, against my weakened side. I looked down. The back of his hand was pressed against the back of mine, but I had no feeling there. Had anybody seen, it would have been an innocent mushing of bodies in a cramped pub.

"Why not?" he said again.

And somebody bumped into my back, pushing me closer to him. I felt his warm breath on my skin.

I didn't know how to answer his question. And when the barman put the beers down in front of us, I didn't get the chance. I gripped two in one hand while he picked up the others, and I followed him back through the sweaty pub to the door where a sign said, *Drink like you mean it but remember where you hitched your horse!*

Outside, the cool evening air embraced us. A bank of clouds was stacking up on the horizon and the sun was hidden from us. Across the road, Michael had jumped onto the wall and was waving at us with frantic arms to get our attention. "You'll never guess what," he shouted.

Before we crossed the street, James said, "Let's just stay here on the beach. We don't need to go dancing to have a good time."

I smiled. I still didn't have any words.

When we joined the others and handed over their beers, Michael's words tumbled out of his mouth.

"Slow down," James told him.

Giuseppe said, "There's a shipwreck that hasn't even washed up yet."

"Where?" we asked.

"Beyond the bay," Danny said. "Apparently it's one of those old ships like you don't see any more."

"What kind of ship?"

"I don't know. A big one. Everyone's talking about it. It's just sitting out there in the water, waiting for the tide to bring her in."

James drank from his bottle and stared across the beach to the sun-dazzled water. "If it's not a warship, I wonder where it came from," he said.

"Spanish Armada," Michael said. "Or a ghost ship."

"Hardly likely," James said. Then he turned to me. "We should go."

"Now?"

"Not now. It's too late. In the morning?" He looked at us. "Michael, we can take your rowboat out."

"I don't know," he said. "My dad will kill me if we lose it."

"How are we going to lose a rowboat?" Giuseppe asked him.

"It'll be an adventure," James said. He held his bottle out to be clinked. "In the morning. Deal?"

Danny and Giuseppe touched their beers to his, and the three of them looked at Michael and me. Michael screwed his face into thought before nodding. He put his bottle in the centre with the others.

"Victor?" James asked.

I touched my dead arm and looked at the ocean. I'd never been out to sea before.

"You'll be fine," James said. "Are you in?"

The dark clouds and the vastness of the ocean left me feeling uneasy. But wherever James went, I would follow.

I tapped the neck of my beer against theirs.

"I'm in," I said.

chapter 9

the present

"Shush," I said.

James held the rooftop door open as Giuseppe pulled Danny's wheelchair over the lip, wheeling him backwards until they were clear of the door.

"Keep it down," I said, peering over the wall to the ground below. I could see the entryway from here, the light spilling onto the dark steps.

In a whisper, we sang Happy Birthday and Danny clapped his hands together. Giuseppe pulled a party hat over his brother's head and pushed the elasticated string under his chin.

"How old am I now?" Danny asked.

"Too damn old," James said.

"Speak for yourself."

James gripped my arm as he eased into a foldable deck chair and I lit the candles on Danny's cake before telling him to blow them out. His breath was weak and Giuseppe helped extinguish the last of them.

"Am I ninety-three or ninety-four?"

"Neither," his younger brother told him. "You're ninety-two."

"What does that make you?" Danny asked.

"A spring chicken," Giuseppe said.

James folded his arms. "Not one of us on this roof is a spring chicken."

I didn't say anything. He wasn't wrong.

It was late October and I gave them blankets to drape over their legs. Winter's touch finds a home in aged knees before it worms its way into hearts. I'd worked eleven nights straight because Mrs Conway sacked one of the other porters and couldn't find a replacement, and she promised me a full weekend off as soon as she could hire somebody. But I didn't mind.

Yesterday morning, just before dawn, while I was wheeling an occupied gurney out to the waiting coroner, James had called to me from his room. He caught a glimpse of the shrouded body as Gloria and the attendant wheeled it into the lift, and he said, "Who is it this time?" Death was frequent here.

"Mr Heeley," I said.

I could still feel the chill of death in the corridor.

James said, "It's Danny's birthday tomorrow."

"I'll wish him happy birthday," I said. I'd known it was his birthday. I had all their dates marked on my phone calendar in case I ever forgot them.

"Buy whiskey," James said.

"I can't bring alcohol into a nursing home."

"Why not?"

"Because I'll get fired."

He rolled his eyes. "Sneak it in."

"James," I pleaded.

"*Stephen*," he said, emphasising the name.

And I nodded. I'd had to stop on the way to work this evening at a supermarket, and I got carded at the counter when I bought a bottle of whiskey and a birthday cake in a plastic tub. The woman at the store studied my ID and said, "What's your secret?"

"Oil of Olay," I said. "And the blood of seven virgins."

"Hard pressed to find many of those around here," she said. She handed my licence back and charged me a euro for a carrier bag.

I stored the bag in my locker in the staff room until Mrs Conway said good night and Gloria slipped out the back for a smoke. She always came back stinking of perfume and Trebor mints, but it never masked the smell. I crept upstairs to the roof and hid the bag by the side of the door, then grabbed a few deck chairs from the boiler room. I guess they'd normally be dotted around the garden in the summer months.

When the residents were shipped off to bed, I did a security sweep, made a fresh pot of tea in the staff room and warmed some chocolate chip cookies in the microwave, hoping the smell would entice Gloria to stay downstairs. I waited until after midnight before going to the third floor and rapping three times on James' door. A secret knock.

He opened it instantly, dressed in a suit with his tie done up with perfect attention.

When I carried Danny and his wheelchair up the final

flight of stairs, with James keeping watch at the corridor, Giuseppe said, "Somebody's had their Weetabix."

I flexed my skinny arms, playing along.

When we were settled on the roof, chairs in a circle, and the cake was cut, Giuseppe said, "We should have brought a wireless up."

"What's a wireless?" I asked, fitting into the stereotype of a modern teenager.

"Music," Giuseppe said.

I pulled my phone out and dropped a playlist of 90s music. The 90s was my favourite decade for beats. It was inane and toneless. It helped me sleep.

"That's just noise," James said, as if he was the first person to ever say so.

To appease him, I found a 50s playlist. Songs that actually had lyrics. Something you could shuffle your feet to. Men are informed by the music of their teens. It shapes them. And these men, these old friends of mine, would have been shaped by rock 'n' roll.

"Who sang this one?" Danny asked.

"Chuck Berry," James said, tapping his foot.

I turned the volume down. I didn't want anybody to hear us.

"Where's the booze?" James asked. I twisted the cap off and handed the bottle to him, and before he drank from it, he said, "For Michael."

He poured a splash on the ground and the others were silent for a minute.

"You still look familiar," Giuseppe said to me when the bottle had been passed around twice.

I drank some but kept my mouthfuls small and manageable. There was a time, somewhere around the 1960s, where I tried to drink myself into a stupor. For six days, I ingested bottles of vodka and rum and a bottle of disgusting port that I raided from the back of a shop. My stomach churned and my vomit was thick and black.

But I didn't get drunk.

I took another small swig and handed the bottle to Danny. "I've told you. I just have one of those faces."

Giuseppe said, "Who does he remind you of, James?"

James didn't look at me. "Nobody."

"No," Giuseppe said. "He reminds me of someone."

I said, "We should go back inside before we're missed."

Giuseppe went quiet and I avoided his gaze for as long as I could.

When the whiskey bottle was almost empty, Danny said, "How long has it been now?"

"Since what?" Giuseppe asked.

"Since Michael went."

"Too fucking long," James said.

A bat skittered over the roof and a pair of headlights flashed at the end of the road as a car turned down Walcot Avenue.

The music had turned maudlin and so had the mood.

I kept my eyes on the roof access door, hoping nobody would come through it. Hoping somebody would.

"Victor," James said.

"Aye," Giuseppe said.

They were silent again.

Danny passed the bottle to Giuseppe. "Where did he ever

go?"

"Who?"

"Victor."

I held my breath.

"Left Ireland, last I heard," James said. "He was a cad."

"Such a cad," Danny agreed.

I could see how tightly James was gripping the arms of his chair. He said, "I loved that bastard, once upon a time."

"We know," Danny said.

"What do you mean, you know?" James' words were harsh.

"Hold your piss," Danny told him. "Everybody knew what you thought of him. It didn't have to be spoken out loud."

Giuseppe said, "It couldn't be talked about back then. Times were different."

"Don't I know it."

"He loved you too," Giuseppe said. "Didn't you, Victor?"

I looked at him. But he wasn't staring at me. He was watching the dark clouds. I couldn't breathe. James covered his eyes and cried. It sounded like a cough. Then he sniffed back his emotions and said, "Who's got the damn whiskey? I'm half sober over here."

And Danny said, "What age am I now?"

"Ninety-two," Giuseppe reminded him.

"That's a good innings," Danny said. And I saw three seventeen-year-olds passing a bottle of whiskey around.

I let them finish the drink, and when Danny was asleep, his chin on his chest, I roused him, peeled his party hat off, and carried him down to his room. I stood watch in the corridor while James and Giuseppe hobbled down from the stairwell, and I asked Giuseppe if he needed anything.

"Just my youth," he said. "Like you have yours."

I smiled. "If only I could."

He nodded good night and I closed his door. Danny was already snoring.

I leaned against the doorframe of James' room. He was struggling to get his tie off so I said, "Let me," and I slipped the thin end out of the knot. I undid the top two buttons of his shirt as he stood there with his fingers curled tightly into the palms of his hands.

I was wrong. Old age wasn't wrinkles and bad posture. It was a disease.

"Victor," he said.

I looked at him. Years ago, when we were seventeen, he was taller than me. Now, he was shortened by age, his spine compressed through years of life.

"Victor was special," James said.

"I'm sure he'd say you were special, too."

"Of course he would," James said. "That's Victor all over. A liar."

I opened another of his shirt buttons, exposing more of his thinning, white chest hair, and stepped away from him. "Can you take it from here?" I asked. I backed out of his room. I couldn't look at him.

Because he was right.

chapter 10

1949

The beach was deserted. It was six in the morning and the gulls were angry as they circled over our heads. Behind us, the dawn sun was just a haze, and in the west, across the ocean, the sky was grey and leaden.

Michael wore an orange life vest over his shirt, and the pale legs that jutted out from his knee-length shorts were skinny and dusted in blond hairs. He looked like a child compared to us adults.

"Take that stupid thing off," Danny told him, poking at the straps of his inflated vest.

"What if we capsize?" Michael asked. We had carried his rowboat to the beach from the shed at the back of his modest house and dragged it across the sand to the shoreline.

"We won't capsize," Danny said. "And if we do, we'll just use your big head to float on. We don't need life jackets."

"Do we even know which way we're going?" I asked. The ocean was calm on the surface, and there was no sign of the shipwreck. If it even existed.

James said, "That way." He pointed out to sea.

"Very funny," I said.

We pushed the boat into the water. Getting into it was a two-handed affair and I was struggling against the tide with the water up to my thighs. But from behind me, James nudged his shoulder against my butt to help me over the edge. I muttered a thanks as I righted myself and he winked. He climbed in after me.

Danny and Giuseppe sat beside each other and took the oars to paddle but they were fighting in different directions. Michael had to instruct them.

"Stroke," he said. "And stroke."

"Stroke this," Danny said, making an obscene gesture.

We bobbed and the boat turned.

Michael had a compass. It was a plastic thing, probably from a Christmas cracker, but he pointed and said, "I guess it's that way."

I could feel James on the bench beside me. His leg was pressed against mine and even through our damp trousers, his skin was warm.

I put my mickey on the bench between us and he didn't move away. My fingers were curled and my thumb was twitching, even though I couldn't feel it. Sometimes it itched. Other times it was just dead.

"And I bet nobody thought to bring a camera," Michael said, producing his dad's Kodak Brownie from a duffel bag. He held the black camera box against his chest, looking down at the small viewfinder, and took a photograph of me and James.

"Get one of us," Giuseppe said, still pulling on his oar.

"I've only got seven left."

James pressed his leg firmer against mine, but when I looked at him, assuming he was trying to attract my attention, he wasn't watching me. I eased my leg into his, pushing with gentle force, and a smile played at the side of his face.

I turned my head away, staring at the horizon, and when I glanced at him again, his eyes were closed against the sun.

Michael pointed. "Look! Over there."

It was still some distance away, but sulking on the ocean was the dark shape of an impressive ship, like an old galleon or—as Michael had joked—something from the Spanish Armada.

"Holy hell," the brothers said. They rowed faster.

"I don't like the look if it," Michael said.

"Shut up," Danny told him. "What are you scared of?"

"Nothing," Michael said. Then, "Maybe it's full of convicts."

"Or maybe," Danny suggested, "it's full of Giuseppe's wild bears, and they're starving. I bet humans taste like sheep."

"That's not even funny," Michael said.

There were other boats, other people trying to get a good look at the wayward shipwreck. When we inched closer, under the enormity of its hulking form, a police boat zipped across the water. A voice from its loudspeaker said, "Return to shore. This area is not secure. For your own safety, return to shore."

Other rowboats and small speedboats were navigating around each other to get close enough to the massive vessel. I heard the creak and groan of its timber from here, and the flap of what remained of its sails, high above us, tattered strips of thick canvas that snapped and stuttered in the breeze.

The wood looked black with soot, as though it had been burned, but there was no smell of old fire. At the front of the prow, a figurehead of a strange gargoyle bared its menacing teeth.

"Jesus, Mary and Joseph," Michael said, making a sign of the Cross as he craned his neck and took a photo.

"And the wee donkey," Giuseppe added.

"Return to shore. I repeat, return to shore. This area is not safe."

"We need a closer look," James said.

The police boat had turned and was powering back the way it came, all the way to the far end of the massive ship.

"Quick," James said. "Go that way."

Somebody in another rowboat called to us, but we ignored him. The brothers put their backs into it as they steered us around the end of the morbid ship and out of view of the police. One lone gull circled overhead before it disappeared, and from the far side of the vessel, the noises from the other boats were dull and distant.

I pointed. "There's the anchor's chain."

James said, "We can't climb it. We'll be too exposed."

Something deep within the galleon groaned and splintered. Danny and Giuseppe rowed us closer to the black hull. At the water line, we saw the crust of slime, algae and barnacles that disappeared beneath, and when we were close enough, I reached out and touched the scorched wood. It left black stains on my fingers.

"It's definitely been burned," I said. James leaned across

me to press his hand against it.

Along the side of the hull, which must have been over a hundred feet long, there were cracks and holes that were above the water level. None of them looked very big.

"There," Giuseppe pointed. A hole, right by the waterline, was wide enough for us to squeeze through one at a time. As they drew us closer to it, he gingerly poked his head through the gap. When he righted himself, rubbing the back of his hand on his nose, he said, "Smells rank. But there's a floor about a foot below the opening."

"No way," Michael said. "It's not safe."

But Danny was already tying the rowboat's mooring line to a splintered board at the edge of the hole.

"James," Michael pleaded. "Tell them we're not going in."

"I'm game," James said. "Victor?"

He was smiling at me and his eyes made me brave. I didn't hesitate. Even as Danny was doubling the knot on the sharp piece of hull, I dived headfirst through the narrow hole. I tried not to think about the ancient woodworm-infested floor giving way as I landed on it, plunging me to an icy death, but once my upper body was through, I had nowhere else to go. With my good arm, I hauled myself inside. The floor, although it was black and rotten, was strong enough to hold me.

"Holy shit," Danny laughed. "Look whose balls dropped overnight."

"Piss off," I said, my words echoing in the dark chamber. Their voices were muffled and I was alone. For a second, I thought that if I poked my head back through the hole to the outside, I'd be in Seventeenth Century Spain or France.

Whichever country ancient galleons were from.

I stood up on shaky legs, feeling the ship listing beneath me. I looked around as first James, then the others, wormed through the hole. It was too dark to see anything, but I heard the squelch of my shoes on the wet floor and I'd convinced myself that four hundred rats were staring at us from the dark.

Michael was the last man in. He gripped his life vest and whispered, "We'll be caught. I know we will."

Giuseppe punched his arm.

I knew James was smiling as he leaned out through the hole and brought Michael's duffel bag in. He said, "Please tell me you brought a torch."

"Of course I did," he said. "I'm not thick." He unzipped the bag and the noise it made scratched into the darkness and got lost among the echoes. He held up two torches. They were silver, with bulky lamps and red on/off switches.

James took the torches from him and tested them, then said, "We'll take one." He stood by my side in the darkness, the white beam of light pushing at the shadows that surrounded us.

"Dibs on the other one," Danny said, yanking it from James' hand.

"Hey," Michael moaned.

"All right," James said. "Let Michael have it. It belongs to him, after all. You three go that way. We'll go this way. First team to reach the top deck wins."

James pushed his hand against my back and we stumbled across the rotting floorboards. Something creaked below us and we stopped, waiting to see if the floor would give way.

It didn't.

From across the empty space, we heard Danny say something about the poop deck and laugh.

"Kids," James said. I heard the eye-roll as he said it, but the light from the torch wasn't strong enough to create a splashback to reveal his features.

He pushed the beam of light around. There was a hole where a door should have been, and he eased over the threshold, testing the flooring. It was safe.

We were in a corridor, with a ceiling that crumbled an inch or two above our heads, and it leaked dust and grime from cracks along its surface.

"It's not a warship," he said. "At least not from the world war. And it doesn't look like a Viking ship."

When he slipped into a room, the corridor went black and I had to reach my hands around to find my way. I said, "Where the heck would a boat this old come from? It must've been floating on the tide for centuries."

"Maybe it was submerged and something brought it back to the surface. An earthquake or something."

"Can that happen?" I asked.

He said, "Maybe."

The room we were in had a broken table and the remains of a wooden chair. There was nothing else. Everything was black with soot or green with algae and the air was thick with the dank smell of mould.

We went further down the corridor and we heard the others in another part of the ship.

"Better hurry," James said.

Ahead of us, there was a set of narrow stairs that went up.

"Watch your step."

"I can't see," I said.

James said, "Here." He turned the beam of the torch and held his hand out.

I hesitated. Holding hands is okay when you're being led up the dark staircase of an abandoned—and possibly haunted—ancient galleon. Right?

I took his hand and his warm fingers tightened around mine.

We went up.

At the top, the door was blocked. It was splintered and in pieces, but something on the far side was stopping it from opening. James shone the beam through the narrow gap.

There was a groan of twisted wood from deep within the ship and I realised I was leaning heavily to the left. We were listing.

"We have to push," James said, and when he spoke, we heard one of the brothers laughing. It sounded like they were higher up than we were.

I nodded.

"On three."

I didn't wait. I heaved against the broken door but it didn't budge. We needed to beat them to the top.

We pushed and shoved, and James kicked his foot through the splintered wood. Whatever was holding it in place shifted an inch. "Again," James said.

It moved. James pushed me through the tight gap and he followed.

The flashlight flickered. Somebody whispered something and it wasn't us.

We listened. I couldn't tell if I heard the scratching of rats or the twisting of timber. Everything was echoing inside my head, including my heartbeat.

James gripped my arm. "You all right?"

I nodded. He was standing close to me. Closer than he should be.

His hand was still on my arm.

He lowered the torch beam and I couldn't see his face.

I said, "James?"

He said, "Yeah?"

But I couldn't say anything else. I felt his breath on my face. He was a shadow in front of me. I looked at my feet and in the dull ache of the torchlight, I saw his shoes, one foot sliding closer to me.

He said, "Victor."

I looked up. His face was there, a black mirage in the dark. He leaned closer.

And the ship protested.

It cracked. The floor twisted and I was thrown from his arms.

I fell into the corridor beyond the door and James tumbled backwards, through the gap we'd forced, and I saw the torch beam tumble down the stairs.

"James!"

He didn't answer. Or if he did, I couldn't hear him over the groan of the ship as its hull tore apart. There was daylight above me. The crumbling crack of a mast falling aside.

I was thrown against a black wall as we tilted and yawed.

I smacked my head against something hard, and when I tried to stand, I realised I was kneeling in water. My mickey ached and I cradled it.

"Victor?" I heard James shouting. He was alive.

Something tore. I don't know if it was the ship or the ocean. I was plunged into the water. And I thought: Michael will survive. He's the only one wearing a life vest.

I couldn't swim.

I splashed and kicked my legs, trying to find something to cling to, but the ship was pulling away from me. My face bobbed above the waterline before I was submerged, and then there was only darkness.

Thick, black, unrelenting darkness.

I felt my hair floating above me. Was that weird? I'd never been deep underwater before. I opened my eyes. And then I closed them because it was just as dark.

I was falling. Down? Up? Space had no meaning.

I tried not to let water into my lungs, but I was running out of oxygen. Instinct made me open my mouth to breathe. And a fog came to me. It smiled at me.

And I smiled back.

And then something gripped me. Hands. A body. Big and dark and heavy behind me.

It tugged at me.

No, I wanted to say. Leave me.

But I couldn't.

And I choked. My face was above the water, and I didn't want to open my eyes, but when I did, I saw a cavern above me, a pocket of air inside the broken ship.

"James?" I croaked.

"Shush," the voice whispered. And I knew it wasn't James. I couldn't move. I was wrapped in its embrace.

"Shush," it soothed. "You want me. Do you want me?"

I shook my head. I didn't want this.

I struggled against him. I felt its body at my back, something firm pressing against me.

He said, "Love me."

I said, "Let me go."

And I felt his lips against my neck. Soft, cold, tender lips. He kissed me.

A tingle ran across my flesh. "You're cold," I said.

He kissed me again.

"No," I said.

"Yes," he told me.

And then his teeth grazed my skin. He cut into me. And I wanted it. I felt it. Needed it. Something entered me, or left me, I don't know. But his mouth was at my neck. His arms were wrapped around me.

I was hard. I couldn't breathe, and I turned my head, giving him fuller access to my flesh. He moaned into me. And I gave myself to him.

But the boat yawed again and I snapped my eyes open. The cavern above me was moving, rotating, and the ship was going down.

The thing that had rescued me hissed. His teeth pulled out of my neck and he backed away.

And before I disappeared under the water, I saw his face. Gold eyes shone. And there was black blood on his chin.

My blood.

And as the galleon lurched into the ocean, the morning sunlight filtered through the murky water. I was going down. And my blood mushroomed in front of my face as I sank into the oblivion.

chapter 11

the present

"Where's James?" I whispered. Giuseppe had been asleep in a highbacked chair in the common room and milky saliva had formed in the corner of his lips. "Giuseppe?" I asked.

He snorted in his sleep and I turned. In the chair beside him, Danny gripped a handheld mirror—something the therapy staff had been using with him. Playing *Guess the Face* or whatever. I don't know. For the past few weeks, Danny was slipping out of reality. Or into it. Who's to say?

"Danny?" I crouched in front of him, my hands on the arms of his chair as if he'd escape me given half the chance. It hadn't been that long since we'd celebrated his birthday on the roof.

Danny looked at the face in the mirror. He'd been deteriorating fast.

"Danny, where's James?"

He blinked at himself. Smiled. "Danny James," he said.

"Focus, Danny. Do you know where James is?"

Danny turned the mirror to face me and I didn't like what I saw there. He said, "That's me."

I nodded and patted the blanket that'd been draped over his knees. I'd worry about him later.

When I got to work this evening, the common room had been busy. A visiting guest had brought a karaoke machine and Nancy Williams and Tanner Graham were singing old Wolfe Tones songs. Some of the other residents were on their feet, making shuffling movements that passed for dancing. When Nancy was too tired to sing another one, Tanner held his microphone in a liver-blemished hand and warbled a Dubliners' song without any music.

I'd seen Danny and Giuseppe at the back of the room and figured James had been with them, so I clocked in and did my first security sweep of the upper floors. That's when I'd smelled Death. He'd returned. And he was on James' floor. I stood by the stairwell, staring down the corridor at the dark shadow that skulked near the end of the hall. I couldn't move.

"James?" I called, but my voice wasn't there.

I dragged my feet along the carpet. I needed to see, even if my body wouldn't let me.

"James?"

But the shadow of Death clung outside Albert MacInnis' door, one of the residents that seldom left his room and never had visitors. Albert knew what it meant to be alone.

So did I.

I opened his door. Death hadn't entered yet, and Albert was asleep, his head on a thin pillow, mouth ajar. But I heard

Death's footfalls in the distance. He was coming, and there was little I could do. I closed the door and went to James' room where Death's shadow almost reached.

He wasn't there, so I went downstairs. Danny and Giuseppe were alone and James wasn't shuffling in the middle of the floor with the others. I checked the roof and he wasn't there either.

I walked through the kitchen and the rear corridors where nobody ventured, but James was gone.

I found Gloria on the first floor, putting Nancy Williams to bed. The old woman was still singing karaoke songs through her tiredness.

"Where's James?" I asked.

"Jesus," Gloria said. "Why are you always sneaking around? Give me a hand over here."

"Sneaking up on people is fun," I said. I took Nancy's other hand and helped to ease her into bed.

Nancy stopped singing when my fingers touched her bare arm. She looked at me and said, "Though I freeze, I am fire."

Gloria said, "What was that, Nancy?"

I pulled my hand away from her. "Probably some song lyrics," I said. I felt Nancy's grief on my fingertips that burned with coldness. "The Wolfe Tones never did make sense, did they, Nancy?" At my mention of the rebel music band, the old woman struck up another song.

We tucked her in and when Gloria closed her bedroom door, the look she gave me was a wary one. She said, "She's not long for this world."

I nodded. "Are any of them? Where's James?" I asked.

"He had a heart attack this afternoon," she said. "If you're going to creep around all night, we'll have to get you a cowbell."

Panic caught in my dry throat. "Did he—is he alive?"

Gloria studied my face and I looked away from her, hiding the hurt that coloured my eyes. She said, "He was admitted to Harvest Lane Hospital. You spend a lot of time with him and those brothers, don't you?"

He had to be alive. Death's shadow hadn't pissed on his door yet. "They've taken to me," I said. "What can I say, I'm a devil to be around."

She nodded. "For a kid, you're very ballsy."

"Thank you."

She walked away from me.

I said, "Has there been any news? Since he was admitted."

At the head of the corridor, she turned to me. "Don't get attached, kid. Once they're wheeled out of here, they seldom come back. And if they do, they're never the same."

But I was already attached. I had been for years.

I couldn't concentrate. I helped put the other residents to bed and administer medications—antihypertensives, anticoagulants, antiarrhythmics; anything with "anti" in the name—and I made sure Danny and Giuseppe were asleep before I looked for Gloria. If only there was an antideath pill.

She was in the staff room with a stack of handwritten notes that she was typing up on a clunky old laptop and a mug of cooling tea on the table by her arm. When I went in, I held one hand to my forehead and the other against my stomach.

"I don't feel well," I told her. It was the truth.

"Stay over there," she said. "Whatever it is, I don't want

to catch it. I have a family get-together this weekend and no time for sickness."

I needed to get out of there. "Maybe I should just go home," I suggested. "Get a good night's rest."

Gloria said, "Not a chance. We're short staffed as it is. Take some paracetamol and get back to work."

I coughed, forcing it up from my lungs. I didn't cover my mouth as I hacked into the air. This is how sick I am, my body told her. I poured a glass of water and took a gulp. I knew what would happen.

I vomited into the sink.

"Jesus," she said. "Just stay over there." She reached for her phone, covering her mouth and nose with one hand. "I'll call the agency for a temp. But it's after ten o'clock. You can't leave your post until they get here."

I pushed another cough out and nodded weakly, leaning against the countertop. When she left the room, I checked the time on my phone. I didn't know how easy it would be to find temp staff this late at night.

Gloria called the agency twice before getting an answer and, finally, forty minutes later, I pulled my coat on. I coughed again. "I'm sure I'll be fine by tomorrow."

Gloria held the front door as she held her breath. "Just get out of here. You look like death."

"Thanks," I said. I limped down the walkway to the gate, hunched in my sickness. She was still at the door, watching me. So I coughed again and retched as if I was going to throw up.

And then I turned the corner.

The night was wet and quiet. Clouds tempered echoes like

cotton wool in a dead man's mouth.

I spat, just to clear the taste from my mouth, and I made it from the manor to the edge of the village in no time. As I walked across the village hospital's car park in the dull warmth of tall streetlights, I heard a nearby clock strike eleven p.m.

Not quite the witching hour.

I stood outside the automatic doors of the main entrance and didn't know what to do. The threshold was cold and uninviting, and I couldn't enter. So I edged around the corner of the building and closed my eyes. I listened.

I couldn't feel him—I wasn't a psychic—but I heard him. The pulse of his blood, slow and irregular, but James. I went around the hospital, under a pagoda and past a small chapel. His room was upstairs at the rear of the grubby building and, in the darkness, I knew I couldn't be seen.

I stood on the wet pavement and took my shoes and socks off. The ground was cold, but doing this with my shoes on was difficult.

I floated.

Don't ask me, okay? Nothing I do surprises me any longer.

I looked around, then glided up to his window on the third floor, my hands pressed against the glass, and I watched him in the bed. He was awake, blinking at the ceiling in the darkness. His bedroom door was open, soft light falling at the foot of his bed, and I heard the whisper of breath in his throat.

He was alive.

I needed him to be alive.

My toes, sharp nails that I hadn't cut in some time, scuffed the wall beneath his window.

James turned his head and I pressed myself against the building beside his room.

When I looked again, James was sitting up, clinging to his drip pole. He was staring at the window.

I held my breath. Closed my eyes.

I heard him push his feet into backless bedroom slippers, the kind all old men need but nobody knows how to walk in. And then I saw his breath fog the window in front of his face.

It was dark out, and I clung to the wall. James stared across the night.

When he opened the window of the old cottage hospital, I wanted to slither down to the ground where I belonged. But he said, "You can come in."

He shuffled back to the bed, the creak of his drip pole following him.

I pressed my back to the wall, four floors up, and covered my face with my hands.

He said, "Fine. Stay out there."

So I went in.

I crawled through the window and faced him, my damp feet leaving wet prints on the tiled floor.

"Hi," he said.

"Hey."

He nodded, as if the greeting was enough, and he eased onto the bed, sitting on the edge with his feet a few inches off the floor, still clinging to his drip pole.

My throat was dry and full of words. I cleared it.

The fingers of his right hand were curled into his palm, twisted with arthritis or the need to punch me. His eyes, hooded and tired, scanned my face. There was a flash of something cloudy there, a storm that needed to be free.

"I—" I said. But all my other words were gone. The chill of emotion at the base of my neck made me hunch my shoulders and I rubbed my arm with my right hand, the left one tingling like it hadn't done in years.

My toenails scratched the tiled floor.

He said, "What were you doing out there?"

"Just hanging around," I said. I closed the window. There was a draft and I didn't want him to catch a cold. I faced him but couldn't look at him directly. *Here I am*, my mind said. *Don't look at what I've become*, it screamed.

His smile was wry. "Victor," he said.

It wasn't a question, but I nodded anyway. I could see the strings of thought that crossed his mind, like tangible cords from one conclusion to another.

"Am I supposed to scream now?" he asked. "Call for help or run?"

I shook my head. "I'd settle for a hug."

And James held his arms out. I went to him and he embraced me. Those familiar arms. Those stranger's arms.

He held me.

"I knew it was you," he said.

"How?"

"How could I not?" James said. "I knew it was you all along."

chapter 12

1949

I opened my eyes and screamed. My body ached worse than if I'd fallen from the top of a New York skyscraper. Somebody was jabbing needles into my eyes and I raised my hands, clawing at my face to stop them. But there was nobody there.

"It's okay," Mum said. I heard her voice but I couldn't see her.

"Where are you?"

"I'm here," she said.

I reached for her and felt her fingers on my arm.

"It's okay," she said again. "You're safe." And then, "What the hell were you thinking?"

I had no idea what she meant. I wasn't thinking. It hurt to think. I squeezed my eyes closed and shielded them with the crook of my arm. God, my head hurt. My whole body hurt.

I tried to sit up but couldn't move. "The ship," I said. I

remembered the enormous galleon and—something dark. Dirty.

Why couldn't I open my eyes?

"It's too bright," I said.

Mum drew the curtains and pressed her hand against my forehead. "You have a fever, sweetheart. Here. Drink some water."

I took a sip from the glass that she held for me and it got stuck in my throat. I couldn't swallow it. It dribbled out of my mouth like a fountain and soaked my sweat-drenched pyjamas. I coughed. "Mum," I said, broken, pathetic. Was there blood in the water? It was too dark to see.

"It's all right, son. Get some rest."

"What happened?" I asked.

"You were in another accident," she said. "I'll have to start calling you a klutz."

My left hand didn't ache. Or if it did, everything else ached worse. I couldn't laugh at her lame joke. And even though the room was dark, I kept my eyes closed. My head didn't hurt so much that way.

From the doorway, I heard Aunt Cara. "He's awake?"

"He is," Mum said, and there was the laughter of relief in her voice.

Cara said, "Good," and then she was gone.

I cracked my eyes open enough to see the outline of Mum. I said, "James? The others?"

"The little one," Mum said. "What was his name?"

"Michael."

"He broke a leg in two places and cracked his collarbone. Miraculously, everyone else got out with a few bruises."

"Jesus," I said.

"Language," Mum said.

I patted my good hand over my chest and abdomen. "Am I hurt? I ache everywhere."

Mum said, "Just get some rest, son."

"Am I hurt?" I asked, panicked. I tried to look down at my body but moving my neck made me feel like I was drowning in lava. I had no idea if all my limbs were there. Is that why my mickey didn't ache?

"You're fine," she said. "You're a bit banged up, and your neck is—well. It'll heal. The doctor said you were lucky."

I touched my neck and a memory coagulated under my fingertips. There was a padded bandage there, fat and crisp with dried blood. I heard the echo of a sharp hiss, felt the press of a stranger's body, and I shivered under the thin blanket.

"Drink some more water."

"No," I said.

She patted my chest and kissed my forehead. And then she closed the door behind her.

My stomach churned. I kicked the blanket off and tried to unbutton my pyjama shirt to get some air, but I didn't have the strength. And a second later, I was freezing and clawed the blanket over me again.

I slept. And in my sleep, I dreamt about giant ships filled with clanking ghosts in rattling chains, and black cats clawing at black mice. And a man—a thin man with a white face and a red chin.

When I woke, there was darkness. I couldn't see the faint glow of the hands on my bedside alarm clock. My body was in agony, shivering and sweating, and my sheets were wet.

I had pissed myself and I was too sore to care. I cried. The stench of my urine was rife.

I couldn't call out to Mum and the tears were burning my cheeks. A Crucifix on the wall opposite the window glowed in the darkness—Aunt Cara had hung one in every room, even the bathroom—and I remembered Jesus' last words from when Mum used to drag me to Mass, before Dad was gone. *Why have you forsaken me?*

I lay in my own stink.

And I fell asleep again.

When I woke, my sheets had been changed. There was a swatch of dust mites in the light where the curtains didn't meet and Mum sat in the chair beside my bed. There was a shadow over her shoulder. A man. A thin man.

I screamed and the man dissolved.

Mum said, "Shush, son." She patted my hand. "You're burning up," she said. "I'll make soup."

And as I watched her walk across the room, she left a trail behind her, blue and amber lights that faded when she went.

I was sweating, but it was fresh sweat. She'd bathed me while I'd slept.

The bandage at my neck, when I touched it, was clean and warm, and I couldn't sit up. When Mum came back with a bowl of soup, she sat in the chair and stirred it with a spoon. I said, "Close the curtains, please," and she did. I couldn't open my eyes fully.

She fed me a spoonful of tomato soup and when I swallowed, it burned my throat. But it hit my stomach wrong and it came back up. I choked and spluttered and red soup splashed across the bedding.

I retched and gripped my stomach. "Oh, Jesus," I said. And Mum didn't tell me off this time.

I was cramping and my feet were cold and my head was burning.

And then I shit myself. I cried and clenched my eyes against the agony. I couldn't look at her.

The smell of my excrement made me vomit. And the retching made my stomach hurt.

And Mum stroked my cheek and said, "It's okay, sweetie."

She peeled back the dirty blankets and rolled them into a ball.

As she gingerly tugged my darkened pyjama bottoms off, she said, "No harm."

And I cried. I turned my head, ignoring the pain in my neck, and screamed against the pillow.

There is one thing worse than death, and that is dying.

There are two things worse than death: Dying, and having your mother clean you after you've soiled yourself. I cried through the indignity of it.

And then I slept.

In the morning—evening? I had no idea—I heard the sounds of the grandfather clock outside my bedroom, its tick a drumbeat that echoed my pulse. It was dark; the curtains were pulled. I rolled out of bed, gritting my teeth against the agony of movement, and when I fell on the floor, I lay there, unable to move. My feet were still on the bed and my left arm was dead. If I lay still for much longer, my sweat would harden and glue me to the worn carpet with its maroon and brown swirls that made me dizzy.

I clawed at my knees to pull my feet to the floor, and

then rolled onto my stomach. I retched against the carpet, but nothing came, not even saliva. And as I forced myself up against the nightstand, colourful lights popped in front of my eyes like Christmas bulbs that heralded Satan instead of Santa.

Even the marrow in my bones was sore.

I crawled up the nightstand to my feet and then fell to my knees again. And when I fell a second time, I knelt there, with my head in my hands, weeping like a child.

But I stood again. Forced myself upright. And I swayed, unbalanced, feeling a rush in my ears as gravity fought against me. I stumbled across the room and smacked into the wall. I found the light switch and turned it on, and covered my face when the light was too much. I blinked, tears making me blind, and I pressed my fingers into my eyes until the anger of the overhead bulb was just an ache.

I turned to the mirror. My pyjamas hung on my body like broken sails on a ship. Sweat coated my forehead and upper lip. My left eye was swollen and purple and there was a graze on my right cheek like somebody had taken a cheese grater to it. A gash on my temple shone where it had been glued back together.

And the thick padding at my neck was discoloured and puckered.

I stumbled closer to the mirror, pressed my hand against it to keep me upright, and when I had the energy, I propped my mickey against the wall so I didn't fall over, and I peeled the bandage back.

Tearing the tape away from my flesh was painful. But seeing the mess hidden beneath the bandage was worse. My neck was torn. Puckered pieces of white skin pressed against pink furrows and the black remains of blood had jellied into dark rivers like a map of Death's travels.

I touched the greasy skin and when I did it moved away from my finger. Pus fed from the darkness inside.

I retched and my stomach heaved. And when I covered my mouth against the threat of vomit, I fell to the floor. I lay in a heap, unable to move, squinting against the glare of the bulb above my head that was yellow and as bright as the sun.

And then Mum was dragging me to bed.

I thought I heard a whisper that said, "Love me," and I fought violently against my mum's hands, my fingernails cutting into her flesh and drawing scratches there. She slapped my face to calm me down. And when she got me into bed, I said, "I love you."

She said, "I know."

Her hair was a mess from where I'd clawed at her.

I said, "I'm sorry."

Mum kissed my cheek.

In the morning—evening? I had no idea—Mum came to my bedside and pressed the back of her hand to my forehead. She tried to feed me a banana that was mashed in a cup, and when it hit my stomach, I vomited again.

The ripe smell of the banana on my chin made my stomach churn and I vomited a second time.

She sent for the doctor who poked me like I was a bull at market. He put a cuff around my arm and told me to make a fist and said, "Hmm," while he squeezed a pump in his hand. He listened to my chest and listened to my back and told me to cough. He said, "Has there been any blood in his stool?"

Mum said, "There was some spotting, but not a lot."

When the doctor turned me onto my side, away from him, I couldn't stop the tears escaping my tired eyes. They rolled over the bridge of my nose onto the pillow.

Mum said, "Is he going to be all right?"

And the doctor made noncommittal noises at the back of his throat.

He flashed a light in my eyes and I jammed them shut. "It hurts," I said.

"I don't believe it's a brain injury," the doctor said. "The concussion will be the cause of his headaches, confusion and light-sensitivity."

"And his fever?" Mum asked.

"Keep him hydrated. It'll pass. He needs plenty of bed rest. And when he's able, get a hearty meal into him."

My stomach objected to the thought of food.

From the doorway, Aunt Cara said, "The devil doesn't like a fatty."

The doctor said, "You don't need to fatten him. Just keep him healthy. Open the window. Plenty of fresh air and a cold compress. If he isn't any better in three days, call the surgery."

"You don't open a window for a fever," Aunt Cara said. "Wrap him up; he needs to sweat it out."

"My advice would be to keep him cool." The doctor packed his Gladstone bag and as he brushed past Cara he said, "Try not to kill him."

"Nonsense," Cara said.

"Mum," I said, when the doctor was gone. I tugged at the neck of my pyjama shirt. "I can't breathe."

She unbuttoned it and pressed a damp cloth against my

burning chest, and I remembered when James had done something similar. My skin was splotched with a heat rash. "Drink some water," she said, but I didn't want to. I knew if I did, I'd be sick again.

And in the morning—evening? I had no idea—my flesh was on fire.

Mum came to me and said, "James is downstairs. Are you up to seeing him?"

I rolled on my side, away from her, clutching my churning stomach. I could smell decaying filth from my throat, like a dead cat in an alleyway.

I said, "No."

Mum said, "He'd really like to see you. He brought chocolates."

"Go away," I whispered.

"I'll just let him up for a minute," she said. "It'll be good for you."

"*Go away!*" I screamed.

The light from the doorway made my eyes bleed sticky tears.

I don't think I could cry any more.

Mum said, "Son."

And I held my breath until she left the room.

chapter 13

the present

I listened. Behind the noise of James' pulse, I heard the suck and whine of distant machines keeping death at bay in the small village hospital. There were eleven heartbeats on this floor, and they punched me so much that when James spoke, I barely heard him. God, I was hungry.

He said, "How have you been?"

"Miserable," I said. I pulled out of his heavy embrace. He smelled the same as he always did, and when I looked at him, I still saw James. My James. His wrinkles were just a suit.

I touched his face, running a thumb over the wet sheen beneath his eyes where tears had formed but didn't fall.

"How are you?" I asked.

There was a wheeze in his throat. The back of his hand was black where a needle had bruised him and he looked thinner tonight than he had before. Smaller.

"I got old," he said.

I nodded. I heard footsteps in the corridor beyond his open door and I slouched into the shadows against the wall where the light from outside didn't reach. We both held our breath as the nurse went by.

And then James whispered, "Where the fuck have you been all this time?"

I stayed in the shadows. "Away."

"Why are you back?"

I didn't answer.

"You haven't changed," he said, and I don't think he meant my appearance.

I came out of the shadows. "You haven't, either."

James shook his head. "Help me back into this infernal contraption they call a bed." He raised his arm for me to take it.

When his back was against the pillows, he stopped to breathe, and then said, "I'm too young to feel this old."

I pointed a thumb at my face. "And I'm too old to look this young." We were the same, he and I. I touched the back of his hand and felt his pain. It was black and murky. "Does it hurt?"

He turned his palm up so that my fingers traced the crease of his lifeline. "Sometimes I forget. There's pain and there's not-pain. And in between, there's you." He curled his fingers around mine and the shock of its sting sizzled up my arm. I wanted to take it from him, but it hurt too much.

"But you're okay?"

"It was just a heart attack. My heart was beating worse the first time we kissed."

I let him hold my hand until it burned and then I turned

from him. "I'm sorry," I said.

James said, "Everyone's sorry when it's dark. Why are you here?"

"To see you."

"But why?"

I didn't know. "Because I'm tired," I said. And I meant it. I was tired of everything. These days, I could barely keep my head up, it was weighed down with exhaustion. I had never known what heavy eyelids felt like until recently. I thought it was just an expression, but gravity—and life—was pulling at my lids with careless fingers.

James shuffled on the bed to give me space, and he patted the area beside him. "Lie with me."

I lay down next to him and he rolled onto his side to face me. When he smiled, it was seventeen-year-old James who blinked at me.

"I've missed this," I whispered. I closed my eyes and breathed him in.

He said, "Why did you leave?"

It took a moment for the words to come out. "Look at me. People would have noticed if I'd stuck around."

James brushed an age-gnarled finger over my temple and cheek.

He was silent.

So I said, "Aren't you going to ask me?"

"Ask you what?"

"About this." I indicated my face, my eyes that shone back at me from inside his wide pupils.

"Would it do me any good to know?"

"No," I said.

"It was that damned shipwreck, wasn't it?" When I nodded, he said no more. He tried to smile but grimaced and turned onto his back. "I can't sleep on my side," he said.

"You never could."

James said, "My organs are dying."

"I wish I could stop them." I meant it. I was cursed to watch him die and I didn't have the capability to intervene.

James found my hand, my mickey, and squeezed it. He raised it to his face, my fingers no longer bruised and damaged, and he turned my hand over to inspect it. Then he kissed the knuckles with a reverence I hadn't felt in years. He said, "When you left, I . . . I thought you hated me."

"Never," I said. "Why would I hate you?"

"I thought I loved you too much. In a time when it was wrong."

"What we had wasn't wrong," I said. "You told me that, a long time ago."

He looked at me, my hand still in his. "If things were different," he said, but he didn't finish his thought. "I got married," he said instead.

I smiled. "Somebody needed to look after you without me around to wipe your nose. Was she good to you?"

He swallowed and nodded. Somebody in the next room was snoring. "She was," he said. "Will you stay with me until I fall asleep?"

"Sure."

We lay in silence, James on his back, staring at the ceiling as I studied his wrinkled face. He whispered, "I can't sleep with you watching me like that."

So I turned onto my back beside him.

He laughed like a kid and when I asked him what he found so funny, he said, "This. Us. After all this time."

I said, "I thought about you every day."

James covered his face with a hand and cried. "Me too," he said.

And when he fell asleep, I kissed his cheek and whispered, "I'll stay with you forever."

I slipped out of the window before dawn and found my socks and shoes where I'd left them by the wall. And I lingered, sensing a greying in the east against the bleak darkness of pre-dawn, the imminent rising of the sun. I held my breath and closed my eyes, and then I chickened out.

I ran through the shadows.

And when I was home, I slammed the door behind me and pressed my back to it. I wanted to vomit and expel whatever pain was in my stomach, but I knew it wasn't physical. I took a shower. I never sweat, but I enjoyed the sting of the water on my pale flesh. The water was hot and I held my face under it until it felt like I was drowning. And then I huddled at the base of the tub and wrapped my arms around my knees until the drowning sensation became a feeling of freedom.

I didn't towel-dry my body. I went to bed, my skin wet, and remembered that thing all mothers tell their kids when they're cold and soaked.

"You'll catch your death."

If only.

I shivered. And I laughed because I'd forgotten what shivering felt like.

When sleep threw its blankets over me, I was neither warm nor cold. The only feeling I had was in my shrivelled heart.

And when I woke, somebody was hammering on my front door.

It was seven p.m. and the sun had been down for a couple of hours. I'd forgotten to set my alarm and sleep had held me longer than it needed to.

I pulled a robe on. My skin, from my neck to my knees, was spattered in gooseflesh and my blankets were on the floor.

Whoever was at my door was insistent. They pounded again.

I went downstairs without turning lights on, and when I opened the door, I recoiled. Nurse Gloria was shining a torch in my face. It had a daylight-white bulb.

"Jesus," I said. "What are you doing?"

She shifted the light of the torch away from me and illuminated the hall behind me. The grandfather clock—it was the only thing of Cara's that had survived all this time—spoke between us with its hollow ticking like an admonishing uncle. I'd moved it down from the top floor when I bought the house.

Gloria said, "I was worried about you." And I heard in her voice that she wasn't.

"You shouldn't have been."

"Are you feeling better?" she asked, moving the light back to my face.

I clenched my eyes. "Why aren't you at work?" I didn't start until eight o'clock but Gloria seemed to be there twenty-four hours a day.

She stepped over the threshold without an invitation. "Night off. I thought I'd check up on you." When I backed away from her torch beam, she said, "Haven't you paid your electricity bill?"

I flicked the light switch, if for no other reason than to make her turn the torch off. Who even carries torches these days? She obviously didn't know about the flashlight on her phone. But as she put the torch away in her handbag, I saw the small pepper spray canister dangling from the end of it. Every tool is a weapon.

I pulled my robe tighter. She had no right to be here. "I'm sick," I said and gave her a dry cough. "But I'm not dying."

"With those pasty legs and sunken eyes?" she said. "You could have fooled me." She walked into the lounge and I followed her.

"Please, Gloria. I just need some rest. I'm sure I'll be back at work tomorrow night."

She found the light switch on her own and studied the room. There was a couch in it, and a large TV standing on the floor with a PlayStation beside it. The rug was old and worn, and there was nothing else. I looked poor.

She said, "Is this it?"

"I'm," I said, and I had to remember what age I'd told Mrs Conway, "twenty. I like playing video games. What more do I need?"

"You live alone?" she asked. "No parents? No housemates?" If she'd twisted her neck around any harder as she investigated my home, she'd have snapped it. And I'd have laughed over her corpse.

I said, "How did you get my address?" I was grateful the sun had gone down and she didn't feel the need to pull the curtains open. I couldn't imagine how she'd react seeing the mess of me in the sunlight.

Gloria walked around the couch and kicked the corner of the rug that was curling up in disgust at her arrival. She didn't answer my question. "Sit down, child; you look so weak you're about to fall. Is the kitchen through here? I'll put the kettle on."

She unbuttoned her winter coat.

"There isn't any tea," I said.

"Coffee?"

"Can't stand it myself," I told her.

Gloria nodded. When she walked into the kitchen, I followed. She flicked the light switch and I was grateful that the overhead bulbs didn't light up. I never cooked. If the lights had worked, she'd have seen how dusty the countertops were, how rusted the stove was. She pumped the switch like a piston as if doing it repeatedly would make the lights come on by magic.

I said, "I've been meaning to replace those bulbs but I've been sick. As you know."

"How's James?" she asked, fishing in her handbag for something.

I took her elbow and turned her back towards the lounge. "Who?"

I had to use force because her feet were planted on the tiled floor. I didn't go into the kitchen often, but when I did, I saw James at the back door, pressing a damp cloth against my neck.

"You didn't go and see him at the hospital?" she asked.

"Why would I?" I lied. "Is he okay?"

In the lounge, Gloria shrugged and pulled a herbal teabag

from her handbag. I smelled her. Underneath the scent of perfume and cigarettes, there was no fear. And that scared me.

I feigned a dizzy spell and said, "Gloria, I'm sorry, but do you mind? I've been throwing up for twenty-four hours; I just want to go back to bed."

"I'll keep you company," she said, pulling her coat off.

"Gloria!" I smiled. "There's more than a couple of years between us."

"Don't be disgusting, child. That's not what I meant."

"Then why are you here?" I was nervous now. Why was her heartbeat so steady?

Gloria sat on the couch. She said, "I've looked you up."

"On the company database?" So that's how she got my address.

But she said, "On the internet."

I had no words. I stood barefoot on the rug in front of her and curled my toes into the thin pile. I listened to her pulse and stared at her face.

Gloria put her handbag on her lap and gripped it like a shield. She said, "I was worried about you. So I looked for you on Facebook."

"I'm not on Facebook."

"I noticed. You're not on Instagram or TikTok, either. Which, for a kid, is unheard of."

"I'm not a sociable person," I said. I tightened the knot of the robe's belt at my waist.

Gloria smiled. "You don't exist, do you?"

"Excuse me?"

She sat back on the couch, running her hand over the ancient fabric as if she was admiring it. She said, "When I couldn't find you on social media, I dug further. And as it turns out, Mr Victor Ballinger didn't exist before four months ago."

I clenched my fists as I smelled the strength in her. I was running out of last names to use on official documents.

I said, "What are you insinuating?"

Gloria stood up. "Who are you?" she said. "And I'm not leaving without the truth."

chapter 14

1949

Mum's skin was sliding off her face like melting wax. She said, "How are you feeling?" and I could see her cheekbone protruding through the rotting flesh. When she touched me, her fingertips ignited the hairs on my arm and orange flames blazed over my skin.

I screamed.

And then Mum wasn't there. Dad sat in a rocking chair in the corner of the room, smoking a pipe—which was weird because he only ever smoked unfiltered cigarettes. He said, "Fernuttin's got a mickey just like yours."

I couldn't look at him. My skin wasn't on fire but my brain was. "Who's Fernuttin?" I asked him.

"You're good fernuttin'," Daddy said. He inhaled from his pipe and the dank smell of it made me retch.

Then Mum dragged a damp flannel across my forehead

and smiled a gummy smile with no teeth. And when I realised Dad shouldn't have been there, I said, "Mum, who's that man in the corner?"

Mum said, "Your Da's come to take you home."

Oh God, why was my skin on fire? I tugged at the neck of my pyjamas and they were soaked through. The paisley pattern bled into a blur. "What time is it?" I asked, kicking the blankets off.

Mum said, "It's ten past three," and she put the bedspread over me again.

A month later, I said, "What time is it?"

"It's still ten past three," Mum said.

There was a thick paste in my eyes so I couldn't crack them open. And I knew the sheets were wet but I didn't care if it was sweat or blood or worse.

Aunt Cara's voice cut through the crunching noises in my head when she said, "He's delirious." And when I looked, Dad and his rocking chair were gone and Mum's flesh wasn't molten and shedding from her skull.

She smiled a normal smile in a normal face. "He's going to be all right," she said as she dampened my forehead and cheeks with her cloth.

And in my agony, I said, "Kill me."

At night—I knew it was night because there was an owl sitting on my dresser, blinking at me, and owls only come out at night—there was a cooling breeze from my open window. I gasped at it, trying to swallow the freshness, to ingest the cold. The owl hooted and scratched the wooden dresser with its talons. It turned its head a full rotation and when it spoke again it said, "Who-oo is he?"

I heard horse hooves on the road outside, quiet at first, coming closer, and I wondered if it was James on his milk float coming to rescue me like Rapunzel. I twisted my head to hear better, and then my face was inside the pillow. I swallowed feathers and choked.

But I wasn't inside a pillow. I couldn't be. I knew I was delirious, even though the word had no meaning to me.

"Del-eerie-us," I said and the owl agreed. I hadn't noticed he was wearing trousers.

The sound of the horse's hooves was louder, closer, and it stopped below my window. I listened.

Something crunched in the dirt outside where Aunt Cara's geraniums were. And I laughed. I held my hand over my mouth to silence myself in case I scared him away.

It was James. James had come to see me.

And something tapped on my windowpane, a quiet fingernail offering solace.

"James?" I whispered into the palm of my hand.

"Love me," the voice said. And I knew it wasn't James.

Del-eerie-us. I looked at the owl but the owl was gone. A feather—from the owl? From my pillow?—floated to the carpet.

"Let me in," the voice said. It was sharp and soft and high and quiet. "Let me in," it said.

I shook my head. And I laughed. I clamped my lips shut. "Shush," I whispered.

"Can I come in?"

"Shush."

"Let me in," he hissed. "Do you love me?" he asked.

I said, "I love James." And I screamed into my fist. How

could I say that out loud? There was sweat in my eyes.

The thing outside said, "I can love you better. Let me in."

The shadows in my room coalesced into a gargoyle. It crept across my carpet before dissolving in the light of the streetlamp outside. The curtains billowed in the breeze.

"I love you," he said.

"No."

"I will always love you."

"No."

He tapped against the window again. "I can take away your pain. Just let me in."

My body was in agony. What if he *could* take away my pain? I sat up on my elbows and when I looked at the window I saw...something. Him. It.

But it ducked below the windowsill and said, "Don't you love me?"

"Who are you?" I asked.

"I could be James."

"No," I said.

"I could be better than James."

"Never," I told him.

The thing was quiet. A horse whinnied on the ground below my second-floor window and I heard the rustling of leaves on the summer-ripe trees of the apple orchard at the end of the street. I listened. Was he gone?

"Are you there?" I whispered.

The seconds of silence felt like years before he said, "Can I come in?"

"Are you going to hurt me?"

"I'm going to love you," he said.

And I said, "Okay. You can come in."

I watched as he entered, one slender leg, a foot with no shoe on, owl talons for toenails, and black trousers that were tapered and velvet. And then an arm, long and thin. His hand touched the floor before his other arm entered, and then a head, a final leg. He creaked upright and I heard the snap of his bones beneath his thin skin. He towered over me, seven foot tall or twelve, smiling and frowning at the same time.

I reached up. "Who are you?" I asked.

"I am Amaral," he told me. He came to my side and traced my cheek.

And I gasped. His touch sent a spark of electricity through my skin, a jolt of lightning that was pain as much as it was love. And my throat didn't feel as tight as it had a second before.

"Is that nice?" he asked, and when I brought my fingers to my cheek, he pulled his hand away.

The shadow-gargoyle hunkered at his side, twisting in deformity.

"Touch me again," I begged.

The man brought his face to mine. His eyes were fire, dark and red, and his nose was a sharp cliff over the soft ocean of his lips that were moist and glistened in the streetlight that stole into the room.

"Amaral," I said, tasting his name.

"I can heal you," Amaral told me. "I can make you whole."

He smelled like soil, damp and rich, and his fingernails were blackened. I saw his words leaving his mouth like colourful refractions of dust. They settled on my bed beside my face.

"How can you heal me?"

"You have to want me."

"I want James," I said.

Amaral grew angry. "No," he spat. He put his hand on my throat, his thumb pressing into the padding of my bandage. "Forget James," he said.

"I can't."

"You must," Amaral told me.

I tried to pull away from him but I was too weak. I was trapped under the heavy bedspread, glued to the mattress with incontinence. Shivering with exhaustion, I turned my head.

Amaral turned it back.

"I can make you," he said.

"Make me what?"

"Make you mine."

"No," I cried. "Leave me. Go away."

And then Amaral peeled the blankets from my body, he pushed his hands under my neck and knees and lifted me from the bed.

"Where are we going?" I asked and my voice was weak.

He shushed me as he cradled me in his arms. He exposed a nipple and pressed my head against his narrow chest. His skin was clammy and the thin hairs around the dark areola caressed my cheek.

He held me.

He was strong.

And when my burning tears touched his creamy skin, he sighed.

"Amaral," I said.

He lowered my legs so that I stood on the floor, but he

kept me in his embrace. He turned me to face the mirror, and in the darkness of a flimsy night, I couldn't see him standing behind me.

He pressed his mouth against my ear. "Do you want me?"

I shook my head and his tongue tasted the tender flesh behind my earlobe.

He said, "Love me."

"I can't," I told him. I knew that if he let go of me I would fall at his feet.

He peeled the bandage from my neck and let it skitter to the floor. I saw the dark stretch of skin where my wound was barely healing. And he kissed me there, where it itched.

He held me tighter. And I let him.

When he opened his mouth, I felt no breath on my skin. Only a stink that I wanted to know better. He locked his jaw around the wound and he bit into it. He tore the flesh with his teeth.

I moaned. My neck was on fire. And my erection was painful. I tried to cover myself.

But Amaral gripped me tight, clamping my arms to my sides. He drank from me.

An itch of terrible lust folded inside my stomach and I pressed my trembling body against him, my back to his chest. My butt against his crotch.

I let him hold me. And eat me.

And when he let go, I dropped to the floor.

I wept. My body tingled and the air around my open neck was charged with a lightning sizzle of energy.

"More," I cried.

Amaral leaned over me, his hands on my cheeks. "No

more," he said.

"It hurts," I told him.

"I can take it away."

"Hold me again, Amaral."

His voice was harsh. "Do you want me to take away your pain?"

"The pain is all I have."

"Will you join me?" he asked.

I shook my head. I wanted James, not him.

"Tell me you love me," he said.

I cried. "Kiss my neck."

"Tell me you love me," he commanded.

But I could not.

And Amaral pulled up his sleeve. He tore the flesh from his wrist with teeth that were coated in the blood of my neck. He ripped his arm open but nothing oozed out of his wound.

He held the arm over my face. "Drink from me," he said.

"No," I told him.

"Drink."

I clamped my mouth shut. Amaral squeezed my cheeks to force my lips apart. I couldn't scream. I had no energy. Dad was—somewhere? Dead. Mum was in her room. Why wouldn't she come to me? Didn't she hear my pain?

"Drink," Amaral said.

A thick, viscous, black sludge began to weep from his wound. And he pressed it against my lips.

It was copper pennies and aniseed. It leaked into my mouth and I choked as he pressed his arm harder against me. I swallowed his darkness with my bile.

I screamed against his open flesh.

When he removed his arm and lowered his sleeve, he came down to me and held his cold forehead against mine. When he kissed my mouth, I felt his teeth scratch inside my lips. His tongue was thick and rank against my own.

And then he said, "It is done."

And he was gone.

chapter 15

the present

Nurse Gloria broke me.

I couldn't get out of bed for the next three nights. I wasn't pretending to be sick anymore, now I *was* sick. When Gloria stood up from the couch—clutching that stupid handbag like it could protect her from my wrath—and said, "Who are you?" I panicked.

Sometimes I didn't know who I was.

I said, "I'm me. What kind of question is that?" I was stalling. She didn't know the truth. She couldn't.

Gloria pointed at the TV and said, "A twenty-year-old with an Xbox and nothing else. You're living alone in a big house, with no social media presence and a night-shift job that puts you in the company of some seriously old people who've never been closer to death than they are right now. I know you're not who you say you are and I want the truth."

I didn't know what to say, so I said, "It's a PlayStation, not an Xbox."

And her laughter fell between us like a barricade.

I couldn't move. My toes were curled into the thin pile of the rug and Gloria looked like a stoic armoured tank as she faced me.

"I told you," I said. "I'm a very private person. An introvert. There's nothing exciting in my life that warrants posting on Instagram, and I'm new in town so what friends would I share my non-exciting life with anyway? And don't mock me for enjoying my job with the elderly. You work there, too."

Gloria smiled. "I have a purpose at Lakeshore Manor. You—you're a succubus. I can smell it on you."

"I don't even know what a succubus is," I told her. "Are you telling me I suck?"

"I'm telling you that you're sucking the pain out of the manor's residents. The longer you're around them, the less they have to give." She took a step forward. I swear that peagreen handbag was bigger than my TV. "Whatever you're doing to their lifeforce, you need to stop," she said.

"Lifeforce? What are you talking about?" I didn't think playing dumb was working. I saw it in her eyes.

"Victor," she said. And when she said my name, a chill scratched beneath the skin at my spine. I stepped back.

Gloria faced me and her neck—that gloriously alabaster neck—was the last thing I ever wanted to taste. It was a hideous neck now. I never wanted to look at it again.

"Gloria," I said, but my exhausted voice couldn't match her treble.

"What are you?" she demanded.

I swallowed. In that moment, I didn't know what I was. Human? More than human?

Something altogether less?

"Gloria," I said again. It was a whisper. Mice speak louder than men.

I tried to focus. But I couldn't concentrate. She had no pulse now. Where was her pulse? I listened and heard nothing. And my feet were stuck to the rug. I knew if I tried to move, I'd fall over.

I felt Amaral's essence fighting inside me, willing me to lash out at Gloria. But my hands were useless. I'd forgotten what my mickey felt like—I hadn't felt it in years—but both of my arms were heavy and broken in Gloria's presence.

"What are you?" Gloria said again. "Banshee? No, you don't have the strength of voice for that." She scanned me from head to toe as if she was trying to determine my origin. "Strigoi? Jiangshi?"

She advanced on me with such swiftness that I had no time to react.

Nurse Gloria dropped her handbag and gripped my throat. Her fingers were ice and I felt the energy evaporate from my limbs. I was frozen and couldn't grip her hand to remove it from my neck, paralysed and useless against her touch.

She was like me. But not like me. I got no sense of humanity from her. Gloria Pinto was something else.

Something darker.

I couldn't breathe. Her fingers were like vines around my throat, tightening and constricting. Her eyes were black and her breath was fire against my face.

She crept inside my eyes, my head, and I felt her stir the

velvet corners of my isolation. I tried to lock her out but I didn't have the strength.

Her grip tightened around my neck and I couldn't breathe. I didn't want to.

And then she released me. She was Gloria again, with that hideous neck and pale eyes that were as cold as they were friendly. She picked up her handbag and flicked the back of her fingers against it like she was trying to brush the dirt off it.

I gasped, inhaling a deep breath that swelled in my fragile chest. My burning lungs felt like they were ninety-two years old at last.

Nurse Gloria said, "I see. Now I know the truth of you."

I touched my throat, expecting to find welts there, but it was smooth, an adolescent's skin that matched my appearance but belied my soul. "What are *you*?" I asked.

Gloria smiled. "I'm a nurse," she said. "Stop interfering with my work. And get some rest. You look like shit."

As she turned to leave, I coughed and said, "Do I still have a job?" My voice was weak.

I felt the force of her presence, the darkness that followed her movements. If I was normal, could her touch have killed me? And could she do it again?

At the door, she turned. She said, "Mrs Conway doesn't need to know a thing. We all have secrets, Victor. Yours; mine—who's to say which is more dangerous? I'll tell her you're still not feeling well. When you come back—and you must come back—I'll be watching you. And if you disappear," she said, "I'll find you."

She didn't ask if I'd agree to her terms. She knew I had no

choice. She opened the front door and left, and I watched her walk down the garden path, over tiny white pebbles that had darkened with age. She gave me a small wave over her shoulder when she reached the dark edge of the garden where the streetlights didn't reach, and then she was gone.

What the hell was she?

Apart from Amaral, I'd never met anyone like me. But there was something about her. Something ancient.

And it scared me.

I paced my house for the rest of the night. It felt like years since I'd visited James in the hospital and I longed to touch him. Or warn him—not that I knew what he needed warning about. Your nurse is a nightmare trapped in the body of a thirty-year-old woman? Says the nightmare trapped in a teenager's narrow frame. It wouldn't wash.

I went for a run to clear my head. It was three a.m. and the neighbourhood was dark, streetlights dropping liquid gold on pavements, the distant drone of motorway traffic beyond the confines of the village, and the soothing pull of waves on the shore in the opposite direction. When I ran along the walkway at the top of the beach, I remembered playing football on the sand with James and the others. Memories of wrestling among the dunes and losing my ice cream in the sand. These moments that were so insignificant at the time now fell on me with such weight that I couldn't run any longer.

I stopped, flexed my tired muscles, and stared across the beach to the dark ocean. The moon was caught behind a heavy cloud, a weak halo unable to light the sky, and although I couldn't see them, I heard the hum of ship engines far out in the Atlantic.

A fox stepped out of the bushes behind me and sniffed the air. I whispered, "The night is yours now. It doesn't belong to me any more." And the fox disappeared into the night, screaming like the banshee that people of old must have mistaken them for.

I wanted to catch my breath but I had no breath to catch.

So I went home, weak in mind and weaker in body. I couldn't shake the image of Gloria's black eyes when she gripped my neck. I didn't know what she was, and the more I thought about it, the sicker I felt. I retched into the porcelain toilet but nothing came up, and I cursed Amaral for blinding me to death.

I tried to drown myself once, the first time I came back to this miserable little village, long after Mum had died. I went to her graveside and touched the marble of her headstone, my fingers tracing the letters of her name, and I tried to weep in her memory. But tears don't come easy now.

Then I stood outside James' house, knowing he wasn't there. It had been sold many years before and James was long gone.

And I cursed the building that he grew up in.

That night, somewhere before dawn, I went to the beach and walked into the water. I left no note, no neat parcel of clothing. I waded out until my feet didn't touch the seabed and then I dived beneath the freezing surface. I swam to the ocean floor and sat cross-legged among the dark algae and darker fish. And I stayed there for two days, the sun's crisp rays goading me from above but too weak to penetrate the water and hurt me.

The sea is salty from men like me who cry their pain into

oblivion.

And when my life did not succumb to the icy dark, I came out of the ocean under a waning moon and screamed until I was hoarse.

Now, standing at the boarded window of my bedroom, I peeled back one of the thick planks and waited for the sun to rise. I dragged an uncomfortable kitchen chair up and sat in front of the window for two hours. When the first shard of sterile sunlight filtered through the gap in the boards, it struck the dusty floor like a javelin. I watched as it inched closer to my bare foot.

But I was chicken and pulled my leg away.

I paced around the sunlight, studying it as it slid across the floor and up the bed where, if I'd chained myself there, it would hurt me. Was I brave enough to do that?

Hardly.

I reached a hand towards the beam of light and even before my fingers touched it, I felt the burn. A blister formed along the edge of my index finger and the smell was like a pig in a tin pen.

I cowered in the corner of the room until the sun went down and I hammered the board back in place. And then I curled up in bed with the memory of Gloria's eyes, the strength of her hand around my neck, and the kiss that James had left on my knuckles before he fell asleep at the hospital.

A few nights later, I had made up my mind. I got out of bed, showered and coated my pale skin in heavy cologne, dressed in a pair of clean trousers and a plain white shirt, and I went to work.

I stood on the lawn outside, next to that forsaken fountain, and Gloria faced me from the open doorway.

She said, "You came back."

And I said, "I'm not here for you. I'm here for James."

chapter 16

1949

When I woke, I felt nothing. The agony of my fever was gone, but so was the firm touch of the mattress under my back. The sound of a cracked voice lingered in my memory from the night before. "Love me," it had said.

I touched my body. My limbs were present and accounted for, but still I felt nothing. When I turned my head, there was no pillow behind me.

I was hovering in the air, a foot above the bed.

When I realised it, I opened my mouth to scream, and my body dropped down with a smack. The pillow curved around my ears to soften the fall. Maybe I was still delirious. That must have been it. People don't float; they drown in the current of their own fears.

I tried to inhale but a dank breath caught in my throat. I hacked up a clot of blood or mucous and spat it out and when

I did, I felt everything, heard everything. My senses rushed alive. In one breath, I felt the weight of my body on the mattress, the cold press of the blankets beneath me, and the moist air from the open window. It was raining outside.

There was an astringent scent of damp earth mixed with the acrid tang of my stale sweat. I heard birds berating the weather, insects buzzing like atomic bombs inside my head, and the distant traffic, voices, music, laughter, footsteps, electric hum, and Aunt Cara's radio two floors below.

And that clock, that damned grandfather clock outside my room, struck my senses with its clanking tick and its grating tock, second by second, hammering inside my head behind the blinding light that flared across my vision and made me cover my face with my hands.

And I screamed.

I bucked my body on the mattress, writhing against the pain of it all, every rustle of the blankets under me, the gurgle of water in the bathroom pipes, the creak of the floorboards settling, and the fingernails on my hands that grew so loud that I could hear the scraping of their ceaseless advance.

I screamed so hard my throat hurt.

Mum exploded into my room, her footfalls excruciating as she ran to my side, her voice thumping inside my head like the violent words of a jackhammer.

"Make it stop," I wanted to say, but I couldn't contain the scream as tinnitus deafened me to everything but its piercing cry. I was blind and deaf and mute with my torment.

Mum's warm hands pressed against my cheeks and the light that fucked its way in from the window glared across her face so that I couldn't see her. I shut my eyes tight but I was still blind. Her voice was an echo, somewhere behind the ringing in my ears.

"Cara, call the doctor," she shouted, a hundred miles from me, right beside my head.

When he came, I was still screaming and covering my eyes and my ears. I was thrashing around the bed so hard that Mum and Aunt Cara had to hold me down while the doctor injected me with something. Without time to assess my condition, he pulled open his Gladstone bag and filled a syringe. He had to give me the maximum dose. I felt its cold river slithering inside my veins, and as the world and all its sounds fell away from me, I lay against the pillow, staring at my mother's worried smile. My chin quivered as my lower lip trembled—just once.

And then there was blessed silence.

I swam in the darkness and there was nothing, no sound to injure me. Not even my heartbeat.

When I woke again, it was dark out and the noises of the night were fewer than in the day. I kept my eyes shut and my hands over my ears, and I tried to concentrate on one sound at a time. I allowed my hearing to tune into the buzz of the electricity in the walls. I heard it sizzling along the cables from one outlet to another.

It was dark, but the world had a strange green glow to it, as if I was seeing the soul of everything, a single aura that connected all things. And in that instant, I recognised myself in the fabric of the earth. I was part of it, and it was all of me.

I was different. When I pressed my hand to my chest, there was no thumping heart. But there was a gurgling in the pit of my stomach that cried out its ravenous hunger. I sat up in bed, expecting my muscles to protest and my bones to seize, but I moved with a fluidity that felt unnatural.

A moth flittered through the open window and danced around my head. I clapped my hands together to kill it, and when I blew the dust of its wings from my palm, I stopped. My mickey was gone. In its place was a normal hand, unblemished and pink with newness. The fingers that were once darkened had filled out, and the nail on my thumb had a pale half-moon that I hadn't seen since before the accident. I curled my fingers into a fist and then stretched them wide. The bruising on my wrist was gone and the fine hairs on my arm stood up against the breeze.

I got out of bed, testing my weight. My pyjama legs had twisted around my knees and I jittered my legs to loosen them. I don't know how long I'd been lying in bed—was it days or weeks?—but my muscles were strong and my limbs were free from stiffness.

My stomach groaned. When I opened the bedroom door, I heard Mum across the landing, the slow beat of her heart and the quiet draw of air in her throat as she breathed in her sleep. I brought my concentration back to the electricity in the walls that eased my senses with its white noise, and I went downstairs. At the bottom, I bounced on the balls of my feet. I couldn't understand how loose I felt after so long in bed.

In the kitchen, I went to the pantry. There were soil-covered potatoes in a metal bucket on the floor, packets of flour and sugar on the shelves, and an uncut loaf of bread in a basket beside cans of peas and Aunt Cara's jars of homemade jam. I picked up the loaf; it was dark on top, almost burned, just how I liked it.

I didn't bother with butter but tore a chunk from the edge and stuffed it into my mouth, chewing and smiling as my stomach cried out for food. But when I swallowed, I retched. My stomach heaved against my will and I dropped the bread, turning to the sink to empty myself. The water that I rinsed my mouth with didn't help and I retched again.

I slid down the side of the cupboard and sat on the cool floor until my stomach settled. It gurgled for something, but it wasn't food that it wanted.

I heard rodents clawing around inside the walls and I wondered how I was ever going to sleep again with all this noise. It took all my effort to concentrate on one sound and drown out the rest. At least there were fewer noises at night. From now on, I'd sleep during the day if I had to.

I stood up, knowing the only pain in my body was the hunger in my stomach, and I opened the back door, standing on the step that overlooked the yard. The grass was overgrown and the rear hedgerow needed to be trimmed. Now that I was better, Cara would put me to work on it the second she saw me out of bed.

I wondered what James was doing. Sleeping, of course, like every other sane person alive. I heard the breathing and snores of the neighbours and as I focused my attention from one nearby house to the next, I was convinced I could find my way to his bed with my ears alone.

And yet the one sound that was missing was the rush of blood in my veins, the pulse that promised life.

A bat chased its buddy across the sky and I saluted them before going back inside. I pressed my fingers to my neck where my carotid artery was, just above my wound, but I felt nothing. I'd worry about it in the morning.

When I went back to bed, I told myself that the delirium of the night before was just a bad dream. The bandage from my neck wasn't there, but I must have accidentally peeled it off in the night. I found it on the floor, crumpled and bloodied. But the tightness in my neck where the skin had knitted back together was gone. I couldn't remember much about the accident, but I must have torn it on a piece of the sinking galleon as it went down. Michael was right—we should never have gone aboard.

I closed my eyes. But I wasn't tired.

I listened to Mum's breathing from the next room, and the whimper of Cara's old-lady snores from the floor below, and I put my hands behind my head. The sensations in the fingertips of my left hand, my mickey, were as intense as those in my right. I couldn't explain how it was healed. And Mum would freak out. So I put my glove back on to hide it. Just in case.

When the night yielded to the sun, the bright greyness of dawn punched through my window so hard I couldn't see again. I clenched my eyes and struggled to close the curtains against it. I guess I'd been in a darkened room for so long that the daylight was too much for me to take.

An hour later, tossing around in bed, unable to sleep, there was a knock at the front door. Mum had got up a little while ago and eased my door open to check on me. I pretended to be asleep; I wasn't ready for conversation. She closed the door and went downstairs without a word.

Now, when she greeted the visitors, my hearing picked up every word.

"Oh, boys," Mum said. "He's still asleep."

"Isn't he better yet?" Giuseppe asked.

"The doctor said it would take some time. He just needs rest."

"Can we see him?" James asked.

I sat up in bed and listened. I wanted her to say no. To say yes. I was terrified of facing James when the last time I'd seen him, in the dark hold of the ancient galleon, I was certain he was about to kiss me. If only that damn ship hadn't torn apart and ruined my chance. But if it hadn't, would his kiss have ruined my life?

"I don't know if that's wise," Mum said.

And I heard the laughter in James' voice as he slipped past her in the doorway. "It'll do him good. We won't stay long."

There were footsteps on the stairs.

"Victor?" he shouted. "Vic?"

"What's all this racket?" Aunt Cara cried.

"Morning, miss," James said, and he continued up the stairs. "Victor?"

He hadn't been in my room before. I stood at my bedroom door and opened it, wishing I'd had time to change into dayclothes, but there he was, a handful of stairs below, looking up at me with wide eyes and a wider smile.

He came to me and threw his arms around my neck, pulling me tight. "You're alive," he said.

I kept my arms by my sides. I let him hold me, but I couldn't hug him back. I inhaled the scent of his skin and heard the beat of his heart as he squeezed me. I didn't know what to say.

And then the others, Danny and Giuseppe, were coming

up the stairs behind James. Danny patted my back in a macho display of friendship.

"Hurry up, slowpoke," Giuseppe said over his shoulder, and Michael came up to join us. He leaned against the banister and used a crutch to help himself up. His leg was plastered from the knee down and there was the faint trace of a yellowed bruise on his cheek and neck.

"What is going on?" Aunt Cara said from below us.

And Mum said, "Victor's friends are staying for breakfast. And that's final." I heard the smile in her voice.

The boys pushed me into my room and Giuseppe closed the door behind us.

"Why are you here?" I asked.

Although he'd released me from his hug, James' arm was still around my shoulders. "To see you, of course."

"That's a lie," Giuseppe said. "We're only here to see your gorgeous old aunt. Do you think I've got a shot with her?"

Danny punched his arm.

I looked at Michael who was standing by the door, leaning on his crutch and looking weak. "Are you all right?" I asked.

He shrugged. "If I'd known how much attention the ladies give you when you're injured, I'd have broken my leg years ago."

"How did you get out of the ship?" James asked me. "We looked for you everywhere. We thought you went down with the wreckage. Danny managed to get Michael's boat untied before the ship disappeared, but we couldn't find you."

Michael said, "James dived under the water to look for you but it was too dark. And bits of the ship were everywhere."

"I nearly drowned," Danny said.

"I don't know what happened," I told them. "I woke up and I was here. I was starting to think the shipwreck was just a bad dream."

"Maybe it was," Giuseppe said. "Maybe this is all an illusion."

"Illusion or not," James said, tightening his arm around my neck again, "I'm glad you're okay. I'd have blamed myself if you'd died."

And I laughed. "I'd come back to haunt you if I did."

Danny reached for the curtains to open them, but I shouted at him not to. They looked at me like I was insane.

I said, "My eyes are still a bit sensitive to light. The doctor says it's normal. Must have got too much saltwater in my noggin."

Giuseppe said, "At least that will fill up the space where your marbles used to be."

"How long has it been?" I joked. "I forgot how much of a funny man you are."

It was nice, seeing them again. Seeing James. When I sat on the edge of the bed, he sat beside me. When I stood, so did he, as if he was my protector, his hand reaching towards my back in case I was going to fall.

But I was strong. Stronger than ever.

The only falling I was doing was for James.

chapter 17

the present

I pulled James' wheelchair over the threshold of Lakeshore Manor. "Whatever happened to Michael?" he said.

The question came out of the blue. We'd been sitting in the garden near the dead fountain and I was wearing a huge winter coat to pretend I could feel the cold. The red tartan blanket over his knees reminded me of picnics and beaches, and the yellow beanie on his head would have looked out of place even on a kid. But at least he was warm. We'd been sitting in a comfortable silence, his wheelchair parked beside a wooden bench, and for a while he held his fingers to his mouth and breathed frost as if he was smoking a cigarette. A bronze plaque on the bench said, *Agnes O'Shea. In memoriam.* The bench wasn't new, but the plaque was.

Back when we'd first met, in 1949, smoking was cool. Newspaper advertisements included pictures of doctors with a cigarette in hand and captions that told you smoking was good for your digestion. It's amazing how things change.

I don't miss the rancid smell of cigarette smoke. I don't even miss food. Except bacon. If you're looking for God, you'll find Him in bacon.

"When did you quit?" I asked James. The sky was bruised by a single purple cloud and the night air was damp.

"My wife made me give up. March thirty-first, 1988," he said, without hesitation. Since he came back to Lakeshore Manor from the hospital, sometimes his mind went blank, and sometimes he could tell you how many raindrops it takes to fill a five-gallon drum.

"Ah, the eighties," I said.

He nodded. "After the hedonism of the seventies, but before the terrible fashion choices of the nineties."

We'd fallen silent again, and when I asked if we should go inside where it was warm, he shrugged. He didn't speak again until I pulled him over the lip of the entrance when he asked what happened to Michael.

"I don't know," I said.

Michael was one of those boys you'd never forget. Short for his age, attractive in a boyish way, and he had a wicked grin that sent the girls wild. But he was also a stickler for truth and the law. I don't think he'd ever been with a girl, despite his bragging on the beach.

I wheeled James into the common room. He could walk—slowly, with a cane or a frame—but I felt better with him in the wheelchair, where I could look after him. Since his heart attack, I think he'd lost at least ten pounds. He said, "We weren't the same after the shipwreck." He pointed towards

Danny and Giuseppe in armchairs that were positioned beside each other. Both brothers were asleep. "None of us," James added.

"I know," I said. The only one who hadn't changed, I thought, was James. Michael had become paranoid and seldom left a three-mile radius of his home. Danny never stepped foot in the ocean again, though it took me a while to notice. If we'd spent the night on the beach, he'd stand with his toes digging into the sand, inches away from the tide, drinking from his beer bottle, but he wouldn't go in.

And Giuseppe had a twitch that I'm sure was imperceptible to the others—or so I'd thought. His right cheek muscles would shudder from time to time, causing his eye to squint, and when I mentioned it once, he'd denied it. "What twitch?" he asked, twitching.

I kicked the brakes on James' chair opposite Danny and Giuseppe, and I dragged a stool close to sit on. We sat in their passive company, saying nothing, listening to their heavy breathing and the chatter of nurses with tired residents.

Gloria, who I'd been keeping away from as much as I could since she gripped my throat and made me choke, was throwing a soft foam ball to Fiona Gordon, a resident whose motor skills were weakening. The ball dropped in the old woman's lap and she ignored it.

"Pass it back, sweetie," Gloria encouraged. "Can you throw it?"

James shook his head. He whispered, "The time for playing catch is when you're eight, not eighty."

I kept Gloria in the corner of my sight. I zoned through the heartbeats in the room and singled out hers. I know she didn't have one in my home when she threatened me over the top of her enormous green handbag. How could she turn it on like that? That would have been a bonus over the years. But the more important question was what kind of being she was. She terrified me. But she let me keep my distance and treated me as she always had—with mild disdain and a superiority bred from years of nursing. Young kids like me were just butt-pimples in her world.

Whatever world she was from.

Danny snorted in his sleep and James said, "We should dress this place up as a mausoleum for Halloween. It wouldn't take a lot of effort."

That's when I noticed a blur skim past the window on the outside. Mr Buckley. In the buff.

I pulled the blanket from James' knee. "Can I borrow this?" I asked, but I didn't wait for an answer. I kept my speed down, careful not to alarm anybody, but when I dashed outside and around the corner after Mr Buckley's naked ass, Gloria was already there, standing in front of him with her arms wide to block his path and her eyes averted from his nudity.

"That's quite far enough," she said.

"I'm on the lam," Mr Buckley told her.

I wrapped the blanket around his waist and held it in place against his protestations. "How did you get outside?" I asked.

"Let go of me, you pervert," he cried.

I turned him towards the building as Gloria said, "I ought to tie your *thing* to your headboard. That'll stop you from escaping."

"I've got him," I said.

"He's touching me!" Buckley said to Gloria. "You're my

witness. It's inappropriate."

"He's doing his job."

I nodded at her. And before leading him inside, I said, "You got out here fast." I was sure she was still in the common room when I ran outside.

Gloria smiled. "Never underestimate a good pair of plimsolls."

I shivered. I was fast when I needed to be. But the only way she could have beaten me here was to morph through the glass windows and bypass the corridor and the foyer.

Was that possible?

I marched Mr Buckley back to his room and closed the door. I threw the tartan blanket into the laundry chute, and when I went back to the common room, Gloria was playing catch with Fiona as if she'd never left.

I would read her employee file if I thought it'd do me any good.

When I went back to James, his head was drooped forward, his hands in his lap, and he was wheezing in his sleep. I heard the rattle in his lungs. He tired easily, napping more often during the early evenings instead of demanding we play bridge, and he was getting more forgetful.

My presence wasn't helping. Sometimes, he'd look at me as though I was a stranger, and other times he'd talk to me like we were still seventeen. I couldn't walk away from him—not again—but part of me knew that seeing me as the seventeen-year-old Victor from his past was messing with his mind. I was just grateful that Danny and Giuseppe were often too far out of it to know who *they* were, let alone recognise me.

"Can I get a hand?" I asked one of the staff, and he helped me rouse the brothers long enough to get them to their room.

I wheeled James' chair towards the lift, hoping he wouldn't wake, and when I backed into his room, I eased him out of the seat with one arm behind his shoulders and another under his knees. I slid back the covers of his bed and lowered him into it, and as his head touched the pillow, he opened his eyes, blinking at me with milky memories.

"Victor," he mumbled.

"I'm here."

He smiled. "See you on the beach."

And as I pulled the blankets over his frail body, I said, "See you on the beach, James."

I held his hand, drawing in his pain, but I couldn't touch him for long. The contact made me dizzy. But the rattle in his lungs was gone.

For now.

The pinkie and ring-finger on his right hand were curled tightly into his palm, stiff with arthritis, and although it hurt to take more of his pain, I did it anyway, until there was some give in his digits. I couldn't tell why taking James' pain was hurting me the way it did, but I didn't want to think about it.

In his sleep, he said, "Poor Michael."

And I slipped out of his room, easing the door closed behind me.

At my back, Gloria said, "I told you not to get attached."

I turned. Although her voice had sounded like it came from the far end of the corridor, she was standing beside me. She was holding the yellow foam ball that she'd been tossing to Fiona earlier.

Her eyes drilled inside my head, searching, but she found nothing. I felt her enter my brain and withdraw just as fast.

She said, "Every door has a key."

I cut a smile across my lips. "Good to know."

Gloria handed me the foam ball, and when I didn't take it, she said, "It's a gift, Victor. Just a gift. Nothing more."

I took it. A faded stamp across the side of it said, PROPERTY OF LAKESHORE MANOR. I held it up. "Are you trying to tell me something?"

"Am I?"

"Property of Lakeshore. The residents. You're saying they're yours, not mine."

Her grin was huge. "Top of the class." She drew something in the air. "That's a smiley face for your permanent record." And she walked away.

I wanted to throw the ball at her. Instead, as she stepped into the lift and turned to face me, I said, "Death takes them sooner or later."

As the doors closed, I thought I saw her true form. Just for a second.

And then I was alone with a yellow ball that reminded me of the sun, something I longed to see but never could. Parents tell their children not to look directly at it, but it's all I wanted to do.

The following night, while Gloria and some of the other staff were hanging Halloween decorations from the ceiling, I sat with James and the brothers at the card table. The green felt was ratty and worn. James dealt a round of crazy eights, but his hands were shaking and he fumbled the deck.

He said, "Might as well have dicks for fingers."

"You'd have too much fun," Giuseppe told him.

Old men were crass. That was the impression I'd formed since working here. I stooped under the table to pick up some of the fallen cards and Danny gave a cheeky whistle.

"That's enough," I said. "Can we get back to playing so that James can finish bankrupting us before supper?"

"I can't help being a winner," James said, and he wheezed.

"Card shark, more like," Giuseppe said.

"Isn't that the same thing?"

"What are the rules, again?" Danny asked.

"Of what?" Giuseppe said.

"Whatever we're playing."

"What *are* we playing?"

"Crazy eights," I said.

And Giuseppe said, "Michael would know the rules."

"I know the rules," James said.

"You don't have to sulk," Giuseppe said, "just because Victor won the last round."

"Who?" Danny and James said together. James was covering for me; he was the only one that knew who I was. But Danny looked confused.

"You know who I mean."

"Victor's gone," Danny said.

Giuseppe looked at me and then at Danny. He pointed to my face. "Well, who the bloody hell is that?"

"Stephen," the three of us said in unison.

Giuseppe's eyes narrowed. "I thought he was called Victor."

"You're going senile, you old bat," Danny said, and he tried to punch his brother's arm the way he used to, but his fist was weak and there was little force behind it.

Giuseppe sulked, but for the rest of the night I had to keep one eye on Gloria and one on my old friend.

Maybe, like Giuseppe had once said, this was all an illusion. Or maybe I was the one going senile.

chapter 18

1949

My gums hurt. I ran my tongue over my teeth and could have sworn there was something firm, like another tooth, poking through my gum, just above the incisor, but when I prodded it with my finger, I couldn't feel anything. I asked Mum to take a look and I held my lip up while she squinted. I was still struggling to focus on one sound at a time and the noise of her heartbeat competed with Cara's radio as she listened to a Catholic mass service on Radio Éireann.

"I don't see anything," Mum said.

"It's just there," I told her, poking the area with my tongue.

"There's nothing there, Victor."

"Are you sure?"

"If you have a toothache, put some clove oil on it," she said. "And for God's sake, why are you wearing those sunglasses indoors?"

155

I let go of my lip and sucked my teeth. "The light hurts," I said. I could still feel the small bump on my gum. "There's something there; I know it."

In the armchair beside the floor-standing radio, an enormous wooden box with a filigreed speaker, Cara said, "Come here and I'll give you something to cry about. Can't you see I'm trying to listen to the good Lord's word?"

The static was so bad I'm surprised she could understand any of it.

I found a bottle of clove oil in the medicine cupboard and rubbed some on my gums, but it didn't do any good. It just tasted foul. I spent the rest of the afternoon running my tongue over the lump and trying to push it back inside.

I kept my aviators on, even while I lay on my bed with the curtains closed. Dad had bought them last year from a gift shop at a travelling circus. I said he looked like an American fighter pilot. Dad said he was better looking. He wore them on the construction site when it was sunny, but it had been overcast on the day of the accident, so he'd left them at home. I snatched them from his bedside table before we'd moved to Aunt Cara's house and Mum let me keep them.

They made me feel grown up, which I didn't feel often.

I didn't float any more. I'm not sure if I had been airborne when I woke from my delirium or if I'd imagined it, but now I lay on my bed and closed my eyes, willing myself to rise from the mattress.

But my body didn't move.

The pale face of a tall man called Amaral haunted my waking hours. Was he also a product of my phrenetic fever, like my floating or the trouser-wearing owl? He didn't enter my dreams—I hadn't dreamt since my delirium. I guess that was a good thing. If I did, I'd be plagued by visions of that sinking ship and James' face, drawing closer to mine, my eyes closing, lips parting. And then water filling my mouth and lungs, killing me, tearing me away from him and pulling me down into the blind abyss.

But sometimes nightmares are better than no dreams at all.

By late afternoon, I was bored and restless. James would have finished his milk round hours ago and was probably on the beach with the others. Tom McShane, the dairy farmer, had been informed of the accident and told James that we could take some time to recover. He knew I'd been suffering more than the others. "But not too much time," he'd pointed out, "or I'll have to replace the pair of you."

I stood at the back door and stared out at the glaring daylight, squinting even with Dad's sunglasses on. The world was bleached white. The doctor hadn't said when my sensitivity to light would go away, but I needed it to leave now. I wanted to go outside. I missed the sun. And the beach. And James.

With my eyes half-closed, I stepped onto the path, shielded from the sun by the deep shadows of the neighbour's oak tree, and I couldn't breathe. My chest was tight and the hairs on my arms prickled and curled.

Where the sunlight speared between the leaves, it struck me like a burning onslaught. Something was singeing.

Me. *I* was singeing.

I screamed.

I looked at my arms. They were going red with sunburn and blistered welts bubbled to the surface. The fingernails on my right hand were blackening and the rot was spreading towards the wrist.

The skin flaked.

Viscid puss wept from the blisters on my arms and there was a weight on my head that glued me to the spot. I tried to turn to the house, to get inside, but I couldn't move. I screamed for Mum's help but no sound left my throat.

I was burning. The sun was killing me.

I fell backwards, toppling my weight with willpower alone. And as the top half of my body fell through the doorway, into the shadows of the kitchen, I gasped for air and pulled myself inside, away from the light.

I kicked the door closed, panting and crying in pain. But I clamped my mouth shut. I couldn't let Mum see me like this.

I drew on whatever strength I had in me and stumbled up the rear stairs to my bedroom. Inside, I peeled my short-sleeved shirt off, careful not to burst any more of the welts on my arms, and I inspected my chest and stomach. The skin was reddened and splotched with scorch marks, but because it had been covered by the fabric of my shirt, it didn't suffer as much as my exposed arms.

I grabbed the bottle of clove oil from my nightstand. If it was supposed to soothe the pain in my gums, maybe it would help on my blisters. I sprinkled the bottle on my forearm and steam lifted from it like a mirage from tarmac on a hot day. It burned worse than the pain I'd already felt.

And Mum was coming up the stairs. I could already recognise the sound of her heartbeat. Outside my room, she said, "Did you find the clove oil?"

I pressed my red back against the door, hoping she

wouldn't open it, and I gritted my teeth. "Yes, thanks. I'm all better now."

"Dinner's at six," she said.

My voice squeaked. "Okay." I breathed through the pain of my burning body.

I would never go outside again.

But I had to see James. I sat on the edge of the bed and blew cool air on my arms. And the longer I stayed in my room with the curtains closed, the more the pain eased. I poked the blistered welts until they burst and then used toilet paper to mop the sticky spills. And in time, my arms and face were returning to normal, healing faster than they should have. Apart from the dry, fractured skin where the welts had been—skin that peeled like sunburn when I tugged at it—nobody would be able to tell the sky had tried to murder me.

At dinner, I wore a long-sleeved shirt, and the broken skin on my face looked as innocuous as acne.

Cara said, "Must he wear sunglasses at the dinner table?"

"Can't you take them off for a little while?" Mum asked.

"My eyes hurt from the light," I said. "If I take them off, I'll cry blood all over my potatoes."

"If you're unable to control your mouth," Cara said, "you can excuse yourself from the table."

"He's sorry. Tell Aunt Cara you're sorry."

"Why should I?" The bravery left my mouth without me noticing it. And it felt good.

Mum slapped her hand on the table and Cara flinched. "That's enough, Victor. You're not too big for a smack. Apologise to Aunt Cara and eat your dinner."

I glared at Cara, wondering if she could see my eyes

through the sunglasses, and then I relented. For Mum's sake. "Sorry," I mumbled. I pushed my fork around the plate. In the past few days, unable to keep anything down, I had become adept at making it look like I was eating. I picked up a forkful of mashed potato and held it to my mouth, putting it back on the plate untouched, scraped it around, forcing gaps in the food, mushing peas into carrots and flaking pie crust across the meal. I left pockets of indentations and holes in the food.

And then I said, "That was delicious."

"You barely touched it."

"I ate enough," I said, and my stomach growled with hunger. But I knew food was never going in my mouth again.

That night, I waited for the sun to go down. If I couldn't go out in the daylight, could my skin handle the cool glow of the moon? If not, I'd be trapped here forever, at Cara's beck and call, a slave to her whims. But it was August and the day was bright until nine o'clock.

I stood by my bedroom window, flicking the curtains every so often to check on the daylight. Although the sun had dropped below the horizon, the sky was still a wash of orange hues. When it finally greyed enough into dusk, I put a heavy coat on, pulled the hood up, and put on a pair of gloves. I slipped down the rear stairs and out of the back door in a hurry. If I took my time, I'd chicken out.

A quarter moon was suspended in the grey sky, and in the west, the final rays of sunlight were petering out. I braced for the pain, but although the remnants of light forced me to squint behind my sunglasses, it didn't burn. I waited, but nothing happened. And as the sky grew darker, I grinned.

With my body covered in protective layers, I ran to James'

house. I was fast, my limbs loose and my muscles taut, and when I stood on the grass outside his home, I saw his parents through the living room window. They sat in armchairs beside each other, her with a book, him with today's *Irish Times* and a cigarette burning in an ashtray beside him. I heard their words as if I was standing in the room with them, heard the crackle of his tobacco and the turn of her pages as she licked her finger to pull the corner of the paper.

But I didn't hear James. There were three heartbeats in the house, but one was small and fast. An animal, like a cat or a gerbil.

When James' mum looked at the window, I slipped behind a rosebush and hid. And then I closed my eyes, listening. I reached out with my hearing, beyond the neighbours and the barking dogs, the sporadic traffic and the hum of the ozone. And I listened to the heartbeats of a village winding down for the night. I cocked my head, turning to the left.

James.

I knew it was him.

I ran, following the sound of his heartbeat. I'd recognise it anywhere.

I found him at the top of the beach, smoking a cigarette and walking along the path for home. He was alone.

"James," I said.

He froze. "Jesus! Where did you come from?" In the dim light, the glowing embers of his cigarette was like a sun to me.

"Sorry," I said. "Where are you heading?"

"Home."

I fell into step beside him, still listening to the beat of his heart. Seagulls cried to each other over the ocean that was black like ink and rippled like linen on the breeze.

James grinned at me. "You feeling better now?"

"Like a new man."

"I liked the old one," he said.

I stopped walking. "Did you?"

He turned to me, sucked on his cigarette before tossing it onto the sand that was brushed across the path, and said, "Of course. What's not to like?"

"What do you like?" I asked.

"Everything."

"Specifically."

He shrugged. "What are you asking me, Victor?"

I was emboldened by the darkness. His skin shone under the faint moonlight and I buried my eyes in the rich blue of his irises. I said, "Do you remember, on the ship, just before it went down?"

James stepped closer. "Yeah."

"And you said my name."

"Victor," James said.

I nodded. I felt the heat of his voice. "Like that. And then—I don't know—I thought maybe you were going to say something. Or do something."

He took another step, into my aura. He looked around before saying, "What would I do, Victor?"

"James," I said.

He nodded. But he just stood there.

I looked down. His arms were by his sides. And we were alone. I eased my hands towards him, brushing my knuckles across his. Then I linked two of my fingers with his, curling around the warmth of him.

I flattened my lips out of the smile they were forming against my will; his heart skipped a beat and then quickened. I heard him swallow.

"James."

He nodded again, like a nervous tic. "Victor."

I kissed him. Hard. I pressed my lips against him, unsure of what I was doing, but doing it anyway. He leaned forward, into me.

And then he pulled back, his hands still in mine. We were standing on the path beyond the beach in the dark, under the weak light of a waxing moon. He pulled his lower lip into his mouth like he was tasting me there.

He said, "What if somebody comes?"

"Nobody's coming," I said.

"How do you know?"

I listened to the air around us. Apart from the gulls, we were utterly alone. "I just know."

I kissed him again. I don't know where my bravery came from, but I liked it. And when James' tongue tested the space between my lips, I felt the pulse in his mouth, the erratic swiftness of it, rising to meet the heat of our moment.

I smelled him. Clean skin, mixed with the faint tang of a day's perspiration. And the smell of his blood in his veins, rich and metallic, pulsing through his neck, just below his jawline.

There was a renewed pain in my gums, a lump pushing against my incisor.

James opened his mouth wider for me.

And I nicked his lip. I bit him.

It was an accident.

He stepped back from me, his fingers probing the corner of his mouth. "Shit," he said.

"Sorry," I breathed.

"It's okay," he smiled.

But it wasn't okay. The deep red blood that trickled over his lip glistened in the moonlight. He wiped his knuckle over it.

And the pain in my gums exploded as whatever was inside, above my teeth, wanted out.

I shook my head. "I'm sorry."

"It's all right."

I backed away from him. I smelled his blood on the air and my stomach rumbled.

And I ran.

"Where are you going?" he called.

But I couldn't answer him. My gums were on fire. And the taste of his blood lingered in my mouth.

chapter 19

the present

The scrape of the razor along James' cheek was loud. He pinched his mouth closed, stretching his upper lip, and tilted his head to let me shave under his nose. The nurses dry-shaved him with an electric razor, but he'd begged me to give him a closer shave. He sat on the edge of his bed with his gnarled fingers twisted in his lap, and I swirled the barber's blade in a bowl of warm water before scraping it across his prickly skin again.

His heartbeat was slow and weak, thin blood making its languid journey through age-toughened arteries. I didn't know what he was thinking as he stared across the room at nothing, and I pressed my thumb against his chin, turning his head towards me so I could shave his sideburns. His glassy eyes locked with mine.

"Hi," I said.

His face was full of confusion for a second. Then he said, "Did you ever think you'd be shaving me?"

"Not in a million years."

"You may live that long," he said.

"I hope not." I swirled the blade in the water again, but I didn't bring it up to his face. I said, "How are your hands?"

He looked at them. "Cut them off and I'd have better dexterity." He flexed the fingers that he could, the others curled into his palms. I put the razor on a towel and gripped his hands. "Don't," he said.

"I want to."

"But it hurts you."

"Better me than you," I said. I closed my eyes and drew in some of his pain, and I could feel the darkness seeping into my veins, blackening my wrists temporarily. It stung. I didn't know what was different about him, why his pain itched inside me like a gut-punch. But I didn't care. I'd take what I could, as often as I could, until all of his pain was gone.

When I chewed on my lower lip in the agony of his misery, James pulled his hands out of my grip. "Enough," he said, and even his voice was stronger. He flexed his fingers. He couldn't straighten them, but there was more movement than before.

I didn't speak for a second. I lowered my head so he wouldn't see the darkness in my eyes, but James knuckled my chin, forcing me to look at him.

"You shouldn't take so much."

"I want to," I said.

"You're a wonder," he told me.

I smiled. He'd said the same words before, in an apple

orchard, under the cover of dark where he couldn't see the fear in my eyes at having him so close to me, his fingers connected to mine and his chest pressed against my side.

I wanted to kiss him, but I knew I couldn't. If anybody walked by his open door, they'd see an old man, arm in arm with a teenager. Me—another old man—I saw two teenagers. I wondered what I'd look like if I'd aged the way James had. Would I be stooped and wrinkled too? White-haired or bald? And would he love me just as much?

He was about to speak, but I stopped him. Something was coming: Death. And he was travelling fast, unexpected.

I stood up.

"What is it?" James asked.

I ignored him. Death was already on this floor. "Stay here," I said. I stood in his doorway, staring along the corridor, and there was a darkness two doors down.

Mr Buckley.

"Victor?"

"Shush," I said.

James was behind me. "What's wrong?"

I stepped into the hall. "Close your door. Don't come out." If death saw him, would he take him too? I couldn't take that chance. "Close it," I said, and he did.

The corridor was quiet. I listened. Most of the residents were downstairs in the common room, and Mr Buckley's door was ajar. When I stood in front of it, I listened. There was no heartbeat inside, but I could smell Mr Buckley's scent. And something else.

I pushed the door open. And leaning over his bed, her fingers poised to close his eyes that had been frozen open in death, was Gloria.

She looked up at me. "We're too late," she said. She straightened up.

I couldn't sense death anymore. He was gone.

Gloria said, "At least he was wearing his pyjamas, at last. I'll call his next of kin. Can you alert Mrs Conway? She'll need to start the paperwork."

"How did you get to him so fast?" I asked.

She paused before answering. "I sensed his distress. I got here as soon as I could."

Her heartbeat had returned, as though she was putting it on for my benefit. I still couldn't figure out how she was doing that.

"He was gone when you got here?" I asked.

"He was," she said, but it didn't sound like a complete sentence, like she was about to say something more.

I nodded. "Do you want me to stay with him?"

"I'll stay," she said, pulling her work-issued mobile phone out of the pocket of her green scrub-tunic to call his next of kin.

I backed out of the room and passed James' door just as he cracked it open. James said, "Is he dead?"

Gloria was watching us from Mr Buckley's door.

I nodded at him and mouthed, *Close your door.*

He did.

Downstairs, Mrs Conway had already left for the night. In her office, I sat at her desk and picked up the phone's receiver. The manager's home number was pre-programmed on one of the speed-dial buttons. She answered after only one ring, as though she'd been expecting the call.

When I told her Mr Buckley had passed away, she said, "The poor tyke," like he was a little kid. "I'll come in early tomorrow to fill in the paperwork. Have you called the emergency services yet? They'll need to make an official declaration of death. And then we should call the next of kin."

"Gloria's handling that," I said.

Mrs Conway said, "Then Mr Buckley's in good hands. Good night, Victor."

I put the phone down and swivelled in the chair to face the window. The night was black and windy. And then I sensed death's presence again. In a panic, I dashed upstairs. Would he take two in one night?

I knocked on James' door.

When he opened it, I closed my eyes in relief. "Stay here," I said.

"Make your mind up," James scowled.

I went back to Mr Buckley's room and Gloria was sitting in a chair beside the bed. Except she wasn't Gloria. She had a bowl of water in her lap and a damp cloth in her hand. Her skin was glowing, a bright blue-white, stark against the dull shine from the bedside lamp. Her hair was floating, like she was underwater.

She pressed the cloth against Mr Buckley's face, his neck, and then she lifted his hands, cleansing them. She said something to him, but I couldn't catch the words.

And then she sensed me behind her. She snapped her head around. Her floating hair followed. And her eyes were black.

Her voice was dark when she said, "Leave us."

I couldn't speak.

Gloria returned to her work, daubing the cloth over Mr

Buckley's skin with reverence. The light that shone from her body fluctuated, shimmering around her. And I knew what she was. I smelled it.

"Death," I said.

Gloria pressed the cloth into her bowl and wrung it out. Water droplets rose towards the ceiling. Her hair twisted in its sorcery.

"Leave us," she said as she returned to her task of preparing his body.

I backed out of the room and closed the door. I couldn't explain what I'd seen, but I knew there was no malice in her actions. She was being tender and respectful, and deserved her privacy.

Later, when I helped James down to the common room and we sat with the brothers, he said, "I can't believe it. Didn't he try to escape last night?"

Giuseppe said, "Didn't he try to escape every night?"

James chuckled and nodded.

"The naked wanderer," Danny said.

We were silent. I'd see many people die over the years, but the feeling of loss was always the same.

James tried to get out of his seat but couldn't. He pulled on his walking frame with one hand and stretched the other to me. "Don't just sit there, help me up."

"What are you doing?"

When I helped him to his feet, he said, "Come on," and he shuffled across the floor.

Giuseppe stood and unclipped the brakes on Danny's wheelchair. "Where are we going?" he asked.

James said, "You'll see."

In the quiet hallway outside the common room, he leaned against the wall and kicked his bedroom slippers off. He popped open the clasp of his belt and his trousers fell around his ankles.

"James," I said. "What are you doing?"

"We're giving the old man one last run."

"You're doing no such thing," I said. "You'll get me in trouble."

But with the freedom I'd given his fingers, he was already unbuttoning his shirt. And Giuseppe was grinning as he peeled his cardigan off.

"Stop it. That's an order."

But Danny said, "Will somebody help me out of this damn shirt?"

I couldn't watch. I turned my back, hoping none of the staff would come out of the common room and catch them in the act. And several minutes later, the grunts of old men struggling out of their clothes stopped. And three pasty white asses trudged past me, James with his walker, and Giuseppe pushing Danny in his chair.

They stumbled up the corridor, whooping and hollering, and somebody in the common room cried out in shock as the three naked men breezed past the glass partition. A stampede of elderly residents and young staff rolled into the corridor to watch and laugh.

If I could blush, my cheeks would have been red.

A ripple of applause chittered through their audience as James, Danny and Giuseppe reached the far end of the corridor, turned, and raised their arms in the air in triumph.

Old ladies averted their eyes. Old men cheered.

And the staff didn't know where to look, hiding their smiles with fingers of embarrassment.

But then Gloria appeared behind the naked runners. She was just Gloria now, a normal woman, her anger stifled under folded arms. "That's enough," she said, her voice booming.

The staff disappeared into the common room, wheeling residents with them or coaxing the others inside.

And when Gloria marched my friends back down the corridor, I had picked up their clothes and handed them over. Gloria opened the office door and said, "In there. Get dressed and don't dawdle." When she'd closed it behind them, she turned to me. "Your doing, I assume."

I couldn't hide my smile. I was proud of them. "It was their idea," I said. "One last naked run for Mr Buckley."

"I'm not a monster," she said. "I can see the funny side of things. But that was inappropriate. Do we need to have words?"

"About what?"

"About that. Or anything else," she said.

"We do need to talk, don't we?"

She lowered her voice. "You know what I am."

I nodded. I didn't need to say it.

"It upsets you?" she asked.

I matched her quiet tones. "You could have told me."

"You are not my keeper."

James and the brothers came out of Mrs Conway's office, fully dressed, and shuffled between us, into the common room, with their heads bowed in mock shame. James offered me a low-five as he passed.

Gloria closed her eyes. She checked her watch. "I have a

lot to do. Keep your friends in check, please."

"Wait," I said, as she walked away from me. I chased after her.

"You have no right to question me, Victor," she said.

"No questions," I promised. "Just a favour."

She stopped walking and turned to me, an unspoken question on her face.

I paused, searching for the words, and then I lowered my voice. "I want you to kill me. Once James is gone. Don't make me go on without him."

Her face turned into a scowl. "Kill you?"

I nodded. "I can't do it myself."

I thought she was going to do it where we stood. But then her lips cracked into a smile.

And she laughed.

chapter 20

1949

I hid under my bed like a burning corpse.

My skin was on fire and it wasn't from the sun. It was passion that swelled in my veins, itching my muscles like a flood of exploding fireworks. I tasted James in my mouth, the tang of his blood. Why did I kiss him? I would never do it again. I ran home from the beach where I'd left him and I threw myself under the bed in my room, clenching my eyes and my jaw. I gripped the bedsprings above me and licked my lips. He was still there, the sharp taste of his blood.

I'd only nicked him, a minor cut. But when his blood eased against my lips, a hunger ignited in me that had me wanting to grip him tight and taste him for hours.

That's why I ran.

That's why I was going to hell.

Homosexual.

It was illegal. And disgusting. But if it was so vile, why didn't I care? I wanted to kiss him again.

But I couldn't. Not any more.

I melted against the shadows under the bed and cried. My stomach growled at me and I punched it. I wasn't normal—this wasn't how my life was supposed to go. I lifted my shirt up and scratched my fingernails across my belly. They were sharp where I hadn't cut them in weeks and they left broken skin, pink in the darkness of night, thin ladders of my jagged life.

I scratched again.

And in time, a sleepy chill drew itself under the bed with me and I closed my eyes. The window was open; the fresh breeze was sweet with the scent of geraniums and campanulas. The fine down of adulthood on my cheeks was tickled by the soft air and lulled me to sleep.

I did not dream.

When I woke, I was still under the bed. Mum was moving around downstairs—I heard the shuffle of her feet and the beat of her heart—and Aunt Cara was in the parlour. The scratch of her fountain pen against a sheet of paper was loud inside my head. The sun was up and I couldn't force myself out from under the bed to draw the curtains. I would die there under the shadows of a thin mattress, and nobody would find me for days.

When Mum knocked on my bedroom door to tell me breakfast was ready, I called out, "Close the curtains, please."

She cracked open the door. "Where are you?"

"Under here."

"What are you doing under there?"

Dying, I wanted to say. But I didn't. I said, "Close the curtains, please."

When she did, making sure one drape overlapped the other, I didn't come out from my hiding place. She got on her knees and leaned down to see me. "Why are you under there?"

"My eyes."

"That's it," she said. "I'm calling the doctor."

"No," I told her.

She touched my arm, her warm fingers like burning flames against my skin. "I'll call every doctor in the world until you're fixed."

"I'm not broken," I said, even though I knew I was.

She pressed her hand over my eyes. "You're cold," she said. "And I'm your mother. If you're hurting, I'm hurting."

"Please don't call the doctor."

"What would you have me do, then?"

I shrugged. She took her hand away.

She said, "You can't go on like this."

"I know I can't."

"Who should I call?" she asked.

I looked at her. "Call James."

Mum closed her eyes. "He's a doctor now, is he?" She patted my shoulder. "I'll get you some eyedrops from the chemist. If that doesn't help, I'm calling the doctor."

"And James," I said.

She nodded. "I'll call him after breakfast."

When I was alone, I crawled out from under the bed. I took a roll of tape from the drawer in my desk and taped the curtains closed. Mum brought up a plate of sausages and scrambled eggs, and when I couldn't look at it any longer, I flushed it down the toilet, leaving a few scraps on the plate to make it look like I'd eaten.

She told me James was still at work, but she'd left a message with his mother asking him to call when he was free. I wasn't sure he would.

When the phone rang an hour later, I pressed my lips tight to the memory of his blood, and I listened as Mum answered it in the hall downstairs. But it wasn't James, it was one of Aunt Cara's church friends.

I waited in my room all day, but he didn't call.

Only when the sun went down, did I relax. I kept the curtains closed and the lamp off, and I sat on my bed in my day clothes, with my knees pulled up to my chin and my arms wrapped around them. There was something calming about the night as the earth's crust cooled from the day's heat and a chorus of crickets filled the darkness outside.

I was getting better at focusing my hearing on one thing at a time. But when I heard the scuff of feet outside, loud above the yammer of insects, I recognised them instantly.

A small stone thwacked my bedroom window and I smiled.

I eased my head under the curtains without tearing the tape off and I looked down. James saluted me from the garden, and when a light flickered downstairs, he shrunk against the shadows.

"Are you coming down?" he whispered, "or do I have to climb the rainspout?"

I laughed and then lowered my voice. "Wait there." When I faced him in the garden, I said, "Why are you here?"

"Your mum called."

"She called this morning."

He nodded and took a step closer to me. "I waited for dark. Because of your eyes." Then he turned and walked back to the gate. "Come on."

"Where to?"

I saw the shrug of his shoulder as he pulled the gate wide. "Does it matter?"

"No," I said, and I followed him. When I fell into step beside him, we were silent, walking down the dark street in the verdant shadows of summer-thick trees. High clouds pocked the sky and I couldn't see the moon.

James pushed his hands into his jacket pockets and kept his gaze on the slope of the hill before us. The high flick of his hair bounced as he moved, and a lock of it fell across his temple where I saw, even in the dark, the throb of his pulse.

We passed the orchard with its high walls and heady scent of green apples, and James tested the gate to see if it was open. But the chain that was wrapped around it was thick and fastened. At the corner, he said, "Give me a boost."

I leaned against the wall and threaded my fingers together, and James put his hands on my shoulders, his foot in the stirrup of my hands, and I launched him to the top of the wall. He reached down to help me, but I swatted his hand aside. I jumped, gripping the lip of the wall, and pulled myself over.

In the leafy darkness on the other side, James whispered, "Where did that acrobatic manoeuvre come from? I know you can't be Superman because he draws his strength from the sun and you haven't been out in the daylight in weeks."

I tried to flex the muscles in my arms. "I've been stuck at home all this time. I've been doing push-ups."

We walked among the trees. He hadn't mentioned last night's kiss or the haste in my feet as I ran from him.

He plucked an apple from one of the trees, rubbed it on his jacket, and held it to me. When I didn't take it, he said, "If it wasn't for Eve, we'd all be naked."

"How do you figure?"

He bit the apple, juice spilling onto his lips like the devil's nectar. "She was told not to eat the fruit, but she did it anyway. And then they had to use fig leaves for clothes."

"Women, eh?" I said.

He punched my shoulder. And then he said, "Why did you run away last night?"

My mouth ran dry. I stared at his lips. "I didn't mean to hurt you."

"You didn't."

"But your lip."

He took another bite from the apple before speaking. "It healed up fast. See?" He held his lip out between his thumb and finger and I leaned in to look at it. I smelled the apple on his breath.

His heartbeat was steady and the crickets in the roots of the trees serenaded the silences in between the beats, where death resided alongside life.

He let go of his lip but he didn't pull away from me. There was a light in his eyes that defied the darkness among the apple trees. I looked at him and he was looking back.

His voice was barely a whisper when he said, "I never noticed before."

"Noticed what?" I matched the softness of his words.

James said, "The flecks of gold in your eyes. They're so

bright. Why have I never seen them before?"

There was no gold in my eyes. Or there wasn't—before. I had no words.

James parted his lips, moistened them, and then swallowed. He said, "Are we alone?"

I nodded.

And he said, "I want you to—"

I kissed him, covering his words with my silence. I don't know what he was going to say, but I hoped it was, "Kiss me." So I did.

And then I heard the sound of the apple falling from his hand and felt his arms wrap around my thin waist. He leaned into me and I pressed against him, cupping his face in my hands and tasting his tongue.

When we stopped kissing, he didn't let go of me. He held his forehead against my shoulder.

"James," I said.

He put his lips to my neck.

"James."

His thumb traced the line of my jaw as his tongue eased across my pale flesh. I opened my mouth to say his name again, but he pressed a finger against my lips. The sound of his heart was in my head. It would always be in my head.

His teeth grazed across my neck and ended with a soft kiss below my Adam's apple. And I wanted to do the same to him.

I waited for the pain in my gums to return, but there was no hunger in my stomach, no smell of blood on the fragrant air.

James linked his fingers with mine and he tugged me to

the ground where we lay among the leaves and fallen apples. His lips found mine again, searching in the dark across my cheek until they locked together.

I had no words any more. I didn't need them.

He pressed his body against my side and I dragged my fingers through his thick hair as he breathed into me, his chest swelling over mine. And his hand slipped down my arm, across my stomach.

Lower.

Tender.

I gasped. And I felt him smile against my mouth.

We lay there for an eternity, wrapped in the night, shrouded in the lust of Eve's downfall. And when the sky turned a hazy grey in the distance, I covered his mouth with mine and told him I needed to leave.

"Stay," he said.

"But my eyes."

He took his jacket and draped it over our heads, securing us in darkness.

I kissed him. But then I stood. I offered him my hand and he tried to pull me down, but I was too strong, so he came to his feet.

We hopped over the wall onto the street. The sky was growing brighter but the sun hadn't risen over the hillside yet. It was almost five a.m. and only farmers were awake.

James took my hand and we walked back home to the applause of birdsong.

When we stood on the pebbles of the garden path that we'd laid an eon before, he said, "I want to do that again."

"Stealing apples?" I smiled.

He grinned, moving closer to me and grazing his knuckles over the back of my hand. "I want to steal all the apples."

"Tonight," I said.

He nodded.

And when I went inside, I swear I was floating again. I dashed to my window, putting my sunglasses on before looking out as the sun broke through the morning clouds. And I watched him walk down the hill.

When he got to the orchard wall, he stopped, turned to face me, and he waved.

I blew him a kiss just as a tractor came around the corner at the far end of the orchard. And James laughed. He popped his collar, hunched his shoulders against his neck, and he ran.

The tractor grumbled up the hill. And I couldn't remove the smile from my face.

chapter 21

the present

Gloria pushed through the rooftop access and took a deep breath. She held the door while I followed, and then we watched it close on its slow hinge. She tapped a finger against it to ensure the catch had clicked into place, and then she pulled a pack of cigarettes from her tunic pocket. I couldn't see the brand, but they looked foreign. She shook one out, gripped its white filter with her lips, and offered me the pack.

I shook my head. "Those things will kill you."

When she'd lit it, the red ember lighting up her alabaster face, she inhaled, held it, and released. "Ha!" she said, the single word a humourless punctuation that cut across the night sky with a sharp crackle.

I watched her silver breath float towards the clouds and, for a second, I let the noise of everything flood in—the birds and insects, the distant drone of traffic on the N18 that bypassed the village on its west, live music from a bar down by the beach, and the slow beat of Gloria's heart. I almost missed it at first, its beat was so slow. I listened to it, watching as she stepped towards the edge of the rooftop, and I counted. Three beats per minute. How was she doing that?

Gloria said, "Why do you want to die?"

Straight to the point. Good. I can answer direct questions better than pussyfooting around loosely connected topics about mortality.

I stood beside her in a cloud of her cigarette smoke and looked for the silver linings in the sky. There were none. "I'm tired," I said.

"You're young," she told me.

"How old are you?" I asked, and I knew a man wasn't supposed to ask a lady her age, even if times had progressed beyond such rigid gender stereotypes.

Gloria finished her cigarette and lit another one from the glowing butt of the first. Her hands were thin and there were grubby yellow stains between her index and middle fingers. I'd never spotted that before. She said, "How long is a piece of string?"

"What does that mean?" I asked.

The cigarette smoke turned through the air like it was acknowledging me before falling upwards. "You don't know what tired is," she said. "I have no age. I came before and I will continue after. You? You have a beginning. And you'll have an end. One day."

"I need that day to be soon."

"You care for him, don't you?" she said.

"I love him."

"But you also care for him, Victor. I've seen how you are with him. More so than the Brothers Grimm."

"Why do you call them that?"

She laughed, mirthless but light. She ignored the question. "Tell me again why you want to die."

"Because I'm tired."

"That's not enough. You can't turn the light off just because you want to close your eyes. Try again."

I thought about my answer. Not because I didn't know the reason, but because I was having difficulty putting it into words. I buried my hands in my trouser pockets even though I wasn't cold. Red and gold leaves skittered across the lawn and the trees that bordered the perimeter were almost bare, like my soul.

I said, "I don't want to go on without him. I loved him before I became . . . this. I thought, at first, that it would fade over time. When all my other emotions left me—fear, sadness—those things disappeared. But James did not. I've watched him grow old. And I know what's going to happen. When he's gone, my heart will ache. And that can kill a man; I've seen it. But I'm cursed to live on, with a blackened organ in my chest that beats for no one. And the pain will be excruciating."

Gloria nodded. "That's what love is. Excruciating."

"Are you speaking from experience? Have you loved?"

Gloria sucked on her cigarette. "Yes."

"I tried not to love him," I said. "In the sixties, I fell into any bed I could. In the seventies, I pumped myself full of every intoxicant known to man. But I couldn't get him out of my head. I can't live without him."

"But you must," Gloria said.

"I can't."

"And yet you will." She stubbed her cigarette out on the low wall that bordered the roof, slipped the pack back into her pocket, but then thought better of it and lit another one. "James' passing is his alone. When it happens, you can't go with him."

"Not by my own hand," I said. "But you can help me."

She shook her head. "That isn't something I can do."

"You have to."

"You're asking the wrong questions," she said.

"Then tell me the right ones."

Gloria turned from me as she breathed her cigarette smoke across Ireland. She didn't speak for a long time. Then, her voice a whisper, she said, "There is an order. The universe is structured. But when you step outside that structure, you are no longer bound by the universe's laws. You become unnatural. *You* are constrained by new laws, whether you know them or not. And those laws are not mine. You're not looking for comfort, Victor. You're asking me to break the universe's natural rules. And I can't."

"Can't or won't?" I asked.

"You're still asking the wrong questions."

I raised my voice. "Then help me!"

"No," she said. "I cannot give you the answers you're looking for. Death—it's part of nature. When will man understand that?"

"But you are death," I said.

Her smile was brief. "I don't take lives, kiddo. I merely guide them into the Next."

"The next what?"

"It is the Next. That is all."

"If I wanted cryptic answers," I said, "I'd have asked Yoda." Gloria turned on me. "What is time?" she asked. "You can start there."

"What is it?"

She turned from me again, a constant dance between facing me and facing the world. "Time is nonsense; that's what it is. I blink and a thousand years go by. Come to me when you have existed for millennia and neither of us will have aged. That is time."

"I don't have that long," I said. "James doesn't have that long."

"No. He doesn't."

"You know when he will go?"

She stubbed another cigarette out. "Soon."

"Please, help me."

"I can't."

I balled my fists. "Dammit, Gloria. End me."

And she lunged. Her eyes glowed like black fire and her hair swirled as her body rocked towards me. She gripped my throat, her fingers constricting my larynx. Whatever languid blood wallowed in my veins was swelling in my head. My eyes bugged as she tightened her hold on my neck.

Her lips moved and although she spoke, her voice was inside my head.

I am not your maker. And I cannot be your undoing.

I choked. My limbs were weak and a blackness swept across my vision until the only thing I could see were her onyx eyes. I had no breath, no strength to fight against her. My chest spasmed. Something inside me was crying. The pain radiated from my neck to my body. My left hand was darkening like it was back in 1949, and I heard my father's voice, his laughter. And my mother's.

I heard the universe.

And it rejected me.

When Gloria let go, I fell to my hands and knees, gasping for the stale breath I was used to. I was weak, unable to stand, and it took all my effort to look at her.

She covered her face like her head was sore. And in the silence, I heard her weeping.

She said, "You see? There is no end for you. Not by my hand."

I struggled to my feet. "I don't fit into your nature," I said.

"You don't fit into *any* nature."

I sat on the wall when I thought I might fall, and I drew the damp air into my heavy lungs. "And yet I exist," I said.

She sat beside me, shaking another cigarette from her pack. "Is existing so bad? You're a butterfly."

"You're not so ugly yourself," I said.

But Gloria said, "You used to be a caterpillar. Now you are something else."

"Not all butterflies are beautiful."

When she breathed her smoke out, she waved it away from us and then said, "You may be unnatural, Victor, but I can tell that, inside, beyond the blackness I see in you, there is a glimmer of light. A hope."

I didn't know what to say to that. As my strength was returning, I stood up, bouncing on my toes to shake the decay out of my limbs. "Why does death have to separate us?"

"I don't know," she said. "Death only bothers the living."

"You can't help me, can you?"

She shook her head, dropping her cigarette and crushing it under her plimsole. "I wish I could." She stood. "Your friends don't have long. If you do not wish to see their end, you should leave."

"And go where? Without James, I am nothing."

"I cannot say," Gloria said. "But there is a light at the end of your tunnel. You just have to find it."

"I can't face the light. And I can't leave."

"I know," she said.

As she turned to the door, I said, "Where will James go when he's gone?"

She looked at me. "Everywhere," she said.

And then she left.

I looked across the night. I was never going to escape it. I was bound to darkness, unable to exist in the light and too afraid to try. My mother had spent a lifetime searching for my cure, dragging me from one specialist to another, even after I was diagnosed with solar urticaria, a rare allergic reaction to sunlight. But she didn't know the truth. Nobody did.

I had no cure.

This was my life. My death. My immortality.

I went to James' room. Where else would I have gone?

He was asleep, his heartbeat pulsing at a languid sixty-four beats per minute. There were no telltale signs in that beat to indicate his imminent end. And yet Gloria had said his time was almost up.

I brought the chair in the corner of his room across to his bed and sat in it, watching him sleep. Old age mocked me. I could only watch it, never exist in it.

I cried, tears streaking my cheeks and flushing my shirt. And when James sat up in bed, I couldn't speak.

He cleared his throat. "Victor?"

My tears came harder. A pain was wedged in my chest.

James pulled back his bedsheets and motioned to me.

I crawled in beside him, drew my back to his chest, and let him wrap his arms around me. And when he pressed a kiss against my cheek, I breathed in his scent. His arms were strong, young. He held me tight.

And when I was exhausted, too weak to keep my eyes open, I fell asleep in his heat.

The last thing I heard him say was, "I still love you. I always have."

chapter 22

1949

They were waiting for me on the wall. I heard their laughter even before the sound of the Atlantic. The brothers waved as I approached, and Michael, head-locked in Danny's armpit, said, "Help, Victor." He held his hand out, asking me to tag him. His crutches were discarded on the sand and his plastered leg stuck out behind him.

I slapped Michael's hand, tagging myself into the fight, and jumped on Danny's side, knocking him into the dunes and freeing Michael, who skittered to his crutches with a laugh. I knuckled the top of Danny's head until he begged for mercy. His pleads to Giuseppe to tag in went unanswered as Giuseppe drank from his stumpy bottle of beer and spat on the sand.

"I give up," Danny said.

I bore my knuckles into his head. "Who's your leader?"

"James," Danny said.

I dug harder. "Who's your leader?"

"You," he conceded, his voice strangled. When I released him, he said, "Where's all your strength come from?"

I stood up, dusting sand from my trousers. I had to open my shirt and flap my undershirt around to get the grit out from beneath it, and when I did, I felt James' eyes taking in the shape of my stomach, the glassy sparkles of the sand dust under the streetlamps at the other side of the wall that lined the dark road beyond the beach.

As I buttoned my shirt again, I looked at him. "All right?"

He dropped his cigarette and stubbed it under his shoe. "All right."

Across the beach, a group of teenagers were gathered around a campfire, drinking and singing.

When the others were around, James and I tried to act normal. But by pretending as though I hadn't had his tongue in my mouth every night for the last week, we had cooled off in the presence of the others enough that Micheal had asked me last night, "What's up with you and James?"

"Nothing. Why?"

"You're acting like you hate each other."

"No, we're not," I'd said. I'd mentioned it to James later that night, on the floor of the apple orchard, and we'd agreed we needed to find a balance between normal and intimate.

"So I shouldn't do this around the others?" he'd asked, kissing my throat. "Or this?" he said, pulling my waist closer to him.

"And we definitely shouldn't do this," I said, unfastening the catch of his belt. He sighed into my mouth when my cold fingers found the heat of his body.

"But I love it when you do that," James said.

"Oh, really? What if I was to stop?" I teased. I pulled my hands away from him, holding them in the dark air, and I knew the soft breeze was playing over his skin because I saw the goosepimples that scratched across him.

"Don't stop," he whispered. And I couldn't tease him any longer.

Tonight, when I'd rescued Michael from Danny's grip and acknowledged James, I tried to make it sound natural, friendly. But Giuseppe looked from me to James and back, and said, "What's this? What's going on?"

"That's what I said," Michael told him.

"What's up with you two?" Danny asked.

"Nothing," we both said. I tried not to smile.

"Something's up."

"Nothing's up," James said. He came off the wall and stood beside me, nudging his elbow into my arm in a playful way that suggested everything was fine. I was still wearing a glove on my left hand because I didn't want anybody to know it had healed.

Giuseppe stood in front of us. "Who said what to who?"

"It's 'whom'," Michael said.

"Whatever."

"Guys," I said. "There's nothing wrong. Honestly."

Giuseppe poked his finger in James' face, then mine. "I don't like it," he said. "Whatever's wrong, you'd better kiss and make up. Got it?"

James shot an arm around my neck and made wet kissing noises as I fought to get out of his grip. "Eww, get off," I laughed.

I think we'd convinced the boys that we were okay, but later, when the village hall clock chimed two a.m. and the night's dew was forming on late summer weeds, James scaled the orchard wall, found me under our tree, and said, "Eww?"

"What?" I smiled. "It worked, didn't it?"

"My kissing technique isn't up to your impeccable standards, is that it?" I knew the scowl on his face was for show, but it had found its way into his voice as well.

"Not when you smack your lips like a humble hooker," I said.

He laughed. "What's a humble hooker?"

"I don't know," I said. "A lady of the night that knows she's no better than we are?"

He knelt on the tartan blanket that I'd laid out for us and he faced me. "We're better than everyone."

I took his hands. "Hiding under a tree in the dark? Skulking around in the shadows like criminals?"

"We're not criminals," he said.

Noel Albermaine from the city was imprisoned two years ago for the very thing we were doing now. He was a local GP, found rutting in an alley with another man. It made all the newspapers and the national radio broadcast. He got eighteen months for gross indecency and the other man, a known rent boy, was beaten to death the following night. His murder received a single paragraph on the bottom of page two, a negligible column inch.

Albermaine was pictured in the papers on his release just two months ago. His hair was unkempt and his face was gaunt, dark eyes sunken into his skull at either side of a disjointed nose. That image would be burned in my mind for all eternity.

And neither James nor I wanted a one-inch story to run about our own deaths. That's why we stayed in the shadows in the dead of night, in a place with high walls and no way to find us. When I kissed him, I always had my hearing tuned to the air, listening for the sound of heartbeats or footsteps. Queers knew how to be quiet when they needed to be.

"You worry too much," James said, tugging me down to the blanket.

He was right. But I wasn't worried for my safety. "We have to be careful," I said. I could never be responsible for his imprisonment. Or death.

James opened my shirt, and as the buttons came free, so did my thoughts. Newspaper print and hard labour were replaced by the warm drag of his fingers across my taut stomach as he lifted my undershirt over my head. And when his lips found mine in the orchard darkness, I wasn't thinking about Noel Albermaine or the nameless rent boy or anything other than the beat of James' heart inside my head and the tug of his body that drew me into him with force.

Later, when he rested his head against my chest, I knew he was listening for my heartbeat. So I shifted, drew his face to mine, and distracted him with a kiss. His heart was beating for both of us now.

The next day, as I waited for the sun to go down, I sat at the dinner table with Mum and Aunt Cara, a plate of mashed potatoes and green beans in front of me. Mum slid a steak beside them and the greasy blood washed against the potatoes like an ocean wave. Mum and Cara's steaks were charred and blackened, overcooked—the Irish way—but I'd learned that rare meat was edible. Almost. I was able to keep it down for longer than anything else, but it still came up, forcing me to rinse my mouth with Listerine, spitting the amber liquid into the toilet bowl after the meat. But the iron-like taste of rare steak satisfied the burning hunger in my stomach.

A few days before, when Mum was rolling ground beef into balls with the palms of her hands, I kneaded some of the mince between my thumb and forefinger and tasted it raw. It was sickly and tangy but I wanted more.

Aunt Cara watched me drag a sliver of steak across the plate, gathering up its red juices, and said, "You're an animal. Meat is supposed to be cooked like the good Lord intended. And take those damned sunglasses off in the house. I've told you before."

I didn't argue this time. Cara had been pointed with Mum for days after the last incident at the table and my pride wasn't worth the aggression. I took the sunglasses off, squinting in the glare of the late afternoon, and mopped up the spill of blood on my plate. I wilfully chewed with my mouth open, masticating the meat like I wanted to do to her throat.

I don't know if Cara had spotted the changes in me, my leaner muscle and my bolder attitude, but she didn't bite back.

When I got to the wall by the beach, twenty minutes after the sun went down, the boys were in their customary spot, opposite the pub on the corner. James was across the street, on his way into the pub, and he threw me a wave, making a drinking gesture to ask if I wanted a beer. I gave him a thumbs up and joined the others instead of clinging to his side.

"It's his birthday tomorrow," Danny said.

James hadn't told me. I don't know why.

"We should plan something," Giuseppe said.

Michael got down from the wall, slipping his arms over his crutches, and said, "I get my cast off tomorrow afternoon, so whatever we do will have to be after."

"We should have a party," I said, knowing that I'd never be able to attend until dark.

We had nowhere to host the celebration, so it was decided to hold it here, on the beach. "After sundown," I reminded them.

"We'll need supplies," Danny said.

"I have some banners and streamers from my last birthday," I told them. James was coming back across the road with his hands wrapped around some beer bottles.

Giuseppe whispered, "We'll come to yours in the morning. You don't have to step outside, just throw everything at us from the doorstep."

When we had a moment alone on the wall, sitting beside each other while the brothers wrestled in the dunes and Michael was hopping down to the shoreline for a pee, I sipped from my beer bottle and then said, "It's your birthday?"

James nodded. "Who told you?"

"They want to do something fun tomorrow," I said.

"Not without you."

"I'll be there. After dark. Why didn't you tell me?"

James shrugged. "Slipped my mind."

"How does your birthday slip your mind?" I asked, but James didn't have the opportunity to respond as Michael slinked back towards us. I whispered, "Tell me later."

"Stealing apples," James mumbled.

When I met him in the orchard, watching the moonlight

shimmer in his eyes, I asked him again. "How come you didn't tell me?"

He tried to shut me up with a kiss but I wouldn't let him. James sighed. "I don't want to talk about it."

"But it's your birthday. It's a big deal."

"Shut up and kiss me," he smiled.

I kissed him, once, before saying, "Don't you love me?" I didn't mean to say the L word, but there it was, hanging between us like a tear in someone's upholstery, small enough that he could have patched it up if he wanted to.

But he tore it wider when he said, "Of course I love you."

If anything was going to jumpstart my heart, it should have been that.

I took his hands and said, "I love you too."

And James said, "But."

I loosened my fingers. "But?"

He nudged my chin, staring into my eyes like he was searching for something. He said, "But I'll be eighteen." He checked his watch even though we both knew it was after midnight. "I *am* eighteen."

"Happy birthday," I said. "But so?"

"I'm one year closer to being considered an adult. And the courts aren't so lenient when you get to my age."

The age of majority was twenty-one. I had images of Noel Albermaine running through my head. But James was right—there were already cases of eighteen-year-olds being tried in Dublin and Cork. And small-town whispers were a lot louder than cities. Our little fishing village had a population of less than six hundred people; if only one found out, they would all know.

"We can stop," I said, pulling him down to the blanket.

"But I can't," James told me, with a kiss that proved it.

"Me either," I whispered against his flesh. I found his jaw with my lips, the hollow beneath his earlobe, and then I kissed along his collarbone, already tearing at his shirt. James cupped his hands under my backside as an owl told us off.

But we didn't stop. We didn't know how.

His breath was ragged when he spoke again, an hour—or hours—later. I'd stopped listening to the sounds of the orchard and the quiet streets beyond as I laser-focused my attention on pleasing him. I hadn't even heard the sound of the village clock over the whisper of his quickened heart.

He nudged my shoulder to lift my face off his chest. "It's getting light."

I jumped, fastening my trousers and pulling my half-buttoned shirt over my head. "I need to go," I said.

James propped himself on an elbow as I tried to pull the blanket out from under him. He leaned his head against his fist and said, "Don't go."

"I have to."

"It's my birthday," he said.

I knelt and kissed him. In the east, the predawn sky was turning grey. I felt a warmth pressing on the top of my head.

"Stay."

"James, I can't. My eyes."

He held his fingers over my eyes and I inhaled the earthy scent of his skin. "Stay," he said again.

And then we both jumped. He heard it the same time that I had, the rickety squeak of wooden wheels on the hill, a distant clicking noise, and a whispered voice. I hadn't been paying attention. James had pulled me into his core and I'd forgotten about the world.

We heard Danny say, "Push harder, I can't drag this thing by myself." And Giuseppe grumbled in response.

"Shit," James mouthed.

I put my finger to my lips and whispered, "They're coming to mine to get supplies for tonight."

"Why are they awake so early? I'll hop the wall after they pass," James said.

We listened, my hearing intent on the squeak of their cart as they pulled it up the hill towards Aunt Cara's house. When they were far enough away, I nodded, cupped my hands into a lift, and James climbed to the top of the wall.

"Wait!" I hissed, but it was too late. James was over the wall before I could stop him.

And Michael said, "Jesus. What were you doing in there?"

Where was my hearing? I had been so focused on Danny and Giuseppe that I forgot to consider Michael's presence as he hobbled up the hill behind them on his crutches. That was the clicking noise I'd heard.

"Nothing," James said. "What are you doing here?"

"Going to Victor's," Michael said.

I had two seconds to come up with a plan. When I leapt to the top of the wall, I pretended to be out of breath and said, "Catch." I'd quickly gathered some apples and dropped a handful of them down to James and Michael before easing myself to the ground like a cat.

Michael's features contorted into disbelief. "Victor?" he said.

"Hey. You guys are early."

"What were you doing?" he asked.

James gathered the apples from the ground. "Stealing apples," he said. "What does it look like?"

But Michael didn't answer.

"I'm going to be late for work," James said. "See you guys later."

We watched him disappear down the hill before I heard Danny and Giuseppe at the top, turning the cart into Cara's drive.

"Need any help?" I asked Michael.

"No," he said. He adjusted his crutches before clicking up the hill.

And as I walked beside him, we said nothing.

When we got home, the brothers were waiting by Cara's car, a tarp rolled back over the empty cart, Giuseppe grinning in the darkness before dawn.

I laughed. "When I said I had some supplies, I meant balloons and banners. What do you need the cart for?"

Danny said, "We're going to tie up your aunt and tickle her until she kisses us."

And Giuseppe said, "Where were you?"

With a sour look on his face, Michael said, "Stealing apples."

chapter 23

the present

Sometimes I hated the rain when it crashed inside my head and sounded like a shipwreck in the ocean. Other times it tempered the noise of everything else. Tonight, an hour before Lakeshore Manor's Halloween party, the rain pissed on everyone's parade, and you could feel the sticky heat of autumn coming from the radiators.

I sat in the highbacked chair in James' room, holding his hand.

His breath came slow, stretching on for seconds of quiet torture in between. His face was pale and his wrinkles deep, and outside, the rain battered the window like it wanted in to wash his soul clean.

Death wore a nursing uniform and she prowled around downstairs. But I wasn't going to let her take him. Not tonight.

"It's Halloween," James said. His words were raspy with

dust in his throat.

I nodded, drawing my eyes away from the window where the reflection of James lay in repose on a ghostly bed of white sheets and blue blankets. Reflections are only shadows with colour.

"Yes," I said. "How are you feeling?" I released his hand, curling my fingers against the blackness of his pain, and I waited for the tingling ache to subside, pushing it out of my palm with a massaging thumb. The darkness sought its way up my arm and into my head.

He sat up, slowly, propping himself on his elbows, and his pyjama shirt draped at the front, exposing the cool sweat on his silver chest. I took a towel and pressed it against him. The dewy heat from the radiator by the bed was making the room throb.

He tugged at the neck of his shirt. "Can you crack the window open a bit?"

"Can't," I said. "It's pissing down."

He looked at the window as though he hadn't heard the drum of the rain against it, and the wind screamed across the roof tiles above us.

"You took my pain again," he said. It wasn't a question.

I shrugged.

"It wasn't yours to take," he said.

"You feel better, though?" I asked, as if making him feel well was all the permission I needed.

James eased his legs out of bed. His pyjama trousers had ridden up and I could see the dark blemishes of life on his glossy shins where old age had taken the hairs that youth had given him.

I helped him into his slippers.

"Why aren't you downstairs?" he asked. The bass-filled tunes of a Halloween playlist echoed through the air vents. Most of the residents were gathering for the party in the common room.

"Because you're up here," I said.

He looked at me. "You're not my keeper."

"Why can't I be?"

He snorted in derision. "Because I'm on my way out and you have many lifetimes to live."

"Don't talk like that."

"It's the truth."

I turned from him. "That doesn't mean you have to say it."

He stood up, shaky, and gripped his walker. "Pass me my dressing gown, you old fool. We're going to this party, and there'd better be cake."

"You shouldn't be eating sugary foods," I said, holding his gown as he struggled to get his arms in. I helped him tie the cord before opening his bedroom door.

"What's it going to do, kill me?"

"If I don't bop you over the head and strangle you first," I said. Sometimes, when he speaks, I forget how old he is.

He laughed. "You and who's army?"

I held my hand behind him as he walked, inching down the corridor.

"Where are the boys?" he asked.

"They're already downstairs with everybody else."

James swatted a paper skeleton that dangled from the ceiling in front of the lift, and I pushed the call button. When we got in, I stood beside him and faced the metal doors.

"You're standing there like a bodyguard," he said.

"Does that make you my Whitney Houston?"

"I don't have the voice," he said. "Or the legs."

"I don't know. I've seen your legs. You'd give Audrey Hepburn a run for her money."

"What do you know about Audrey Hepburn's legs?" he grumbled.

I shrugged. "Nothing. I'm only surmising."

"Did you turn straight in your old age?" he asked, and the thick ropes that held the lift in place laughed at his joke.

I hated that lift. It took forever to go anywhere and the creak of its pullies and winches were louder than the gripes of an old man.

"Heaven forfend," I said, my mouth hanging open in shock at his allegations.

He nudged my chin with a warm knuckle. "Put your tongue away before you start catching flies."

Sometimes I imagined what it would have been like to grow old with him. If things had been different. If the world hadn't conspired against us. Would he wake every morning and run his fingers through my slowly greying hair, kiss my lips and call me beautiful? Or would he joke about my wrinkles and tell me I had more lines than *War & Peace*?

I wanted to kiss him, but the doors of the lift opened and Nurse Gloria was standing in the corridor. Her shadow fell across the floor like a pointing finger and I stepped in front of James to protect him. She was wearing a pair of plastic devil's horns as if it wasn't the most apt thing she could have donned for Halloween besides a tinfoil scythe.

"Happy Halloween," she said. She held out a plastic

pumpkin full of Cadbury's Heroes and James took a fudge. I wished he hadn't. In his hand, as he peeled the wrapper apart, I worried that the sweet was a poisoned apple. "None for you?" Gloria asked.

"No, thanks."

I watched her walk away and when she disappeared at the end of the corridor, a renewed barrage of rain smacked against the front door opposite the reception desk. The lights flickered.

"Spooky," James said.

"Old buildings and bad wiring," I told him. I wished I believed that. "Hey," I said, before he shuffled into the common room. "If you feel unwell, you let me know, okay?"

"I'm fine."

"You are now. But later, if you start to feel ill. Or tired. Or dizzy."

"Victor," he said. "I know you mean well, but let me die in peace, will you?"

"Not on my watch." I looked up the corridor and Gloria was standing in the shadows, watching us. When I glanced at James and looked back, she was gone.

Death's energy seeped across the carpets.

In the common room, a disco ball had been suspended from the ceiling, but the lights hadn't been turned down so it was difficult to see the sparkle of the ball across the walls. Bobby Pickett's *Monster Mash* was falling out of the corner speakers and some of the residents were wearing witches' hats or plastic Halloween masks. Their families had been invited and grown-ups stood around with cups of tea or glasses of prosecco, and children were dressed as ghosts and mummies and princesses.

A therapy dog wearing a yellow bandana rolled onto her back between some of the residents and begged for a belly rub.

We found Danny and Giuseppe by the card table, but they weren't playing. Giuseppe was trying to feed Danny a yoghurt and sticky cream coated the corner of his lips. Danny was wasting away. I swear I could see his skull through his skin.

"All right?" James asked like we were gathered by the wall above the beach, ready for a night of beers and shenanigans.

Danny smacked his lips and his sunken eyes were half closed.

"Open up," Giuseppe said. He prodded the spoon against his brother's mouth.

Danny grumbled. He didn't want any more.

"One more bite," Giuseppe said, "or I'll get Victor to hold you down and pinch your nose."

"Stephen," I reminded him.

Giuseppe looked at me with a frown, then turned back to his brother.

The lights flickered again and some of the younger kids screamed. There was too much noise, so I focused on James' heartbeat, keeping a watchful ear on him. If there was any arrythmia, I'd know it.

Danny's head drooped forward and Giuseppe nudged him. "Stay awake or you'll miss the dancing."

I wished I'd had a brother to grow old with.

Or a lover.

James.

Giuseppe said, "Get me a napkin, will you, Vic?"

I reached for some serviettes on a nearby table and said, "Giuseppe, you know my name is Stephen."

"You think I'm senile?" he asked, snatching the napkins from me and wiping Danny's mouth.

"I think you're confused. That's all."

"Now, now, boys," James said. "That's enough bickering."

"If Michael was here, he'd back me up," Giuseppe said.

"Michael's not here."

I didn't open my mouth. We all missed Michael. Sometimes, when I woke, I'd get the sense that Michael's spirit was in my room, watching me. I'd open my eyes and, for a second, he'd be standing in the corner, a kid with floppy red hair and wide eyes. But when I focused, he'd be gone.

Danny raised a frail hand and motioned to the half-empty yoghurt pot in Giuseppe's hand. He wanted another mouthful now. Old men are allowed to change their minds.

His tongue was fat and red when Giuseppe raised the spoon.

Claire Osmonde shuffled over on the arm of a young woman. Claire wasn't much for talking, and any time I'd interacted with her it had been brief but pleasant. Her bedroom slippers were new and fluffy.

The younger woman said, "Mammy wants to know if any of you gentlemen would like to dance with her."

Claire pointed at Danny, and Giuseppe said, "Do you want to dance, old timer?"

Danny's lips moved but words didn't come out.

Giuseppe leaned in to hear him, and then he stood up. He gripped the handles of Danny's wheelchair and kicked the brakes off. "He'd be delighted, was what he said." There was a hint of a smile on Danny's yoghurt-painted lips.

"Charmer," James laughed.

We watched as Giuseppe wheeled Danny into the centre of the room and Claire's daughter guided her along in front of them. The younger woman held on to Claire's elbow as her mother shuffled her feet, and Giuseppe turned Danny's chair back and forward in a box step. Some of the residents clapped their hands in time with the music and others joined the dancing, slippers whispering over the carpet to an unconventional beat.

James rubbed his chest.

"Are you in pain?" I asked, looking around to make sure Gloria wasn't nearby with her devil's horns and deathly stare. I could feel her strength seeping through the walls. Somebody was going to die tonight and I needed to make sure it wouldn't be James. I wasn't ready.

"Will you relax?" James said.

I reached for his hand but he pulled it away from me.

"You can't fix every ache."

"I can if you let me."

"I had an itch," he said. "If I let you scratch it, will you shut the hell up?" But he was smiling. "I'm fine," he said.

"Are you sure?"

He scowled and I zipped my mouth up, twisting my fingers like a lock.

I moved my chair closer and we watched the dancing. Somebody had put party hats on Danny and Claire and the old woman's daughter was laughing at something Giuseppe had said. Probably a filthy innuendo, knowing him.

Later, after I'd asked James if he was all right two more

times, my skin bristled when Nurse Gloria came into the room. A thick breeze followed her that nobody else seemed to feel. I shivered as she passed by. Her trick-or-treat container was almost empty as she walked around the room, touching the backs of the residents that I thought she was marking.

You're next, I thought. And you. And you.

James said, "What time is it?"

"Ten thirty."

He yawned.

"Are you tired?"

"No," he grumbled, but then he checked himself and said, "Yeah."

I stood. "Do you want a wheelchair?"

"I'll walk."

"I can carry you," I said, and he laughed.

"Do you want to out yourself? Who's going to believe a skinny little kid like you could bench press an old thing like this?"

"There's nothing of you," I said.

"I could pick up twelve of you with one hand," James said, and he struggled to his feet, batting my arm away when I reached for him.

He gripped his walking frame and I slid an empty chair out of the way so he could pass.

And then Gloria was in my way. She slipped her plastic horns off and touched James' shoulder. "Have you had a good night, young man?"

James caught his breath from the effort of standing up and I tried to get between him and her, tried to force her hand off his shoulder.

"He's just a little tired," I said. "That's all. Just tired. Nothing more."

"You go on up and get some sleep," she said. "Have you had your nighttime meds?"

"I've got him covered," I said, and I wasn't referring to his medication.

Gloria rubbed his shoulder like a concerned nurse and I saw a glint in her eyes that I didn't like.

"Sleep well," she said.

When we got upstairs, I sat by his bed and listened to the rain outside and the muted thrum of the music from downstairs. And I listened to the quiet corridor beyond his room, making sure Gloria wasn't coming for him.

James yawned when I'd got him into bed. He said, "There's room for you in here beside me."

"I'll be okay here," I said. I couldn't lie down on the job. James wasn't going to die tonight. I wouldn't allow it. Gloria couldn't kill me—and I'd hold her off as long as I could.

I heard the others returning to their bedrooms later, and I brought my attention back to James' soft breath and quiet heart that filled my head with his love. I was lost in a reverie, a memory of James' lips pressed against mine under a canopy of thick trees when, in his sleep, he mumbled, "Stealing apples."

I smiled. Were we sharing a memory? I sat by his bed for hours, watching him sleep.

And then I heard Giuseppe scream.

"Help!" he shouted. "Jesus Christ, I think he's dead."

I opened James' bedroom door just as Gloria swept down the corridor towards us.

"No," I said.

She shook her head.

"No," I demanded.

But Gloria opened Danny and Giuseppe's door. She went inside and closed it behind her.

And Giuseppe's weeping flooded inside me.

chapter 24

1949

The long summer days were shortening as August lost the battle against September. Normally, I'd be morose, miserable at the failing sunlight and the dawn of an early autumn. But the longer nights meant I could go outside earlier, after the sun had cut a path into the ocean and drowned in its crystalline bath.

Soon after celebrating James' eighteenth birthday with beers on the beach—much like any other summer evening—and then a private party, just the two of us, under the sweet scent of green apples, I had stopped noticing the hunger in the pit of my stomach. It was so constant that it became the standard by which my future was set.

I'd taken to sleeping through the day and slipping out to the apple orchard at night to spend a couple of hours in James' arms before he had to go to bed. Although I was unable to return to work, James still had a life to take care of.

"I don't want to go," he said often, under the shadow of the trees, and I'd grip his face with my hands, kiss him with an intense passion, and remind him that we always had tomorrow. And the night after.

"And the one after that," he'd say.

I'd stand on top of the wall and watch him disappear into the night, and then I'd drop to my feet without any effort and run home. I could get from the orchard wall to the front door in under four seconds. I timed it.

It was Amaral's fault.

I had convinced myself that he was real, that my condition wasn't a result of the shipwreck and exposure to the extreme temperatures of the ocean. At least not directly. If it was, how come James or the others weren't affected?

I'd spend the rest of my nights prowling the house while Mum and Aunt Cara slept. I opened the drawers of the bureau in the parlour and read the letters that Cara wrote every evening. Although they weren't letters as I had suspected but quotes from the bible. At least she couldn't drag me to Mass every Sunday like she used to, now that I couldn't go out in the daylight—and she'd have a battle on her hands for midnight Mass on Christmas Eve.

I'd retune the radio to a modern station that played Perry Como and Frankie Laine, the music drifting into the room through the fuzz of static, and I'd dig up the weeds in Aunt Cara's garden not because she wanted me to but because there were only so many things you could do at four in the morning without any friends.

In late August, Mum took me to the first of an onslaught

of specialists. She tried to book the appointment for as early as possible, hoping to avoid the direct sunlight that burned me, but the timeslot they gave her was eleven a.m. and she had to drape a heavy blanket over me as I dashed for the back seat of the car. She bundled me inside and I hid under the blanket the whole way there.

The specialist wasn't called Doctor. Mr Mitchell took me into a dimly lit room and had me take my shirt off while he inspected the skin on my shoulders, back and arms. He pointed out moles and asked how long I'd had them and if they'd changed shape or colour recently.

"And when you're exposed to sunlight, how long does it take to feel uncomfortable, before it gets painful?"

"Instantly?" I said. I posed it as a question because I didn't know what he wanted me to say.

"And what about indirect sunlight?"

"It still burns," I said.

He made me put my shirt back on and then said, "I'm going to put this protective cover over your arm." There was a one-inch square cut in the blue fabric and I was terrified of what would come next. "Then I'm going to shine this UV light on it. You'll let me know if there's any discomfort, won't you?"

I nodded, clenching my jaw and my fist against the inevitable pain.

When he turned the UV lamp on, even before shining it on the open square, I felt the heat of it stinging my cheeks. He turned the lamp around and passed it over my arm.

I screamed. Hot steam rose from the square and blistered welts bubbled to the surface.

"Jesus," Mr Mitchell said. He turned the lamp off and pulled the cover away from my arm. A perfect square of skin was red and pocked. He held my arm closer to his face under the dim overhead lights and marvelled at the reaction. If he was a farmer looking at a prize bull, he'd had whistled in admiration.

He scribbled some notes on his paper and then looked at me. He didn't apologise for burning my skin. "And you say you've had this reaction since you almost drowned at the beach?"

I nodded. I was still gritting my teeth in pain.

He scribbled again. Later, when Mum was brought into the room, Mr Mitchell said, "Without a marine biologist to investigate the waters around young Victor's accident, I can't rule out exposure to something in the ocean—a pollutant or some as yet unaccounted-for microorganism. I've never seen such an aggressive case of solar urticaria. In most instances, a patient might display signs of hives within a minute or two. But Victor's symptoms appear at once."

"Is there a cure?" Mum asked. I was glad she was there, but I already knew the answer.

"I'm afraid not," Mr Mitchell said. "But there are ways to manage the condition. I'd like to refer you to a colleague of mine in Dublin. He's a dermatologist specialising in cases of polymorphic light eruption."

I cradled my arm after Mr Mitchell dressed it, pulling down the sleeve to make sure the doctor didn't see my body's ability to heal itself, and Mum patted my leg like I was a miserable child. She said, "You mentioned ways to manage it?"

Mr Mitchell wrote on a prescription sheet. "I'm prescribing

a course of antihistamine cream to soothe the breakouts when they do occur, but I suggest you also pick up a zinc oxide ointment from the pharmacy. Apply it liberally when you absolutely must go out in the daylight but try to avoid direct sunlight where possible. At least until you've been to see Dr Strauss in Dublin."

"No more construction work with my shirt off, then," I said and Mum nudged my elbow. She didn't like jokes. Not since Dad had died.

We picked up the cream and ointment on the way home but I refused to use them. I knew they wouldn't help. It wasn't solar urticaria that I had; it was something worse. Something terminal.

And it was all Amaral's fault.

As the days stretched into weeks, the dark hunger in the pit of my stomach swelled again. I knew what my body wanted, but I had no intention of feeding that hunger. I was getting weak, my skin pale and fragile, even as my muscles strengthened.

Eating rare steak wasn't enough. I was hungry and thirsty and craving the burning tang of blood. But I wouldn't give in. I couldn't.

And when it got too much for me, when I lay in James' arms under the cover of apple trees and listened to the pulse of blood in his veins, I coughed against his skin and told him I wasn't feeling well. I stumbled away from him in a panic of bloodlust that gripped my jaw like a vice.

I ran to the beach at three in the morning and wailed at the moon. I shouted Amaral's name at the ocean and waited for him to come. But he didn't.

"Amaral, you bastard," I screamed. "Fix me or kill me. I don't care any more."

And the rainclouds washed in from the Atlantic, soaking me with their tears for my plight. I knelt on the drenched sand and cried Amaral's name until I was hoarse.

When he didn't come for me, I slouched through the streets of the village that smelled of smoked fish and brine. I climbed the tree outside James' house and knocked on his window.

He opened it for me and I went inside.

"You're soaked," he whispered, draping a spare blanket over my shoulders and ruffling it through my hair.

I had no words. I cried against his neck, inhaling his scent, and he unbuttoned my shirt and helped me out of my trousers. I stood before him in only my undershirt and pants, my skin glistening under the soft glow of his bedside lamp. He steered me into his bed and got in behind me, pulling the blankets over us and rubbing my arm like he was warming me.

He kissed the nape of my neck with searing lips and I think I was too cold to shiver. Or perhaps I wasn't cold enough. I didn't feel the temperature any more.

"What's wrong?" he whispered. His breath was soft against my cheek.

I closed my eyes, my head swallowed by the pillow that smelled like him, and I opened my mouth to tell him the truth. But the words wouldn't come. Instead, I said, "I'm tired of being sick."

"You're not sick," he said. "You're you."

"I can be me and still be sick."

"Is it your eyes?"

I turned on his narrow bed to face him, blinking in the dark. I could tell he was searching my eyes for the gold flecks that he loved.

"It's not just that. If I go out in the daylight, I'll die."

"You won't die."

"I will," I said, and he pulled me tighter, offering me a kiss on my forehead.

"You're freezing," he said.

"Am I?"

I felt his strong hands on my back as he tugged the blanket tighter around us. He said, "You've never been in my room before."

I looked over his head at the nightstand with its lamp and a snow globe of Dublin, a knackered chest of drawers with the front of the bottom drawer trapped at an angle, and a wooden chair with yesterday's clothes dumped on it. His socks and underwear were kicked under the chair on the floor.

I touched the lapel of his pyjama shirt, drawing my thumb across his chest. I smiled, sniffed back the tears I'd stopped crying, and said, "Why isn't this on the floor with the rest of your clothes?"

He hurried out of his bedclothes, kissing me as he pulled my undershirt off, and his hands kneaded my skin while his teeth dragged against the pale flesh of my chest.

In the morning, he woke me with a kiss and his breath was minty. I stretched knotted limbs and looked at him. A thin towel circled his waist and his thick hair was damp and tossed.

"Morning," he said.

I bolted upright. "What time is it?"

"Relax. It's still dark. I have to get to the dairy." He turned from me, dropping the towel to pull on a pair of underpants, and I studied the contours of his body, the pale fuzz that cupped his cheeks. "You talk in your sleep," he said.

I sat up, planting my feet on the floor and searching for my socks. "What did I say?"

"I don't know," he said. When he turned to me, I saw the trail of dark hairs that led from his navel to the waistband of his underwear. I wanted to dig my fingers under that band. "Something about owls wearing trousers and . . . a name. I couldn't make it out."

"I don't dream," I told him.

He pushed me back onto the bed and pinned me down with his weight, his thighs either side of my waist. "I don't know about that, but you were talking up a storm."

I linked my fingers behind his neck and drew him down. I kissed him and rolled on top.

The air whooshed out of his lungs and he laughed. "It's like that, is it?" He tried to roll me off him but he couldn't, so he resorted to tickling me. But I don't tickle. Not any more.

He squirmed, kicking his legs to throw me off, and as he wriggled, he bumped the nightstand with his knee and the glass snow globe toppled. It smashed and he jumped.

"Shit," he whispered. He covered my mouth for silence and listened. But we hadn't woken his parents. A cat meowed outside James' bedroom door.

And even over the fresh scent of his silencing fingers against my lips, I smelled his blood.

I stood up, backing over the broken glass. "You're cut."

He twisted his leg to look. A trickle of blood snaked through the fine hairs on his shin. "It's just a scratch."

I held my breath. The tangy smell of it was making my stomach growl. My gums were swelling. "There's glass in it," I said. I could see the glint of it even in the predawn darkness.

He held his leg up. "Can you get it out?"

"It's tiny," I said. I didn't want to touch him.

"You have longer nails than me," James said. "You can pick it out better."

"James."

"It's just a little blood. Come on, Vic, I'm going to be late for work." He wriggled his toes. "Don't you like my legs?"

"James," I laughed.

"Please?"

I knelt. Gingerly touched his leg. Watched as the blood eased around the curve to his calf. I tried to ignore it, focusing on the tiny wound. The glass shard was miniscule, but I had no problem seeing it in the dim light. I think my eyes were glowing.

I reached out, dug my teeth into my lower lip to distract my brain, and picked the glass out. I dropped it.

There was blood on my fingertips.

"Did you get it?" he asked.

I didn't answer him. I brought my hand to my nose and inhaled the tang of his blood. I sucked a finger into my mouth and tasted him.

It was heaven's nectar.

I cradled his leg. And I kissed the hairs where the blood had formed. I kissed again.

And I sucked.

I drew his blood into my mouth, swallowing the warmth of it.

James inhaled sharply, and then let the breath go. I looked up, my lips clamped to his shin, and watched as he threw his head back.

"Victor," he said.

I moaned against his skin. The blood had stopped. The cut wasn't deep and the air was healing it. But I wanted more.

My gums cracked. I felt something weeping inside my mouth and a sharp pain stabbed above my teeth.

I let go of him, stumbling back onto the floor on my ass. He stared at me. "What the fuck? What was that?"

"What was what?"

"Are we blood brothers now?"

"I have to go," I said. I stood up. "It's getting light."

I opened his window.

"Victor," he said.

I turned. I could still taste him in my mouth. "I'm sorry. Will I see you tonight?" I crawled through the window onto the thick tree branch.

He nodded.

And I skidded down the tree to the ground. When I looked back, he was watching me from his window. There was something in my mouth, either side of my incisors. I ran my tongue over them, and as I did, they disappeared back inside my gums.

chapter 25

the present

Giuseppe sat beside Danny's open casket. The faint warble of orchestral music with a deep cello sadness draped around the corners of the room from invisible speakers. It was after ten p.m. and the room was thick with the fragrance of flowers.

"Are you okay?" I asked him.

Giuseppe didn't acknowledge me.

"You should get some sleep. I'll take over."

He looked at me, eyes blinking, confused, as though he didn't know who I was. His tie was at an awkward angle, strangling the shirt around his thin neck. His fists were in his lap, clutching a handkerchief, and I saw the silver glare of Danny's watch on his wrist. He'd put it on during the night after Danny had passed and now, two long nights later, he checked it religiously, as if knowing the time was the most important thing in his life.

"Giuseppe?" I asked.

He blinked again.

The funeral home was warm, with soft carpets and velvet seats. It was the one place a cherrywood coffin didn't seem out of place. Even the white satin inlay was inviting, although I couldn't look directly at Danny's ashen face. I still had the echo of Giuseppe's screams in my head from when Danny had passed away and the look on his face now made me want to hold him and never let go.

Danny was his world.

Giuseppe checked the time, tapped the dial with a crooked finger, and then pressed it to his ear.

He said, "The date's wrong. What day is it?" He fumbled with his thick fingers on the winder and I offered to help him with it.

I wound it forward, the small number rolling over to the second of November.

When I looked at his face, adjusting his shirtsleeve over the watch, he said, "Is it right?"

"It's right."

"Good." He put it to his ear again.

"There's a car waiting outside, Giuseppe."

"Where's it going?" he asked.

I touched his shoulder. "It'll take you back to Lakeshore Manor. You need a hot meal and some sleep."

"I'm all right here," he said.

"Danny's not going anywhere," I told him, and I didn't mean it to sound as dire as it felt. "I'll watch over him," I added. "I'm here for both of you. All right?"

He nodded. "Where's James?"

"At the manor."

"And Michael? We'll have to tell Michael."

I smiled, offering him what little comfort I could. "Michael's gone, Giuseppe. Remember?"

"I know," he said. He stared at Danny's face. His brother's hair had been combed neater than usual and, although he no longer looked like my old friend, I had to admit the makeup they'd applied to his cheeks and forehead was professional and left him looking warm and at peace.

"The car is ready," I reminded him.

He nodded again. "Nobody calls me Joe these days."

"We haven't called you Joe in a long time," I said, realising that, by saying *we*, I was giving him my secret.

"Do you know where the name Giuseppe came from?" he asked.

I waited for him to answer his own question.

"Danny gave it to me one day out of the blue. I have no idea why. I used to rack my brains, trying to figure it out. Giuseppe Meazza, maybe—the footballer. Or Giuseppe Farina, the racing driver. He never did tell me."

"Isn't Giuseppe Italian for Joseph?" I asked.

"That'll be it," he said, "but it still doesn't explain why. We should wake him up and ask him." He looked at me then, his eyes studying my features. "Do you want to wake him up now?"

I didn't know what response he wanted. I said, "I can't."

And he nodded. He stood up, shaky, and gripped a walking cane that I hadn't seen him use before. I don't think he'd eaten in two days.

He put his hand on the side of Danny's casket and looked

in. His fingers shook when he touched Danny's wrinkled, sunken face.

"Victor," Giuseppe said.

Under the circumstances, I didn't have the heart to lie to him. "Yes?" I asked.

"You could have saved him." He didn't look at me. And I didn't have the energy to ask him what he meant. He said, "You could have made him live. The way you lived. You could have saved us all."

I couldn't speak. I opened my mouth and nothing came. But I shook my head and forced the words out. "What I have isn't a life. And besides, I don't have that ability." I couldn't. Whatever Amaral did to me, I couldn't do to others. I knew because I'd tried. Once.

Giuseppe nodded when a male nurse opened the door and cleared his throat.

"Watch over him, will you?" Giuseppe asked.

"I will. I'll stay with him all night."

"And you'll come to the funeral? None of this daylight disappearing act?"

I felt something in my chest. A weight. I said, "I'll be there."

Giuseppe hobbled to the door where the nurse was waiting for him. When he took Giuseppe's arm to steady him, my friend turned back to me as I stood by Danny's coffin. He said, "I get it now."

"Get what?"

"Why you're here."

I looked at him with a question on my face.

"You're here to say goodbye, aren't you? To Danny, and me.

And James. Before it's too late."

I ran the ridge of my lip under my teeth.

Giuseppe checked the watch on his wrist and pressed it to his ear for a second. Then he said, "What about you? When are you going to get some rest?"

"Soon," I said. And I meant it.

Giuseppe nodded and let the nurse lead him outside.

I sat down in the chair that Giuseppe had left empty. Then I stood up. My limbs were tingling with raw pain at the thought of attending Danny's graveside in the morning. But I knew I needed to be there, just as Danny had been there for me often enough.

They all had.

I leaned over him and kissed his cold forehead. I caught Gloria's scent on his skin and I wondered what words of comfort comes with death. Does she whisper the way to the afterlife? Does she tell a dirty joke?

Death *was* a joke, a cruel prank that the universe plays on her subjects. But did it really have a punchline that I'd never get?

"Help me," I said to Danny's empty face, watching his closed and sunken eyes. And if he lifted his hand out of the coffin to comfort me, I wouldn't have been surprised.

I stayed by his side until dawn, and in the morning, I called the manor and asked to speak to James. "I need a favour," I said.

"No sweat," he said.

I sat beside him in the funeral parlour the next day. Sunlight streamed in through the high windows above us and shone against the far wall. I watched it slink down the brickwork as the celebrant spoke, and I curled my toes when it slid across the dark blue carpet.

James was stony faced. When he sat down, I'd moved his walking frame out of the way. We were in the front row beside Giuseppe, who was hunched over in his seat like he didn't have the strength to hold himself upright.

"At ninety-two," the celebrant said, "one must only imagine the life Daniel Grainger had, what adventures he shared with his friends." James gave a quiet grunt. We didn't have to wonder; we were there. "He leaves behind his brother, Joseph, affectionately known as Giuseppe. And of course their dearest friend, James. Danny was cared for lovingly by the nurses and staff at Lakeshore Manor—Lisa Conway, Gloria Pinto, and others, who all had a great many words to say about how much of a charmer Danny was."

I didn't mind being grouped in with the others. The patch of sunlight eased across the floor, darkening as a cloud passed over it.

James read a poem when Giuseppe couldn't, and I held both of their hands as the casket's lid was closed and the pallbearers carried Danny outside to the waiting hearse. Giuseppe cried.

We all did.

It had started to rain when we got to the cemetery, the sun shielding its eyes from Danny's burial behind dark clouds. I was grateful for the dull winter morning that was already stinging my eyes. I wore a long black trench coat, buttoned to the neck, and a pair of gloves. I'd wrapped a scarf around my face and pulled my cap low, all of which James had brought for me—the favour I'd asked him.

Before we got out of the car, James said, "Are you good?"

I nodded. I'd have to be. For Giuseppe. For Danny.

I opened the car door, held my breath against the sunlight, and stepped out. My limbs were trembling. I unfurled an umbrella over my head to further protect me from the light, but my skin was already smouldering. I could feel it growing red. I gritted my teeth against the unbearable pain, trapping the scream at the back of my throat.

But it was a pain I deserved. I felt the weight of the sun even though it was hidden behind the clouds.

"Vic?" James whispered.

I shook my head. I couldn't speak. My face was on fire.

James let go of his walker and took my elbow. "Can you walk?"

I nodded, but I wasn't sure if I could. I was singeing. I knew it. I moved a foot, sliding my shoe over the gravel, too weak to lift it off the ground as the stabbing needles burned inside me. But with James' help, we inched to the open graveside. He kept me upright when I almost fainted. Where the rain hit me, it was cooling. I couldn't see, couldn't think.

The priest said something and Giuseppe nodded.

I forced my head up, looking around at the few people gathered with us. Gloria was there, a black coat over her green tunic, a clear plastic umbrella over her head. I focused on her face. She was staring at me, and although my eyes were squinted and my vision clouded in fear and pain, I recognised the expression in her look. *They'll all be here, one day*, it said.

I was weakening and James knew it. There was a dark noise at the back of my throat that I couldn't help, a pain that shrivelled my organs. I felt his hand on my back and I moved the umbrella so that I didn't have to look at Gloria any longer.

I couldn't breathe. My body was being crushed, and I looked down, making sure I had no exposed flesh, nowhere for the sun to get to me if the clouds were to disappear.

Wishing they would.

Wanting to throw myself in with Danny and be done with it.

The priest asked if anybody had some words.

Giuseppe cleared his throat but didn't say anything.

And James gripped my elbow tighter as he took Giuseppe's hand. He said, "The love we give away is the only love we keep. It's through this love that we become immortal in the hearts of those we touch."

I don't know if he made it up or if he was quoting something, but even Gloria nodded in appreciation.

And the sun clawed through the clouds overhead.

Danny's coffin was lowered into the earth. I wanted to comfort Giuseppe when he cried, but I couldn't move. Tears burned my cheeks. James pulled Giuseppe into a hug, the three of us huddled under my umbrella.

And when they squeezed me, I winced. I still couldn't speak. My eyes were on fire and the world was turning amber, and my skin was flaring red and blistering around my cheeks.

Giuseppe said, "Victor? It's the daylight."

James nodded. And between them, they helped me back to the car. And Gloria was there. She peeled her coat off as she jumped into the back seat beside me, and she draped it over my head.

"Get in," she told the others.

"He has a condition," James said.

Gloria nodded. "I know." She put her hand on top of my head, keeping me covered, and when James and Giuseppe were in the car, she told the driver to go.

"Quickly," she said.

And I was never so grateful for Death.

chapter 26

1950

"Three!" we shouted. "Two!"

We didn't get to *one*. James pulled me into the tightest hug, one arm around my neck, his other hand at the back of my head, with his fingers sweeping through the soft waves of my unruly hair. He pressed his cheek against mine, for the briefest second, and his hot breath warmed my ear. "Happy new year," he shouted over the noise, his lips dangerously close to my skin, and then he released me, turning to Giuseppe to drag him into an awkward New Year's embrace.

Danny was in the centre of the dance floor as tickertape confetti tumbled around us, but he was oblivious to the world. Danielle McClean, with her hair swept back into a tail, had all but disappeared between his arms as he engulfed her, kissing her so passionately that we had to blush on her behalf.

I shook hands with Michael, whose suit jacket was so big

it made him look like he was playing dress-up, and then I pushed my hands into my trouser pockets to stop myself from looking awkward as all the boys kissed their girls and the doors of the dance hall were thrown open in the tradition of letting the old year out and the new one in. Heavy sleet swept across the threshold and the cold wind was a welcome relief from the stuffy, lover-infested dance hall.

The band started up again and James slipped into place beside me, crossing his arms as everyone stood in a circle to link hands. The confetti coated us like promises as we sang *Auld Lang Syne*, and when I looked at him, James was grinning at me, singing at the top of his voice.

I loved him more in that moment than I had in all our private passions. His eyes were wet with glittered stars and when he sang, he was singing to me. When the song ended, he drew me into another hug. He bounced on his toes with excitement. "Happy new year," he said again. He was tipsy—they all were—and I faked a hiccup in what I hoped looked partially inebriated. The effects of alcohol didn't work on me anymore except for getting me sick to the stomach, just like anything else I ate or drank for the last five months. I still couldn't work out if that was a gift or a curse.

James gripped my shoulders and shook me. His grin was enormous. "1950," he said. "This is our year. This is Day One of the rest of our lives. What are your new year's resolutions?"

I hadn't thought about any resolutions. I had everything I needed—my health (I was stronger than ever, could run faster, react quicker), my family (Mum spent the week between Christmas and New Year cleaning Aunt Cara's house and singing Christmas carols as though she didn't have a care in the world), and James: the rock on which I built the foundations of my new life in the darkness.

I shrugged and said, "I don't know. I guess I'll resolve to find a good job. Something I can do at night."

Behind me, Michael leaned in and said, "I'd have gone with finding a cure for your sensitivity to light."

"Bugger," I said. "Can I pick that instead?"

"Too late," James laughed. "You only get one wish."

"Hey, that's not fair."

He threw an arm around my neck and knuckled my head lightly. "Fine. Second choice wishes come with extra resolve."

"What about a girlfriend?" Michael asked. "If you're talking about wishes, the pair of you should be thinking about that." Sally Byrne stood beside him, looking contrite. She'd given up her summer infatuation with James when he hadn't replied to her milk-bottle note and he hid every time she passed us on the beach. Michael had won her over with his goofy mannerisms and boyish charm. He was closer to her age anyway, and now that James was eighteen, nobody thought he'd ever have the time of day for a fifteen-year-old. She'd celebrated her birthday a little over a month ago and Michael had turned up on her doorstep with a bunch of flowers and a packet of Bolands Mikado biscuits. According to Michael, she ate every last mallow biscuit and didn't let him have one. But he still took her to the dance that night and now they were going steady.

"I'm keeping my options open," James said. "Who wants to get tied down to one girl?"

I had tied him down the night before—with fishing rope—and he hadn't been complaining. But I couldn't say that to Michael.

"And I don't have time for girls," I said. "What with sleeping all day and being awake at night."

"Stealing apples," James said and he snickered.

Michael scowled. He took Sally's hand and said, "You'll never settle down at this rate. Come on, Sally. Let's dance."

James turned to me. "Was it something I said?"

I shrugged. "I think Sally's trying to force him into popping the question."

"But they're fifteen."

"He's nearly sixteen," I said. "Do you want to get out of here?"

He smacked my chest with the back of his hand, flicking my tie up. "I thought you'd never ask."

Outside the dance hall, we turned our collars up and ran through the frozen rain towards the boathouse by the beach. When we got there, James' cheeks were red and our hair was soaked. We'd upgraded from the apple orchard when the weather turned sour, but we still referred to our alone time as stealing apples. Because it was cute.

We crept around the back of the boathouse where the padlock on the rear door was busted, and before we slipped inside, I kept watch as James removed the lock and creaked the door open. It was dry inside, despite several leaks in the roof, and we'd set up a narrow bed in the corner, made from old blankets and a tarp to cover us. So far, we hadn't been discovered.

It wasn't easy. Sneaking out of the house at night was tricky because Aunt Cara would get out of bed to use the bathroom at least twice a night. Once, she'd caught me coming home and I said I was just getting a glass of water, but she didn't buy it.

"You were outside."

I had to think on my feet. "I needed to pee," I said.

"In the yard?"

"You were in the bathroom so I used the old outhouse."

"That old toilet hasn't flushed in years. Wash your hands. I won't have you touching yourself and then handling my good China."

I washed my hands. But at least I'd got away with it.

Soon, I had figured out how to slip out of my bedroom window and scale the latticework at the side of the house without hurting myself. It's like my feet found the footholds with no effort. And as the weeks turned into months, I'd timed my escape and return based on Mum and Aunt Cara's slow and steady heartbeats.

James and I huddled under the tarp in the boathouse and held each other. His skin was burning next to mine and when he was slick with sweat, I would run my tongue from his navel to his chin, conscious of the drum of his heart and the catch in his throat when I dragged my lips over his dark nipples.

"You're freezing," he said.

The wind wailed against the side of the building and it reminded me of the screams I'd made the night I stumbled down to the beach to cry out Amaral's name. I still had the memory of James' blood in my mouth from that night. Every time I kissed him, I tasted the iron of his essence. I was hungry for him, but I was careful never to let him cut himself.

He had come to me at two in the morning with a dried shaving nick on his chin once or twice and I feigned illness and left. I couldn't be around him—or anyone—with that tang on the air. When the hunger got too much for me, I ate the soft flesh of rodents, the bitterness of their blood satiating the gnawing agony in my gut. And then I'd cry over their corpses, with their blood on my chin and a thickness in my stomach that was both satisfying and repugnant.

I buried their carcasses under Cara's geraniums, a sad cemetery where flowers grew more vibrant because of it.

But when I wasn't thinking about blood, James and I would spend hours together in the quiet of night. He did that for me. He'd go to work before dawn, sleep through the afternoon, and spend time with Danny, Giuseppe and Michael when they weren't hanging out with their girlfriends. Then he'd meet me under the moon with a smile.

We'd make love in the boathouse and walk along the beach, our hands linked and our feet kicking up wet sand. And he'd hug me from behind, his arms around my waist, as we watched the moon play hide-and-seek through the clouds. With his chin on my shoulder and his cheek against my ear, he'd cover my eyes and say, "Do you love me?"

And I'd lean back against him and say, "Of course I love you."

He'd laugh. "So love *is* blind."

Later, walking through the park before the dawn greeted us, he'd punch my arm. "Tag, you're it." He'd laugh and run from me, darting between the trees where he thought I couldn't see him in the darkness.

But I could smell him. I'd hear his heartbeat and creep up behind him, pinning him against the tree with my body and kissing him hard.

When the new year resolutions were forgotten about and the nights were getting shorter as March bowed towards April, James took the keys to his dad's car. We drove along the R445 to Limerick where we found an all-night roadside café that serviced the early morning traffic. The owner sat behind the counter while we drank milky tea at four in the morning and played footsie under the table. And then, on the way back home, we pulled over at a lay-by and climbed into the backseat.

We had to speed home to beat the sun.

It was weird, sitting in the car outside Aunt Cara's house as the dull April morning turned grey in the east. James linked his fingers with mine and held my hand above the gearstick. His eyes scanned my face and he smiled. "You moved here nearly a year ago," he said.

I looked at the house, dark against a darker sky. And I remembered Amaral climbing through my top-floor window, and James and the others raking gravel across the path. James pressing a wet cloth to my neck in the summer heat. My weeks of delirium that felt so long ago. I nodded. "A lot can happen in a year."

"Like falling in love," he said.

I looked at him. "Are you scared?"

He squeezed my hand. "Of this? Never." He shifted in the driver's seat and glanced over his shoulder at the empty road. "Of everyone else? Maybe. But you make me stronger. When I'm with you, I know I can do anything."

I wanted to tell him my truth, but part of me didn't know what that truth was. Amaral was real. My bloodlust was real. And my allergy to sunlight was life-threatening. But how do you tell your lover that nothing beats in your chest, especially when it's supposed to be beating for him?

I kissed him. We were surrounded by heartbeats in the neighbouring homes, people asleep or shuffling into their early morning routines. But it was still dark out. If somebody saw his car from a nearby window, they might not see us inside it. We were alone in a sea of pulses.

"See you tonight?" he asked, keying the ignition.

I kissed him again. One day, when I was old enough, I'd have a house of my own where he could spend the night without fear of discovery. And I'd fall asleep in his arms, listening to the echo of his heart as he curled his fingers through my hair.

I stood on the grass and watched the car roll down the hill, past the orchard where we used to spend our nights, and then I slipped around the side of the house to the back door where the neighbours' heartbeats sounded odd. Different.

And Michael sat on the back steps below the door. His duffel coat was bunched up where he huddled inside it for warmth.

"Welcome home," he said bitterly.

The fingers in my left hand tingled. "What are you doing here?"

"Waiting for you." He didn't stand up and I couldn't read the expression on his face.

I shuffled on my feet. "I was just taking a walk." I pointed over my shoulder as if that would explain it.

"I know what you were doing." His voice was hard but also tired.

"I'm allowed to take a walk," I said. "You know I can't go

out during the day."

"It's sick," Michael said.

"Walking?"

He stood up at last, his teeth glinting in the dark. "I was watching you."

"No, you weren't." He couldn't have been. I'd have heard him.

"Why him?" he asked.

"I don't know what you're talking about." I looked around the yard. Cara's flowers were budding for spring and the grass needed to be mowed. The shed door was warped from a winter of heavy rain and the wheelbarrow that was propped against it had a rusted hole on its underside.

"Stop lying," Michael said. "I know about you and James. It's disgusting and it's illegal."

"Michael," I said.

"Stop it. You can't lie to me. I've seen you. *Kissing.*" He spat the word out like it was decayed.

"We're not—it's not like that."

He pointed a finger at me. "You're going to ruin his life."

"No. Michael, you don't understand."

"What's to understand?" he said. "You'll end up in jail, the pair of you. What if you get caught?"

"We won't get caught," I said.

"You already have!"

I shook my head. His heartbeat was loud, fast, and my vision was clouding over. If it got out, it would destroy James. I remembered the news story of Noel Albermaine and the murder of his rent boy. "You can't tell anyone," I said.

"But what you're doing—it's illegal."

"I know," I said. "We'll stop."

"It's too late." He tried to get around me but I stopped him.

"What are you going to do?"

"I'm going to tell the truth."

"To who? Michael, please. Be reasonable."

He looked up at me and the pain in his eyes was dark and violent. "Get your hands off me."

"Please, Michael."

He spat in my face.

And I lunged. An agony burrowed out of my gums and I gripped his head. I turned him around, pulled him into me, and locked my mouth against the soft flesh of his neck. His blood was in my mouth. And his hands clawed at my head. And in that moment, I wasn't me. I wasn't thinking about the consequences of his words. I was tasting him. His strength was entering me and it was sweet in my throat. I moaned against him. He was mine now.

And as he went limp, I held him tight, like a lover's embrace.

I sucked on his open flesh.

Until there was nothing left.

chapter 27

the present

"Are you all right?" James asked.

"I'm fine," I lied. They'd bundled me from the car into Lakeshore Manor—as fast as Death and two old men could bundle anything—and dragged me into the nurses' quarters on the ground floor.

"Give him some space," Gloria said, crouching by the bed and tugging at my sunglasses with one hand and my tie with another.

I winced and sucked warm air into my dead lungs. I blinked. The tears were thick on my lashes and they cooled my scorched cheeks as they tumbled from my eyes.

"What can we do?" James asked.

"I'm fine," I said again, but my throat was raw and my voice was broken.

"What'd he say?" Giuseppe asked.

"He'll be okay," Gloria told them.

She unbuttoned my shirt, pulling the tail out from the waist of my trousers, and as she peeled the sides back, they gasped. I lifted my head off the flat pillow to look down. My chest was red and the skin was broken and splotched with angry welts. The shirt had stuck to me and where it clung to my flesh, there were fibres of cotton embedded there.

"Jesus," Giuseppe said.

"What can we do?" James asked again.

"You can get out," Gloria said, standing and holding her arms wide like a barrier. "Let me tend to him; there's nothing more to be done."

"I'm going nowhere," James said, and I reached up to touch Gloria's trouser leg to stop her from forcing them to leave.

She looked at me and I nodded, and Gloria stepped back.

James shuffled closer, lowering himself onto the edge of the bed to sit by my side. He took my hand and I bit my lip against the pain. He eased the glove off—it was my left hand, what used to be my mickey—and two of my fingernails were still inside the glove when he let it drop to the floor. The skin on my fingers was raw and wet.

He kissed my knuckles.

I smiled at him as best I could. "I'll heal," I said.

"You'd better."

"I will."

I hadn't noticed Gloria leaving the room as I stared into James' eyes. His skin might have wrinkled and sagged over the years, but his eyes were the same. They aren't the window to the soul; they *are* the soul. And in James, I saw the intensity of his love that hadn't diminished with time and distance.

I read him, and in that look, he read me too. I'm here for you, my eyes said. Where you are, I am.

Gloria came back in with a bowl of water and a soft cloth, and when she wrung the cloth out and daubed it across my burned chest, I felt the cool water wash my cuts and it brought tears to my eyes.

James stayed her hand and, even with his gnarled fingers, he took the cloth and worked it against my neck with a tenderness I had missed.

"There," he said. "Just like old times."

I looked over his shoulder at Giuseppe who leaned against his walking cane as though he'd collapse without it.

"I'm sorry," I croaked.

He shook his head. "I shouldn't have asked you to come. I knew about your skin condition and I still wanted you to be there."

"I will always be there," I said.

"I don't know much about your physiology," Gloria said. "What can we do to ease the pain? I can dress you with some silver sulfadiazine, but will that even help?"

I shook my head. "I just need time and somewhere dark," I said. "And I should eat."

Gloria stood up with a determined abruptness. "Everybody out," she said. "Go back to your rooms, please. When he's well enough, you can see him later."

"Not a chance," James said, but she took him by the elbow and forced him to his feet.

"I'm not asking. Leave. Now."

I smacked my lips. My mouth was dry. "Go," I said. "I'll be okay."

She ushered them out of the room and closed the door, and I was grateful that she'd put a barrier between them and me. She had reacted quickly when I said I needed to eat and she wasn't about to let them be the victim of my hunger.

"Thank you," I said. My skin was still on fire.

But Gloria came to me. She rolled up her sleeve. "There is blood in me."

"What?"

"Hurry. Before I change my mind."

"Gloria."

She brought her arm closer to my face. "My blood is tainted with death, but it is still blood. I don't think it will harm you. It may not do any good, either, but you have no other choice."

I eased my hand up to touch the soft skin of her forearm. "A rat. A hare. Anything," I said.

"This is a nursing home, Victor, not a laboratory. If you see any rats running around, you can report us to the health inspector, but for now, I'm all you've got."

I nodded. I could already smell the blood in her veins. "What will it do to me?"

She pressed her forearm to my lips. "I do not know."

And I bit her. Death flashed its violent face at me for a second before Gloria returned, with her eyes closed and her mouth wide in a silent cry.

I sucked from her and her blood was dark and pungent. It was cold as it spread down my throat and throughout my limbs, and there was a tingle of electricity in it. And as her blood pulsed into my head, I saw Gloria as a child, a million years old, a crater that held all of life. That's what death was, I knew: the depression in which life resides.

I clamped my lips around her flesh and drank, and when she tried to pull her arm away, I gripped her tighter. But she slapped my face and ripped her arm out of my mouth.

"Enough," she said, wrapping a towel around her skin.

I gasped. Her essence was inside me and it chilled me.

And I passed out.

When I woke, the room was dark. Gloria must have drawn the curtains. The bowl of bloody water was gone and on the nightstand was a glass of orange juice with a note that said, *Replenish your sugars*. I couldn't drink it, but the thought was there and I was grateful for her.

In a neat pile on the chair opposite the bed were fresh clothes and another note. *These are Danny's. But Giuseppe says you should have them. Velour, am I right? G.*

I eased myself out of bed and inspected my arms and chest. My skin was still red but it was healing and the pain was gone. The clothes they had torn from my flesh earlier were missing, and when I held up Danny's red velour tracksuit, I laughed.

When I put them on, they were baggy and too long in the arm, so I rolled the sleeves up to my wrists and eased my blistered feet into the dress shoes I'd worn to Danny's funeral. I looked like an old man on my way to a Vegas casino as I stuffed my phone and wallet into the pockets.

I don't know what Gloria's blood had done to me, but I felt cold. And I liked it. I hadn't felt the cold in so long that it was a refreshing change. I stood beside the radiator and pressed my hands against it. There were stubs of fingernails returning to my damaged fingers. The clock on the wall told me it was three forty-five and I knew I didn't have long to wait before the sun went down. Winter was tearing up the countryside beyond the window.

When I cracked open the door, worried that my face was a gnarly mess of broken skin and angry blisters, the corridor was empty. I found James and Giuseppe in the common room, still wearing their funeral suits, and although they were facing each other, neither of them was speaking. I cleared my throat from the doorway, trying to attract their attention, and I had to do it twice before James looked up. He nudged Giuseppe's knee and I slipped away from the door before anyone else noticed my broken face.

When they joined me, James let go of his walking frame and pulled me into a tight hug. I winced, more in shock than pain, when his lips kissed my cheek.

"Are you okay?" I asked Giuseppe over James' shoulder.

James didn't release me.

"Are you?" Giuseppe asked.

I smiled. "I would be if James wasn't crushing the life out of me."

"I'm not letting go," James said.

I wrapped my arms around his waist. "That's going to be awkward at dinner time. And what are you going to do when you have to pee?"

He squeezed tighter. "I'm already peeing. Can't you feel it?"

"You're disgusting," Giuseppe said, and James let go of me at last.

"You're okay now?" he asked, holding me at arm's length and inspecting me. Flakes of my skin had rubbed off onto his cheek where he'd held me and I brushed it out of his white stubble.

Giuseppe said, "You look worse in that outfit than Danny ever did."

"Where's Gloria?" I asked. "I never thanked her."

"She's gone home," James told me. "She'll be back for her shift tonight. What does she know about you?"

"Nothing," I said. "Not a lot," I added.

Later, when most of the residents of Lakeshore Manor were in bed, I sat in a deck chair on the roof terrace beside James, with Giuseppe opposite us. He was still wearing his shirt and tie, though it had been loosened and the top button was undone.

Behind us, by the door, Gloria had her arms folded. She said, "Don't stay out here too long. You don't want to catch your death."

I laughed and James said, "What's so funny?"

Gloria turned from us to leave, but I said, "Thank you. For helping me this morning."

She nodded. "You owe me one."

When she was gone, James lifted the bottle of whiskey he'd been hiding and struggled to unscrew the cap. He poured the first splash on the ground. "Danny," he said.

I nodded and looked at Giuseppe, who was studying his hands in his lap. After a moment of silence, he said, "Is he in a better place?"

James said, "What can be better than here, right now?"

"What could be worse?" Giuseppe asked. He looked at me. "What do you think? Where is he now?"

I didn't know.

Giuseppe took the bottle from James and drank. He didn't let up until the bottle was half empty. He wiped a spill from his chin and said, "Fuck you, Danny."

"Hey," James said.

"Fuck all of you. What do I have now? Danny's gone. You two have each other. I don't even have Michael to pick on. What've I become?"

"A cantankerous old fool," James said, reaching for the bottle.

But Giuseppe held it out of his way, taking another drink.

James said, "Getting drunk isn't going to bring him back. Let's face it. We're old. We're all going to die and it's going to happen soon."

"The sooner the better," Giuseppe said. He pointed a finger at me. "Turn me."

"What?"

"Do it. Turn me into you so I can live forever with my pain and the memory of what a fucked-up life I've had."

"No," I said. "I can't."

"Why not?"

"It doesn't work that way."

He handed the bottle to James and stood. "Kill me, then. Danny's dead. You might as well put me in the ground beside him."

"I can't do that either," I said.

"Sure you can."

"Sit down," I said. "I love you too much to do that."

He nodded. "Not as much as you love James."

"That's different," James said. "You know it is."

"I love you both," I told him.

"I'm going to bed," Giuseppe said. "Fuck you very much."

When he slammed the rooftop door behind him, I stood up to follow, but James said, "Let him go. He needs to cool off."

"We should be with him," I said. "He's just lost his brother and best friend."

"He's lost his life," James muttered into the neck of the whiskey bottle. "Mollycoddling him isn't going to ease his pain. He needs to soak in it. At least for now."

I hesitated, but maybe James was right. When I sat down, he passed the bottle to me but I shook my head. "I can't drink that stuff any more."

"You've changed," he said.

"We all have," I reminded him.

James nodded and drank some more. "What *have* we become? Giuseppe is right." He stared across the night. "I wish we could go back. To our youth. To the beach. To the boathouse."

"The past is behind us," I said.

He shuffled in his seat, getting comfortable. "All we have is the past. Danny's in it now. And Michael's there too."

Michael. My skin ran cold. Michael was very much in my present. He always would be.

"Sooner or later, I'll be with them," James said.

And I knew he was right.

chapter 28

1950

"Michael?" I breathed. His blood coated my chin and there was sinew trapped between my teeth.

He wasn't moving.

When I pulled my incisors out of the soft flesh of his neck, he fell to the ground, his arms tucked under him, spring grass splayed across his cheek. I swallowed the taste of him and felt his energy coursing through me. It burned hot in my chest and stomach. I wanted more.

But it was Michael.

"Michael?" I whispered.

The sky was turning orange in the east.

I shook him. "Michael."

I felt the sting of the sun but my brain wasn't working. I couldn't think. When I looked around, my eyes sought something—anything—that my mind could latch onto. Shed.

Garden. Aunt Cara's house.

There was a noise from inside. The whisper of Cara's bedroom door opening had me dropping to the ground beside Michael. I shook him again. "Get up, Michael."

He didn't get up.

I panicked. I couldn't go inside and face Cara, so I ran to the shed. The sun's rays burst through the eastern clouds, pointing its angry fingers at me, and I struggled with the lock, pulled the bolt back, and swung the door wide. It was cool and dark inside, but Michael was still sleeping on the grass.

"Michael," I hissed. I ran to him, my skin burning as dawn broke, and I gripped the hood of his duffel coat. I dragged him inside the shed and swung the door closed just as the back door of Cara's house opened.

"Who's there?" It was Cara's voice. "Victor Callahan, is that you?"

I clapped a hand over my mouth and hauled Michael behind the workbench where I crouched beside him. "Shush," I whispered.

My body was tingling, alive with the power of his blood. Why the hell did I have an erection?

I made a fist and dug my teeth into my knuckles.

"Damn cats," Aunt Cara said, and she closed the door.

I couldn't breathe. In the darkness, I looked down at Michael and the realisation of what I'd done hit me like a rocket to the gut. I put my hand on his shoulder. "Michael? Oh shit, Michael."

I touched his cheek. Was he cold? I couldn't tell. My fingers were numb.

"Jesus," I said.

Michael's eyes were open, staring at the darkness under the bench where a leftover sack of gravel from the garden path was stored. At first, I couldn't see any damage to his neck, and I wondered for a second if I was going mad. But I pulled back the hood of his coat and gagged. Below the ear, dark and mangled, his flesh had been torn.

I stumbled back from him on my ass and skittered towards the far wall, knocking over a jar of nails that shattered and pipe-bombed across the floor. And I watched him as he lay there, unmoving. Not breathing.

My face was wet—blood, tears and snot—and I wiped my sleeve across it, sponging his blood from my chin.

"Michael?"

What had I done? I got on my knees and crawled closer to him. I touched his arm, tugged at him, and he rolled onto his back where his dull eyes accused me.

"No. Wake up. Get up, Michael. It's not funny."

His blood—what was left of it—was already coagulating around the gash on his neck.

"I'll do it," I said. Then added, "No. It won't work." I slapped my face. "It'll work!"

I leaned over him, pressing my fingers to his chin to turn his face to me.

"You'll get better," I said.

I pulled my sleeve up. I looked at my scrawny arm, pale flesh with black veins, and I brought it to my mouth. I could still taste him on my tongue and I spat on my arm, rubbing the ball of my other hand into it like I could sanitise it. I bit my forearm. It was tougher than I thought—tougher than Michael's neck had been.

I punctured the skin and felt the thick bile of my blood work itself out of the torn flesh. And I held it over his face. Black splotches dripped onto the bridge of his narrow, upturned nose, and a drop splashed into his unseeing eye. He didn't blink as it washed across the bloodshot white and the pale grey iris.

I moved my arm closer, black blood oozing onto his lips.

"Drink," I said.

I touched his chin, easing his mouth open.

"Drink," I said, and I pressed my open forearm against his lips. "Come on, Michael. Drink it. Drink me."

He didn't. My blood was collecting in his mouth and it spilled over the edge.

I nudged his chest. My face was wet with fresh tears. His blood was catching in my chest as I breathed and *my* blood was pooling out of his lips.

"Come on. Jesus, please. Just drink."

I struck his face with the palm of my hand and his head twisted, the blood in his mouth splashing across the dusty floor.

I shook him. And then I thumped his chest. He didn't move.

My tears blinded me, and as they fell onto my blood-soaked shirt, I knew he wasn't coming back.

I had killed him. Michael. My friend.

He was gone.

And I couldn't breathe. I retched and turned from him, expelling the black contents of my stomach. The gouge on my forearm was healing, the dark sludge of blood hardening and smelling sour.

It had worked for Amaral. Why didn't it work for me?

I couldn't look at him. I lay on the dirty ground, my back to him, and I wept even after the tears had dried up.

But I felt him behind me, and so I turned to him, forcing myself to look at his blank face. A string of viscid blood stretched between his lips and the concrete floor of the shed. I straightened up, pressing my back against the wall, and I dragged him into my arms, his neck against my thigh, and I cradled him.

My brain was alive. I knew it was Michael's essence—I felt him inside me, his blood violating my rotten insides. And I swear I heard his voice say my name. But when I looked down at him, his eyes were dead and his mouth hung open.

I kissed the top of his head and rocked against him. "I didn't mean it. It was an accident. I'm sorry. I'm sorry, okay? I'm sorry."

Michael didn't forgive me.

And I cried again.

We were still there by nightfall. I didn't notice the time passing, but I absently heard the shuffling of feet in the yard outside the shed. Voices. People I didn't recognise. And then Cara's voice. I didn't catch what she'd said; I wasn't listening—I was scanning Michael's body for a pulse, a heartbeat, but found none.

And then there was silence.

The daylight that had butted through the crack under the door of the shed was gone and crickets chirped their evening song. Somewhere in the distance, lambs were screaming for their mothers.

I wanted to do the same.

I looked down. Michael was still in my arms and I wiped the drool of dried blood from his mouth with my fingers. The wound on my forearm was healed, only a thick scratch remaining, and my stomach felt empty.

"I'm sorry," I whispered, and my voice was dusty and cracked.

He still didn't forgive me.

And then I heard the doorbell sounding at the front of the house. Damn my hearing. I listened.

"Yes?" Mum said.

"Is Victor in?" It was Danny.

"Have you seen Michael?" Giuseppe asked. I held my breath, expecting to hear James next, but his heartbeat wasn't present.

Mum said, "He'll be in his room. Which one is Michael?"

"Little one," Danny said, and I could imagine him holding his hand up to demonstrate how short Michael was.

"He's missing," Giuseppe said.

"I'm sorry, I haven't seen him. Wait here, I'll wake Victor."

I listened as mum dashed up the stairs and I heard her knock on my door before opening it. And then she went back downstairs.

"I'm sorry, he doesn't seem to be here."

Danny said, "He's probably already out looking. If you see Michael, tell him to go home at once."

I heard their shoes crack along the gravel path and the garden gate swing closed behind them.

"He's in here," I said. My voice was weak and quiet. I didn't have the energy to shout. I held him tighter. "He's in here."

But nobody came.

We sat in the silence, Michael and me, and I hated myself. My ass was numb from sitting on the concrete and my mother's voice came to me from a distant memory. *Get off the cold ground, you'll get piles.*

I nodded. But I didn't get up.

I looked at Michael's grey face and I couldn't stand to see his eyes. I covered them with my hand and said, "What am I going to do?"

Michael said nothing, and it filled my head like a scream.

I don't know what time it was when I emerged from the shed. It was dark and the moon was a dull ache behind a black cloud. I didn't blame it for turning its back on me. I picked Michael up, cradling his small, mortised body, and I pressed his head against my chest. "I'm sorry," I said. I started walking.

I stumbled over a tree root and almost dropped him, but I twisted on my feet to regain my balance and gripped him tighter.

"I'm sorry," I said again, and I knew I'd be saying it for the rest of my life.

I lifted his body onto my shoulder in a fireman's lift, and I jumped over the wall of the apple orchard. With my bare hands, I dug up the rich soil among the trees, and I buried him. I straightened out his duffel coat and combed my fingers through his hair before I brushed the damp earth over him, and when I was done, I lay on the ground on top of him and cried.

A bat flapped overhead and a dog barked somewhere in the distance.

The night was thick with oppression.

A rotten apple fell from a nearby tree and thumped into

the darkness, and I knew I could never come back to this orchard with James.

I went home and Mum saw me in the hallway.

"Where have you been? Look at you," she cried. "What happened?"

I held my hands up. Michael's blood was black and coated in soil so that she couldn't tell what I'd been doing. My clothes were filthy, but at least none of the redness of him was visible.

"Michael's missing," she said.

I nodded.

"Did you find him?" she asked.

"No."

I went upstairs, my footfalls heavy on the polished wooden staircase, and Mum followed me. I sat on the hardbacked chair in my room as she heated pails of water to fill the metal tub in the bathroom, and then she steered me by the shoulders.

"In you get," she said. When I didn't respond, she unbuttoned the top few buttons of my shirt. "Get yourself clean," she said. "Victor, do you hear me?"

I looked at her.

"Get in the tub. You're filthy."

I turned, facing the bath full of hot water, and I leaned forward to enter it.

"No," Mum said. "You've still got your clothes on."

She was right. I swallowed the taste of Michael in my throat.

Mum said, "Leave your clothes on the floor. I'll collect them when you're done," and she closed the door behind her, leaving me alone.

I gripped the tail of my shirt, but I didn't remember what she wanted me to do. My hands were filthy and there was a hot bath beside me. So I got into it. Red mud seeped into the water from my clothes.

I pulled my knees up and wrapped my arms around my legs.

Why was I sitting in a bathtub, fully clothed? It made no sense.

Eventually, Mum knocked on the door. "Victor? Are you washed yet?"

"What?" I said, and my voice sounded odd, like it wasn't my own.

"Are you still in the tub?"

I looked at the blackened water. "Yes," I said.

"Hurry up," Mum called.

I got out of the tub, stripped my clothes off, and got back in. My skin was red from the heat but I didn't feel it. I soaked a flannel under the dirty water and wiped my face with it, and when I was done, I felt no cleaner.

In my bedroom, I put fresh clothes on while Mum drained the bathtub, and I sat on the edge of my bed.

"Feel better now?" she said.

I nodded. But I didn't feel anything.

A black tear left a track on my cheek.

"Victor?" Mum said.

I knew my chin was quivering, but I couldn't stop it.

"Is it the light?" she asked, but it was dark out and the curtains were drawn.

I shook my head and then nodded. And Mum wrapped me in her arms. I cried against her hair.

"It's okay," she said.
But it wasn't.

chapter 29

the present

"*Show me the way to go home,*" James sang. He sloshed the bottle in the air as if he was conducting an invisible orchestra. He squinted at me, trying to remember the words to the song. When he couldn't, he said, "I'm dying." He coughed and his breath caught in his chest, a ragged sound that echoed across the rooftop.

"I know," I said. I could hear the slow arrhythmia of his heart.

He looked small in the deck chair, his face hidden in the darkness of night, only his eyes glinting. Below us, the lights in the common room were dimmed and I heard somebody locking the front door. I didn't want to check the time and spoil the mood, but it looked as though James was falling asleep. He rested the whiskey bottle in his lap and it tilted at a dangerous angle.

"You'll spill it," I said.

He nodded. The bottle was almost empty.

When he coughed again, he brought the crook of his arm to his mouth and I saw that his fingers were curled into the palm in an arthritic fist.

"Come on," I said. "Let's get you to bed."

"*I'm tired and I wanna go to bed,*" he sang, remembering the lyrics.

"You and me both," I said. I pried the bottle out of his embrace and sniffed the neck. I'd forgotten what alcohol did to a man. I hadn't been drunk since I was seventeen. James' heartbeat was laboured and, when I listened hard enough, I heard the soft swoosh of his aortic valve telling the rest of his body that it was still alive. I sat the bottle on the wall and took his hands.

"Up you come."

When he was on his feet, he said, "Dance with me."

"James," I protested.

"Dance with me."

"You're drunk."

"Good," he said. "It's just the way Danny would have wanted it."

I doubted that, but I didn't say so. I let him hold my hands for a second as he swayed on his feet, and then I said, "Bed."

"I'm too old for you," he said, and his laughter turned into a cough that hacked in his throat.

"You're too old for your own good," I told him, and he closed his eyes as he caught his breath. I said, "It'll all be better in the morning."

He nodded, slowly, wheezing, and his head drooped. I

curled my arm under his knees and carried him inside, away from the cold night air. In his room, I helped him into his pyjamas and peeled back the bedsheets for him, tucking him in like a child.

James said, "I'm tired."

"I know."

"*Show me the way—*" He didn't finish the lyric as a drunken sleep took him.

I kissed his forehead, and then I closed his bedroom door. I wanted to stand guard there, his protector, but I had the sense that death wouldn't be back tonight.

I stared at Giuseppe's door. The nameplate on the wall still said, *Daniel Maguire, Joseph Maguire.* Somebody would replace it soon, erasing Danny from Lakeshore Manor as if he'd never been here. How soon before all the names were changed? Before all of the residents were gone?

I listened. Inside, Giuseppe's breathing was slow, but I could tell he wasn't asleep. I knocked. He didn't answer, so I knocked again. "Giuseppe? It's me."

I waited. I didn't want to interrupt his grief.

"Giuseppe?"

"Go away," he called. I knew in his voice that he'd been crying.

"Are you okay?" I asked, and I wondered why we insist on asking stupid questions when we already know the answers.

"Go away," he said again.

I nodded, my hand on the frame of his door, and I pressed my forehead there for a second. I whispered, "Good night," and then I left.

Downstairs, still feeling the chill of Gloria's blood in my

system, I unrolled the sleeves of Danny's velour tracksuit top to cover my fists, and I checked the lock on the back door and the windows in the common room. The foyer was empty and, through the glass of the front door, I saw the neighbourhood fox had returned, sniffing around the stonework of the fountain. A shiver cracked the base of my spine.

Behind me, Gloria said, "You can't stop the march of time."

I turned to her. I hadn't heard her approaching and I wasn't sure if that was because she'd tainted me with her blood, or if she'd stopped pretending to be a noisy human.

"I don't want to stop it," I said. "Not any more."

She nodded. "I know what you want to do."

"Do you?"

"You shouldn't do it."

"Why not?" I asked. But Gloria didn't answer. She wrapped her arms around herself just as I also felt the cold, and she turned from me, going back into the office where she'd been counting bottles of pills.

I followed her, but she checked off her list of tablets with such attention that I knew our conversation was over.

And I was unbelievably tired.

"You can go," she said. "It's been a long day. Get some rest."

"Gloria?"

She didn't look at me. "Yes?"

I wasn't sure what I was going to say. So I said, "Good night."

Outside, the cold night air raised the hairs on my arms. I'd only been feeling the cold since this afternoon and already I was sick of it.

I walked along the path, past the fountain where the fox had been, and through the wrought iron gates, and I stood at the roadside, unsure of myself. Michael was still on my mind. And James, Danny and Giuseppe. Once, they had been my life. Now they were my death. And even though two of them were gone, I felt their presence nearby.

They walked along the street with me, and although we were half a dozen kilometres from the coast, I smelled the brine of the ocean from here.

Come on, I imagined Danny shouting.

Slow down, Michael would have called.

When I stood at the top of the beach, I studied the drystone wall that stopped the sand from spilling onto the road. Years of people sitting there had worn the surface smooth and I counted along the larger stones to the spot where James and I would sit in the evenings, watching the sun drink the ocean waves and Danny chase after Michael with a crab in his hands.

I sat on the wall and laughed at the memory. Behind me, across the road, the old pub we would buy our beers from was gone. An art gallery stood in its place with a roundabout outside, and a chip shop stood on the opposite corner. The angled parking spaces were empty.

Tonight, the moon had a halo, and I couldn't see any stars.

I took my shoes and socks off and buried my toes in the dark sand. It was cold and damp. When I closed my eyes, I could hear James' laughter. I left my shoes where they were by the wall and walked to the water's edge, and as a wave slipped over my feet, I cried. The November ocean was icy. And I felt it.

Death, what have you done to me?

I eased myself onto the wet sand, my legs crossed, and I let the water wash around me. I watched a plane soar overhead, on its way to Shannon Airport, and the noise of its engines lulled me. Out on the ocean, too far for anybody else to see in the dark, a whale broke the surface and disappeared.

I slipped my phone out of my pocket to check the time. 3:44. And then I dropped it into the water. I didn't need it. Nobody called me and it was filled with two-factor authentication messages and nothing else.

The water didn't take it, so I nudged it with a finger, offering it to the ocean, and with reluctance it was carried away on the next wave.

I took out my wallet. My driver's license said, *Victor Ashley. Born 2004.* The license I'd had before that said, *Victor Jones. Born 1995.* I'd lost count of the number of counterfeit IDs I'd had over the years. They were easier to fake years ago—just like emotions. Licenses were paper and ink. Now, they were plastic with photographs.

I don't photograph well. I haven't in a long time. The gold flecks in my eyes reacted to the camera lens, making it impossible to see me. So I'd Photoshopped a face that looked like me onto my IDs.

I inspected the items in the wallet. Thirty-eight euros and some coins in the zipped change pocket. An eighty-year-old library card for a library that no longer existed. Bank card, credit card, two store cards. Receipts that were so old the dates were worn off.

I let it all float away in the ocean.

And then I hugged myself against the chill.

I sighed. And then I cried—for everything I'd lost, and everything I'd done.

And everything I was about to do.

chapter 30

1950

I didn't leave my room for two days. When Mum said I should eat something, I told her I wasn't hungry and when she touched my forehead with the back of her hand, she said, "You're not burning up."

I didn't know what I was. I felt nothing but fear. Three times before nightfall, a group of men marched along the street calling Michael's name. They'd camped out at the end of the road, on the corner between the village shop and the road out of town, and when the darkness came, Mum put her coat on and tied the belt at the front instead of buckling it. "Are you coming?" she asked.

"Where are you going?"

"We can't just sit here," she said. "We need to help." She went downstairs, came back with my coat, and threw it on the bed beside me. "I know you miss him, but you can't coop yourself up in your room forever. It's not healthy."

"Mum," I said, my throat tight. "I can't."

"The sun's down, Victor. What will people think if you don't help with the search for your friend?"

I knew she was right. But what would people think when they found out what I'd done? I hadn't meant it. I'd spent the last two days convincing myself that it wasn't me who'd done that thing, it was somebody else. Something else. I tried to remember that moment on the lawn by the back door, as the sun was coming up, and Michael said . . . something. I couldn't remember. I was angry, I know that much. But the only thing I recalled was sitting on the floor of the garden shed with Michael's head in my lap. And there was blood on the ground.

Whatever happened before that, my brain had fogged over it, even if I knew the truth—because Michael was in me.

I tried to convince myself that it was all a dream, but as Mum urged me to put my coat on and voices outside shouted, "Michael?" I couldn't deny it.

I was a murderer.

Or something inside me was.

"Come on," Mum said.

I pulled my coat on even though I didn't feel the cold and I slouched down the street behind her, past the apple orchard whose treetops were glowing in the moonlight, sparkles of murderous lies shining like a beacon across the hilltop. The gate was padlocked and a gardaí officer in his navy uniform was rolling a cigarette under a streetlamp, eyeballing the orchard's name on the wall.

"What can we do to help?" Mum asked.

The officer smiled and I scuffed my shoe in the dirt in front of the gate, with my hands in my pockets.

"Some of the men might like a cup of tea," he said.

Mum smiled. She was never fond of male superiority. She turned to me. "I'll walk along the road as far as the football field. Victor, do you have any idea where he might have gone?"

I couldn't answer her, and the police officer struck a match, which flared and sputtered before he lit his cigarette. "Friend of yours, was he?" he asked.

I nodded, balling my fists inside my coat pockets. I couldn't look at him.

"When did you last see him, young man?"

Mum put her hand on my back when I didn't speak. She said, "He hasn't been well lately. He's been stuck in his room for the longest time. Barely sees a soul."

The officer eyed me with suspicion and nodded. "Thought he looked a bit pale around the gills."

"Go on, now," Mum said, nudging me. "Go and find your friends and help with the search."

"All the young lads are down by the beach," the officer said.

I glanced at the orchard gate and then backed away from them. If I tried to divert his attention from searching inside, he'd know what I was doing and they'd double their efforts to look among the trees. I needed to play it cool. They were going to search it no matter what; with any luck they'd give the orchard a cursory look and move on.

When I got to the beach, groups of men were searching the dunes and along the water's edge with torches. I knew where James was without seeing him. I heard his heart.

As I approached, he waved at me and Danny shouted, "Where have you been?"

Giuseppe shone his torch beam in my face and I squinted, turning from them. It looked like one of Michael's torches from when we boarded the shipwreck.

I scratched the back of my hand. "I had a flair-up from the sun. Been stuck in my room for days."

I fell into step beside them and James bumped his shoulder against me, whispering, "I missed you last night."

"You waited for me?" I asked, my voice low enough that the others couldn't hear us as Danny and Giuseppe inspected the waves like there'd be clues among the seafoam.

"Not for long," he said. "Everyone was out searching and I knew that was more important. Are you okay? After your flair-up, I mean."

I nodded, guilt itching inside me.

Giuseppe said, "He didn't run away."

"How do you know he didn't?" Danny asked.

"Because his rowboat was still moored up. And besides, he only just started dating Sally Byrne five months ago. Have you seen her? She's devastated."

"Maybe he wanted to get away from her," Danny said.

"If you're going to run away," James said, "you don't do it in a rowboat. You do it on foot. Maybe he got the bus to Limerick or Cork."

"He didn't get the bus," Giuseppe said. "Paddy McGovern's dad works at the bus depot. He says the gardaí already quizzed him about it."

"Guys," I said. I wanted to tell them the truth. They'd understand, wouldn't they?

But James said, "Victor's right. He didn't run away. Something happened."

"Like what?" Danny asked.

James shrugged. "I don't know. We're his friends. We should know if there was something wrong."

"There was nothing wrong," I said.

"Right. He was acting normal. But he can't have just vanished."

I put my hand in front of James' chest. "Watch your step," I said.

He shone his torch at the sand to reveal a jellyfish reflecting the light. "How did you see that?"

I shrugged like it was no big deal. Being near him helped to take the edge off the darkness in my nerves. When he looked at me, I saw the smile that twitched the corners of his lips, the soft look that entered his eyes.

Danny said, "What if it was the sheep killer?"

"What sheep killer?" I asked.

"The one from last year. Left a trail of dead sheep across the countryside."

"The wild bear," Giuseppe said.

"It wasn't a bear," James told them. "And anyway, you don't go around killing a bunch of sheep and then come back almost a year later and take one boy."

"Maybe he's just getting started," Giuseppe said.

We were getting nowhere. As we turned at the edge of the beach and walked back on ourselves, I realised that none of us knew what we were looking for. It's not like the water would offer a clue or a trail to follow, in the same way that it spat out a shipwreck last year.

We spent most of our time on the sand, and it felt good just being there, knowing that nothing could be done but trying to feel useful all the same.

We spent the next three nights searching the village, along ditches, among brambles. One of the younger kids thought he found something important, but it was just a woven potato sack, torn against the spring heather. His father clipped him around the ear and the rest of us continued our search.

And when I was unable to sleep during the day, staying out of the way of the sunlight, I hid behind my curtains and glanced down the road at the apple orchard. As far as I could tell, they'd already searched it and found nothing. But there was no guarantee they wouldn't go back.

And with each passing night, the sting in my chest at what I'd done grew stronger. Half of the time, I couldn't cry. And the other half, I couldn't stop. Mum made chicken soup and I ate it, shovelling it into my stomach, knowing it would come back up, and I was satisfied when I spent twenty minutes in the bathroom, vomiting black sludge into the toilet bowl.

The next night, we traipsed across the fields at the edge of the village, through a narrow stream, and shouted Michael's name over the heather-coated hillside. And every time I shouted his name into the wind, something dark cut into my brain.

I should have told the truth (don't ever tell the truth).

It was an accident (you wanted it).

James would understand (he'd hate you).

"Let's get back," James said and I nodded.

When we got to the wall at the top of the beach, we sat down. James stuffed his hands in his trouser pockets and said,

"What if we don't find him? What if we never find him?"

"We will," Danny said. "Like you said, he can't have just disappeared."

Giuseppe yawned. "I'm going home to bed. We can head out again in the morning."

James and I watched as he and Danny walked away, and in the silence that followed, I wanted to scream.

"You look sad," James said.

I tried to smile. "Do I?"

He looked around before putting his hand on the wall, right beside mine. His finger stroked the edge of my hand. "Do you want to go to the boathouse?" he whispered.

I couldn't look at him. I could open my mouth now and tell him the truth. I didn't mean it. I don't know what happened. But those words had no meaning. And somewhere inside, I knew it wasn't true. I knew exactly what had happened. And at the time, somehow, I knew I wanted it, the taste of his blood, cooling the craving that grated inside my body.

I listened to James' reassuring pulse as I watched the waves roll back across the dark sand.

"We don't have to," he said.

But I nodded and James stood up. We didn't race, didn't run to the boathouse, and as we walked along the sand and up the dunes, we said nothing, alone together. He pulled the door open and ushered me inside, but my feet wouldn't move.

"Victor?"

I swallowed. The waves crashed against the shore in the dark. The wooden sign above the door of the boathouse groaned on its hinge. Distant voices of men still searching for Michael carried on the wind. If I went inside, would I tell him the truth?

"Come on," he said, "before we're caught." He took my arm and pushed me inside.

And when I crossed the threshold, my tears came. I stood there, facing him, with my arms at my sides, and I cried.

"What is it?" he asked. He took me into his arms. "Victor, what's wrong?"

"Michael," I said, the word splintering on my lips.

"We'll find him," James soothed. He held me tight and rubbed my back, and for five minutes or five hours I cried against his neck as he kissed my cheek and made soft noises against my ear. "It's okay," he said. "You're okay."

When my lungs burned and the sound of his pulse was all I heard and my sobs had subsided, I pressed my mouth against his neck, just beside his Adam's apple, and I felt him swallow against my lips. His skin was warm and salty, the soft stubble of youth prickling my face.

"It's okay," he said again.

"I'm sorry," I breathed. I inhaled the scent of his skin, and I felt the push of pain in my gums. My eyes stung but I had no tears left. His neck pulsed against my lips as I opened my mouth.

"I love you," he said, and his fingers found the back of my head, pushing through my hair. He tilted his head, extending his neck for my kiss.

And I closed my mouth, forcing the pain in my gums to leave me. I wanted him, needed him inside me. But there were other ways.

I kissed his neck. And then I kissed his mouth, allowing his tongue to taste my sadness.

James pressed his fingers against my eyes the way he often did. "Do you love me?" he asked.

"I love you," I said.

I heard the smile in his voice. "Love is blind," he told me.

"Kiss me," I said, as he lowered me to the blankets on the dusty floor. "I will love you forever."

"Forever and a day," James breathed against my skin.

"For eternity," I told him, and I knew eternity was a long time.

We didn't make love. We held each other and he studied my face, and when he wasn't kissing me, I ran my fingers across his forehead and his cheek and the corner of his mouth. I was memorising him, every detail, every crease and freckle.

He said, "I wish we could tell the world. Show them that our love is real."

"We can't," I said, remembering Noel Albermaine.

He nodded. He was probably thinking the same thing.

"But it doesn't matter what the world thinks," I told him, my fingers tracing the shape of his ear. "We know what's true."

He kissed me. "Even if you pluck my eyes out and put them in a jar of acid, I'd still be able to tell you how beautiful you are."

I made a derogatory noise.

"It's a compliment," he said.

"I know. But I don't deserve it."

He kissed me again. "No one deserves it more."

"Charmer," I laughed. But my laughter was fake. I knew he meant it, but I didn't believe it. I also knew I would never forgive myself for what I had done to Michael. And I would sooner kill myself than do the same thing to James. And I'd been dangerously close to it this evening. I could still taste the salt of his sweat on my lips and the pounding of his heart filled my head with hunger.

I heard the village clock chiming three a.m. and I sat up. I couldn't be here. "It's time," I said.

"I can walk you home," James offered.

"You should go and sleep before work," I said. When we stood up, I drew him into my arms and held him tight. "Will you be okay?"

"Of course I will. Will you?"

I covered his eyes and said, "I love you." Then I stepped away from him and nodded. "You go first," I said, because I knew I couldn't walk away from him.

James cracked the door open and peered into the darkness of early morning beyond, then he pushed it wide and stood in the frame. The moonlight caught the edges of his hair and glinted in his eyes.

"See you tonight?" he asked.

I smiled. I couldn't say it. So instead, I said, "Good night, James."

He blew me a kiss and then disappeared, the door grating closed on its rusted hinges. He didn't know it, but I followed him home, and I stood at the edge of his garden while I listened to him getting ready for bed. And when his breathing slowed and his heart followed suit, I took a deep breath, pushed my hands into my pockets, and walked away from his house.

I found a flat stone on the beach, smoothed from centuries of sea air, and I gripped it in my fist. When I got to the apple orchard, I made sure nobody was around—the group of men who had made the end of our street their search base must have gone to bed—and I jumped over the wall.

I sat in the dark among the trees, beside the careful mound of Michael's resting place that was undisturbed. I took the stone from my pocket and with my other hand I touched the damp soil.

"Michael," I whispered. "I'm sorry. It's all my fault. But I'm going to make it right. I'm going to find Amaral and I'm going to make him pay." I listened when an owl laughed, and then I said, "I hope you're in a better place. And one day, if I ever make it there too, I hope you will forgive me."

The owl didn't respond and I placed the stone on the ground, a marker to remind me that Michael was there, something to show that his life wasn't meaningless. I closed my fingers around the damp earth, scooping some of the soil into my hand, and I put it in my pocket.

"I'm sorry," I said again. And then I left.

I looked up the hill at Aunt Cara's house, a black bastion against the night sky. I heard Mum's heartbeat from here, the gentle pulse of her quiet life, and I knuckled my eyes against the pain I felt. When I stepped through the back door and into the hush of the kitchen, I tried to shake off the darkness that crept with me, but it clung to my side with fierce talons.

Upstairs, I eased Mum's door open and slipped silently into her room, and I sat in the chair beside her bed, watching her sleep. When she stirred, I held my breath; if she woke, I would break.

"Victor," she said, and I knew it was my father she was talking to in her dreams, not me. She turned in her sleep and there was worry behind her eyelids. I felt it. And so I held her fingers to soothe her. I didn't know what I was doing, but the veins in the back of my hand throbbed black against the darkness of the room. I felt her pain enter me, and although it stung, I knew it was better inside me than it was in her.

Mum's stirring eased, and she settled into silence.

And in the weight of her pain, I whispered, "I love you." And then, "I'm sorry." I kissed her hand and folded the blankets over it for warmth.

I took some of the soil from my pocket and I sprinkled it under her bed, begging Michael to watch over her. And then I left, closing her door behind me.

On the floor below, Aunt Cara was snoring. I stood outside her room and listened. And I nodded to myself. "Goodbye, bitch," I said.

I smiled.

Outside, I turned from the house and ran. When I hit the one-kilometre marker beyond the village, I stopped and looked back.

I heard the village clock strike five, a distant clang that would see James waking up to start his day—if he'd managed any sleep since I left him—and I turned east, towards the greying sky.

In seven minutes, I'd run past the six-kilometre marker, and by the time the sun scattered light across the mountains in the east, I had found a shallow ditch in the foothills to sleep in, shaded by a fortress of trees above me, and I burrowed into the underbrush for protection. I took my coat off and draped it over me like a blanket, and I thought about the wild bears Giuseppe had mentioned. But I was certain Michael had once said there were no wild bears in Ireland.

I settled in for sleep and I thought about James. He'd hate me for leaving.

But I knew I couldn't stay.

chapter 31

the present

When I got to Lakeshore Manor the following night, I'd been trying to pull my mood up from the darkness of an excruciatingly long life. My pockets were empty but my heart—it was still inside me; it had to be—was full.

I went to James' room, forcing a smile on my face as I got out of the lift. His door was open and, as I raised my hand to knock on the frame, I saw him lying on the bed.

And Death leaned over him.

"No," I shouted, panic pulling at my gums. I raised a hand, my fingernails already sharp.

Gloria turned to me. "Quit screaming," she said. "You nearly gave me a heart attack."

I looked beyond her and James was staring at me, his eyes widened by my outburst. A white, floor-standing machine beside the bed was thrumming and half of James' face was hidden behind a mask.

"Are you okay?" I asked. "Is he okay?" I knelt by the bed and took his frail hand. I couldn't help myself—my veins pulsed black as I tried to take his pain.

"We had the on-call doctor here this afternoon," Gloria said.

"You should have called me."

"I tried," she said, and I remembered I'd thrown my phone in the ocean last night.

"What's wrong with him?" I smoothed his hair away from his forehead and he blinked, a slow and peaceful action. He tried to talk through the mask but his words didn't come.

"Congestive heart failure," Gloria said and James blinked again as though he was sending me signals. But I couldn't read Morse code. And I felt his pain.

I put my hand on his chest and listened to the rhythm of his heart. It was lazy, tired.

"He's been short of breath for a while," I said. "And tiring easy. I put it down to age."

"I've been keeping an eye on the swelling in his ankles and feet," Gloria said.

"Why didn't you tell me?" I looked at his swollen feet. I hadn't noticed before. Not that I'd have understood the significance of them if I had.

"You're not a nurse," Gloria said.

James dragged his hand up his chest and tugged at the mask, pulling it away from his mouth. "Hey," he said. "My eyes are up here."

I laughed. And James' smile was big and lopsided. I helped him put the mask back on.

"Is he going to be okay?" I asked. I kissed the back of his hand.

"He's no worse off than yesterday," Gloria said. "The oxygen concentrator will help with his breathing." She smiled at him. "But it isn't buying him any more time." She backed out of the room and said, "I'll leave you two alone. But Victor?"

I looked at her.

"I know you want to be with him, and far be it from me to tell you off, but you do still have a job to do."

I nodded and turned my attention back to James. I gripped his gnarled hand in both of mine and closed my eyes. He said something under his mask, but I ignored him as I pulled the pain out of him. It felt like electrified pins and needles coursing through my arms and into my chest. It clogged in my throat like a golf ball before it stung through my cheeks and darkened my eyes.

My brain ached. But I took some more.

In time, James removed his mask and put his free hand on top of mine, breaking my concentration. "Stop," he said.

I lowered my head to the bed beside him. I was exhausted and weak.

"You've taken too much," James said.

I rolled my head back to look at him, unable to lift it as his pain swelled inside me. "I haven't taken enough. I want to take it all."

"It's killing you."

"I'll recover," I said. "I always do."

"Look at you," James said. He touched my cheek with callused fingers. I don't know what was wrong with my face, but if it looked like my hands, the veins were black and popping.

"I'll heal."

"But you aren't healing," he said.

"Give it a minute." I patted his hand and struggled into the chair at the side of the bed. I closed my eyes and breathed, and I waited for the pain to subside and the blackness to dissipate from my limbs. "So this is what 'old' feels like," I said.

James reached out of bed to turn the oxygen machine off, his breathing normal, and said, "There's nothing like dying to make you feel alive."

"That isn't funny."

"It wasn't meant to be."

I exhaled. The pain was leaving me and I was able to perch forward on the chair as James leaned back against his pillows.

"Promise me you won't do that again," he said.

"It only hurts for a minute."

"That was ten minutes," he said. "And you know you can't lie to me."

"I never could."

"That's a lie," he said, but he was smiling. He stretched his hand towards me and I took it. "Promise me."

"I don't want you suffering," I told him.

"I'm dying. There is no death without suffering."

"James O'Carroll, the great philosopher," I smiled.

"Just promise me. Stop taking my pain. It's no good for either of us."

I couldn't fight him, so I nodded. "I promise."

"Even at the end," he said.

"Okay. Even at the end. I won't. I swear."

He toyed with the mask in his hands and I knew his ability to sit up and talk was because of me. If I hadn't been taking his pain, would he be gone already? He stared through the window at the rain beyond it, and then said, "Do me a favour. Go and get a permanent marker." He tugged at his shirt, opening the buttons. "I want you to write on my chest."

"Victor was 'ere?" I teased.

"If you like," he said. "But make sure you add DNR. In big letters. Right across my chest."

"That's not necessary, James."

He coughed. "I might not be of sound body, but I'm definitely of sound mind. Don't break my heart; write on it."

"Do Not Resuscitate? That's not legally binding," I said. "Somebody might still try to bring you back."

"So give me something to sign as well. A napkin. The back of an envelope. I don't care." He looked at me. "But you'll be there, won't you? At the end?"

I gripped his hand tighter. "I will always be there."

"Then you'll make them respect my wishes. I've done my time. Once I check out, I don't want to come back. Please don't let me die twice." The wheeze in his chest was returning and he looked at his mask.

"Okay," I said. I turned the machine back on and helped him with the attachment over his face. The mask clouded as he breathed, and I went in search of a marker pen.

I found Gloria at the back door by the boiler room with a pack of cigarettes in her hand and I followed her outside. I'd forgotten how cold an Irish winter could be, and as we stood under the smoking shelter that probably should have been torn down years ago, I wrapped my arms around myself as the wind licked the earth and the rain sprayed across the pavement at our feet.

"Do you get any enjoyment from that?" I asked.

Her lighter wouldn't catch and she turned her back against the wind until her cigarette glowed. "Standing in the pissing rain, inhaling carcinogens and smelling like an ashtray? No," she said. "But like anything in life, we tell ourselves it's comforting." She looked at me, waving the smoke away from her face. "You were a couple, once upon a time."

It wasn't a question, but I said, "Yes."

"That must have been tricky. Being in love in a time when it was frowned upon."

"It wasn't frowned upon, it was illegal," I said. "We kept it a secret, like every other gay couple at the time."

"Lesbians, too," she said. "And everyone else on the rainbow."

"It's better now," I said.

"It was better before, as well. Ancient Greece, Rome, Egypt. Even Ireland. The Celts—they had no fucks to give. You'd have had fun in the Iron Age." She stubbed her cigarette out and lit another one.

"You were there?" I asked.

She shrugged. "I was always here."

"Here in this village?"

"Just here," she said. "Everywhere." She smiled at me, and it was a sad expression. "You look like your father."

"You took him?" I asked, shocked.

Gloria nodded.

"Did he suffer?" I asked.

She said, "A little. I won't lie. But it was over quickly. Some men tell me that's the best way to go. Not like these guys," she said, looking up at the building. "Lingering."

I stepped back as the wind kicked up, and I felt a shiver paint white gooseflesh along my arms and back.

Gloria said, "You're reacting to temperatures now?"

"Just the cold. Since I . . . you know. Your arm."

She pulled her sleeve up and the skin was intact and unblemished. I guess death doesn't get wounded for long. "I won't say sorry," she said.

"I don't need you to. I'm forever freezing, but at least I'm feeling something. It's good."

"You're more human than you think," Gloria said.

And in reply, I said, "Don't take him."

"I don't make those rules, Victor." She drew from her cigarette until the ash fell from it, and she jabbed it against the wall-mounted ashtray, pulling another one from the pack by her teeth.

"Let him live," I said, one last ditch attempt to stop the inevitable. "I'll take care of him."

Gloria said, "What kind of life would that be, for either of you? Old and infirm. Dying on the inside even as he continues to breathe."

"It would be a life together," I said.

"You can't stop it."

"*You* can."

She shook her head. "I can't. Nobody can. Humans—their hourglass has a finite amount of sand. Every grain might be a second, but when they've all slipped through the waist of the glass, their time is up."

"You can turn the glass upside down," I told her.

She laughed. "I can't Benjamin-Button the life back into anyone, Victor. I wish I could, but I can't."

"Death isn't fair," I said.

"Nor is life. But it can't be stopped." She turned to me. "If I don't do it, another will. I'm not the only one. If you don't know how to die, you can hardly know how to live."

"What does that mean?" I asked.

She smiled again.

I'd heard enough. I braved the dash from the smoking shelter to the back door of the manor and as I pulled it open against the wind and rain, Gloria called to me.

I turned.

"I admire you," she said. "James is lucky to have you. But be warned. He's not the only one at my door."

I waited, thinking she was going to say something more, but she lit another cigarette and turned from me. And as I pulled the door closed behind me, I knew what she meant.

Giuseppe.

I raced upstairs and dashed down the corridor. I hadn't seen him since the night before when he got drunk on the rooftop and asked me to turn him or kill him. I'd been blinded by my love for James that I forgot about my friend.

I hammered on his door. "Giuseppe?" I opened it without waiting for a response.

He was lying on the floor beneath the window. There was no heartbeat. I should have known. I should have heard. "Fuck," I said.

Gloria was already by his side, and her skin was glowing, her hair escaping its knot and breezing towards the ceiling.

"What did you do?" I demanded.

"I didn't do it."

I didn't care how she got there before me. It wasn't the first time. But I watched as she crouched by his body.

"His agony was too great at losing his brother."

I felt his pain in the room, as if whatever he'd done had released it into the air. His face was at peace, and his arms were folded over his chest. There was a tightness in my throat that closed against my will. "Giuseppe," I said, my voice cracking. I couldn't breathe. I leaned against the wall and the room twisted as I slumped to my ass on the floor beside him.

"Heart attack?" I asked. "Or suicide?" I saw her pick something up from the floor and put it in her pocket as her skin returned to normal and her hair fell around her face. I couldn't tell what she'd lifted, but there was no blood, no sheet or belt around his neck. Had she given him pills? Had he stolen them?

"It was grief that killed him," she said, "not his actions. There's a note." She indicated an envelope on his bed, resting against the pillow.

I didn't want to stand, but I forced myself to get up. His cursive handwriting was scrawled across the envelope. *James & Victor*, it said.

How could I tell James? He was the only one left.

Gloria stood up and touched my arm. The smell of cigarette smoke was still fresh on her breath.

"I'll get him into bed before calling the authorities," she said. "They'll want to speak to us. A formality. Go and be with James."

I took my gaze off the envelope and looked at her.

She said, "You don't have long."

chapter 32

1987

What does a seventeen-year-old do in 1987 that he didn't already do in '77 or '67? I rode my BMX around the Parisian streets at night, down by the Pompidou Centre, wearing a Depeche Mode T-shirt and a pair of Levi's over my beat-up Converse.

On my Walkman: a mixtape of music by Indochine, Téléphone and Jean-Jacques Goldman. It all sounded like noise to me, but I needed to fit in. If Laurent liked the poetic lyrics of Indochine, so did we. I made myself a follower. Followers don't stand out, they blend in. In a group of friends, I became popular enough that I'd be invited to parties, but never host one of my own.

That was Laurent's job. He was nineteen and had a small studio apartment, and anything within a fifteen-foot radius of him was apt to smell of weed. His parents owned the apartment, not that he'd admit to it, and he'd filled its walls with revolutionary posters and a life-size cardboard cutout of Siouxsie from Siouxsie and the Banshees. He said it was ironic. He read philosophy at college for a single semester before dropping out because, "The man knows nothing."

Laurent was not the man. Laurent knew everything.

He didn't have his own bike; he'd ride double on the back of someone else's so that we were always the ones putting in the legwork. And when he wasn't hosting a wild party of drugs, alcohol and alternative music, he held court over a group of teenagers who would listen to his words as if he was the new Messiah.

He'd sit on his beatbox after dark in the wide space outside the Pompidou Centre as we skidded down the steps on our bikes, and he'd shake out a cigarette, turn the music off, and say things like, "You see, the world is nothing but a decaying relic of false promises. Broken dreams. The generation before us—parents who were supposed to be our guides—they've done nothing but lead us into a labyrinth of consumerism and hollow ambition."

We'd nod, enraptured, and he'd create a dramatic pause while he flicked his lighter against his jeans, lit his unfiltered Gitanes Brune cigarette, and said, in a voice so soft we had to lean forward to hear him, "Existence precedes essence. That's what they say. We must define ourselves, not by their standards, but by our own. The truth is, there is no inherent meaning in the world—only the meaning we create."

Seventeen-year-old Julien would say, "*Exactement. C'est clair.*" The only thing that was clear was his unrequited love for Laurent. We'd ride home together at three in the morning when he had to sneak into his bedroom before his parents knew he was gone, and he'd tell me, in broken English, "It is love. But it is doomed."

I knew how he felt, though I never told him. Parisian youth were more open to alternative lifestyles than I'd been familiar with in Ireland, but every boy I kissed reminded me of James. I kissed Julien once. He was drunk and handsy, and I was lonely. But he licked the taste of my tongue from his lips and said, "*Désolé*. You are not the one I want."

I'd nodded. "I don't want you either," I said.

I won't bore you too much with how I got here. In 1957, I was in London. In '67 I had a job as a nighttime street cleaner in Barcelona. In the seventies, I spent several years in Berlin, enjoying the underground film scene of gay movies in the back rooms of side-street cafés. The polizei raided those midnight screenings often, and I was caught once. The officers had been built like army tanks and they'd cornered me among the pillars of Brandenburg Gate. The next day, I left Berlin before news of the three missing polizei officers got out. But my stomach was full for the first time in months.

I didn't eat often, and when I did, I tried to stick to rodents and stray cats. But sometimes the hunger got the better of me and, in situations where my life was in danger, I acted rashly. Those three officers, whose bodies I dumped in the Spree, kept me satiated for the longest time, even if the weight of my actions flattened my desire to live.

From there, I spent the early eighties in Newfoundland, chasing ghosts. I'd studied the news for unexplained deaths, men or women with their bodies drained of blood, or the mutilation of sheep and goats in out-of-the-way villages and obscure towns. And I saw him once. Amaral.

Or I thought I had.

I chased him along the bank of Lake Melville, but he was too fast for me and I lost him at the neck of the ocean near George Island. I was on foot and he'd been in a boat—nothing as grand as the galleon we'd seen in Ireland, but large and creaking all the same. He waved at me from the stern, black hair whipping his pale face in the wind, sharp teeth flashing under the moonlight.

Did he know me? I wasn't sure.

But I lost his trail and spent the next few years hunting through microfiche reports from foreign newspapers while I worked as a night watchman at a logging mill a few miles outside the company town of Churchill Falls.

I came to Paris in 1985. There'd been reports of seven unexplained deaths over seven nights, and an outbreak of solar urticaria among more than a dozen residents across the French capital. I wasn't sure if Amaral was singlehandedly turning France, or if he had help, but I boarded the first flight out of Toronto, bound for Paris, with a seven-hour layover in Dublin.

I didn't leave the airport during the stop, but I stood by the automatic doors, breathing in the scents of Ireland that I'd almost forgotten. The accents, the miserable weather.

I exchanged some Canadian dollars for Irish punts and pressed the black receiver of a public phone against my ear. But even with the area code, I was still three digits short of dialling Aunt Cara's number. Her enormous house had been one of the few residences with a phone in 1950.

If I'd called her home, what would I have said? "Does

James O'Carroll still live nearby? Is my mother still alive?" I remember thinking Cara Morgan would have outlived us all.

Instead, I dialled the operator and asked for the number of Mr O'Carroll, County Clare. I told her the name of the village and she said, "I have no listing for that person."

"What about the Grainger residence?" I asked.

She said, "One moment, please."

When the phone rang, I hung up. If Danny or Giuseppe had answered, I didn't know what I'd have said. They'd be in their fifties now. And I had no idea where James was.

The first time I realised I wasn't aging, I was twenty-three but still looked seventeen. Thick stubble never gripped my cheeks. My chest never filled out more than it already had. And my voice was in a perpetual state of being almost grown up, with the petulance of a child's anger behind it. You don't know agony unless you still have teenage acne in your fifties.

It meant I could never stay in one place for long.

So when Julien said, "You haven't aged a day since you came here. What's your secret?" I shrugged, blamed my impossibly awesome genes, and made the decision to leave Paris.

But I still hadn't found Amaral.

Which was why I rode my bike with Julien and the others, listened to Laurent's tirade against the establishment and his views on the fascist rise of capitalism, and I studied the darkness of Parisian nightlife. I'd only been here for two years. I could manage another couple if I needed to.

Amaral was close. I felt him.

A month later, as autumn leaves were turning golden, Julien and I were riding through Jardin des Tuileries, on our way to meet up with Laurent and his disciples. It was eleven-thirty and the Parisian moon was bigger than I'd seen it before. On the corner of Rue de Rivoli and Lemonnier, I said, "There has got to be something better to do with our nights. I know you love him, Julien, but Laurent isn't all that."

Julien didn't respond.

When I looked over my shoulder, he'd stopped riding. He stood on his pedals, balancing naturally, and was looking at the tunnel that went under the Tuileries Gardens before coming up at the Seine.

"Julien. Yo."

He didn't look at me. He said, "Did you see that?"

He nodded, though I hadn't asked him anything, and he turned his handlebars towards the tunnel. I was blinded by the headlights of an oncoming car as I called after him.

But he didn't stop.

I listened, sniffed the air, and thought I tasted something dark that came from the pits of the earth. "Julien. Come back."

When he disappeared into the dark tunnel, I cursed and followed him.

Two more cars came out and as I squinted against the glare of the overhead lights, there was silence. No cars. No buzz of electricity or squeal of the wind. For a moment, I heard the whir of Julien's wheels. And then nothing.

"Julien?" My voice reached forward and then came back unanswered.

I peddled into the tunnel just as the lights above me exploded with a crackle and I was plunged into darkness. I stopped riding, shielding my face from the sparks, and it took my eyes a second to adjust. The night behind me was dulled and lacklustre. I heard the distant honk of a city bus and the clang of a bicycle bell, but the sounds were muted, as though somebody had put a glass bubble over the tunnel and trapped me inside.

"Julien?"

I heard a scratch. A snarl.

I peddled into the dark.

And then Julien's voice broke the blackness. "Shit. Fuck." He always swore in English. But I heard metal scrape against concrete and then, "*Putain de merde!*"

The tunnel wasn't long, but I couldn't see the far end. It was too dark, even with my enhanced eyesight. I slid to a stop and jumped off the bike before it crashed to the ground.

Julien screamed.

And I ran.

There was a shape on the ground, something hunched over it, and Julien's scream had turned into a gargling sputter.

My teeth were out, my fingernails sharp, and I leapt on the man with a roar. "Get off him, Amaral."

But as I landed on the struggle, Amaral's hand shot out and flicked me away like I was nothing. I slumped against the side wall of the tunnel and grazed my face on the brickwork.

"Amaral, you bastard," I shouted. "Let him go!"

He looked at me, his face dripping black-red blood, and Julien was convulsing on the road.

But it wasn't Amaral, and for a second, I hesitated. It had to be him. How could it not be?

The man laughed, wiped his mouth with the sleeve of his tattered jacket, and then tore a chunk from his forearm, holding the arm over Julien's choking face.

"No!"

Thick blood leaked into Julien's mouth and I got to my feet. I leapt on the man again and curled my arm around his neck. He shook me off, swinging his body around, and with a powerful hand, he pinned me to the ground beside Julien, his thick fingers around my neck.

He chomped his sharp teeth and snarled at me.

And then there were footsteps. Julien was gasping for breath, blood coating his face and neck, and the man on top of us grinned like a loon. And Amaral leered over him to stare at me.

"Amaral," I said, my voice weak as the bloodthirsty man was squeezing the life out of me.

Behind him, Amaral was wearing the same suit I'd seen him in thirty-seven years ago, white thread showing at the dark seams, a faded pinstripe that had seen too much wear. He peeled a glove off, staring at me with curiosity, and then he flashed his long teeth, his tongue curling over them.

"Who are you?" he asked in French, and I was confused.

"It's me," I said in English.

Julien choked on the other man's blood.

"One of mine?" Amaral asked.

"You don't know me." I knew it before I said it. He had no clue who I was. I'd chased him for decades, to face him and show him what he'd turned me into, and for what? I was nothing to him. Probably one of hundreds. Thousands.

Julien's hands fought against his assailant, but he had no strength, and Amaral pulled a chain from his pocket, clipping the end of it to a collar around the man's neck.

"Enough," Amaral said, and the man—his damn pet— released us both.

I gripped my throat, easing away the pain, and then I rolled onto my side, pressing my hand against the open wound on Julien's neck.

Amaral studied me like he was inspecting a butterfly whose wings had been pinned open behind a frame. He said, "You smell like mine."

"What have you done?" I asked. I think I was crying, but I can't be certain.

Amaral said, "I did nothing." Then he narrowed his eyes. "Why do you fight your nature? I feel the struggle in you."

I glared at him and spat at his feet.

"Albie," Amaral said, and the man licked my spit from his master's shoe.

I kicked at him.

"I disown you," Amaral told me. "You will not see me again."

He clicked his tongue and Albie turned on all fours. Amaral's footsteps were loud as they disappeared into the darkness.

And Julien coughed.

"Jesus," I said. The smell of his blood brought my teeth out and I forced them away. I pressed my hands tighter against his bloodied neck. A car horn blared as it passed us, and I knew Amaral was gone. "What do I do?" I asked Julien. But he couldn't tell me.

His eyes shuddered, focused on my face, and then he blinked and went somewhere else. Albie's blood was still in his mouth.

"Spit it out," I said. "Don't swallow it." I pulled his head towards me, turning his face to the road, and wedged my fingers in his dark mouth to force his lips open, scooping out Albie's essence. "Spit," I said.

Julien choked and wheezed. And swallowed.

Another car tore past us and I pulled Julien into my arms, crawling against the far wall, tucking him into the dark shadows. I cradled his head in my lap and remembered the last time I'd done that to a friend.

"Julien," I said. "You have to live."

Julien's hand fought against the air and I gripped his wrist, pulling the arm down so he wouldn't hurt himself. And then I forced myself to lift my hand away from his neck. I needed to see the wound.

It was already healing. Albie's blood had entered him.

"No," I breathed. This was not a life. He didn't deserve it.

I rocked him against my chest and wept.

Julien cracked his lips open and struggled to move his tongue. He said, "Laur . . . Laurent."

I nodded. "You're too good for him," I whispered. "He'll be nothing without you."

I gripped his cheeks and he looked up at me. He tried to smile.

And then I broke his neck. I ended him—before he had no life to live.

And I fed.

chapter 33

the present

I stood outside James' room but I couldn't go inside. The door was open and he was lying on top of the bed, fully clothed. The oxygen concentrator hummed and I watched his chest rise and fall as he breathed. The collar of his shirt was loose and the sleeves of his beige cardigan were folded back on themselves, exposing thin wrists with weathered skin like the bark of an ancient tree. There was a tremor in his hand.

I knew him but I didn't recognise him.

I wiped the tears from my face with the back of my thumb and said, "Hi."

He turned his head, slowly, and he blinked. His eyelids were loose and his earlobes were long.

I recognised him but I didn't know him.

He raised a hand and curled his fingers. An invitation.

But I still couldn't enter. I scrunched Giuseppe's letter in my fist and stuffed it into my trouser pocket. I heard Gloria in the brothers' room as she spoke on the phone to the authorities. I was grateful she'd closed the door so that nobody else could eavesdrop.

"Hi," I said again.

I pushed my foot across the threshold as if it would catch fire. In the hallway, I didn't have to tell him the truth. In his room, the truth was all we had.

He reached a weak hand towards me and I knew that the pain I'd taken from him earlier had returned. But I'd promised not to leech any more from him, and that promise was killing me. He inhaled, his chest swelling, the breath catching before he released it.

Behind the mask, his voice was muffled, but I understood him. "What's wrong?"

I shook my head. "Are you in pain?"

He waved his hand. So-so. "What's wrong?" he asked again.

"James," I said. I didn't know how to tell him. I could live for a thousand years and never have the words.

He pointed his gnarled fingers at the chair by the bed and I sat. I looked at him. He was impossibly frail. When he struggled to take the mask off, I helped him with it, silencing the oxygen machine, and in the quiet, I listened to the hearts of all the residents and staff. Even Gloria's regular beat had returned.

James' heart thumped inside his chest, the loudest beat I'd ever heard, echoing in my head like a song I'd never forget.

"Tell me," he said.

I pulled the letter from my pocket, smoothed it against my

leg, and looked at him. My mouth refused to work.

His gaze went to the envelope in my hand and then to my face, searching my eyes for the truth. He stretched a hand out for it.

When I held it towards him, I had been gripping it so tightly that there was a discolouration on the edge of the envelope where my fingers had been.

He read the front. *James & Victor.*

I watched his Adam's apple cut along his throat like a razor, and a tear clouded on his lashes.

He passed it back. "Read it."

"I can't."

"Yes, you can," he said.

I took the envelope and held it in both hands to stop it from shaking. The ink on the front blurred as I blinked back my tears. I tore it open, pulling out the folded sheet of paper. It was Lakeshore Manor stationery, powder blue with the logo and address on the top, and Giuseppe's handwriting was looping and shaky.

"Read it," James said again. And I did.

> *Here we are then. What can I say? I guess I couldn't stand the idea of Danny hooking up with all those beautiful women on his own—Marilyn Monroe, Grace Kelly, Ava Gardner (she's dead right? Don't tell me I've done this for nothing!).*
>
> *If you're looking for a "sorry" from me, you'll be waiting a long time. Danny's gone. What else could I do? Since Mary died on me and Danny took me in, there's not a day gone by without his piss-ass voice in*

my ear. It's been so damn quiet since he went. I need the silence to end.

James—it's not your fault. Nothing ever was, despite what you think. Michael's disappearance. Victor's disappearance. Even that time I broke my arm when I fell over the wall outside the pub and you blamed yourself for some shit-fuck of a reason. It wasn't your fault. It's not all about you, you know! You were a brother to Danny and me in everything but blood. We had our laughs, our fights, and our quiet moments. They're in my heart where they need to be.

And Victor—I knew it was you all along. Everyone thought I was going senile but I'm smarter than all you dumb fucks (I'm going for the world record for how many fucks I can write before I close my eyes again).

The last time I saw you, you were a lanky kid with a mop of hair that looked like it had never seen a comb. And now? Well, you're still that lanky kid, aren't you? Lucky fucker. You've got the same look in your eyes, but I can see you're carrying something heavy on your shoulders. You could have shared your burden. That's what friends are for, right?

Hey, maybe I'll get to see Michael again. Me, him and Danny can have a kickabout in the clouds like we used to on the beach.

James, be good to yourself. Vic, look after him for me.

And Victor, I'm not sure what brought you back after all these years, but I'm glad you came. Maybe *it was fate, maybe it was just dumb luck, but either way, it feels right that we all ended up together again, even if only for a little while (Miss you, Michael. See you soon, buddy).*

Take care of each other. And if you find yourselves down at the beach again, build a sandcastle for me, will you? A fucking big one.

I'm going now. And that's OK. You don't get anywhere in life by dying, but we all do it. Sooner or later.

Joseph 'Giuseppe' Grainger the First.

We sat in silence when I'd finished reading. James wheezed, and I folded the piece of paper, putting it back in its envelope. There was a hint of a smile on James' lips even as molten tears rolled off his lashes.

"Fuck," he said.

"Fuck," I agreed. I needed to burn the envelope and get rid of Giuseppe's suicide note before the authorities arrived, but I held it in my hand like a memory.

And I cried.

James motioned to me and I moved from the chair to the edge of his bed. He reached his arms around me and I leaned into him, the letter crushed between us. His arms were weak but he held me with all his might as I sobbed against him.

"It's okay," he said. He rubbed my back. "Let me take *your* pain for once."

I let him hold me for the longest time, and when his wheezing grew too loud, I sat up and helped him put his mask back on. I adjusted the dial on the flow meter and made sure he was comfortable.

And Gloria stood in the doorway. "I'm sorry," she said. "Do you have a minute?"

I nodded and James gripped my hand for a second, squeezing my fingers. "I'll be right back," I said.

In the hall, I pulled James' door closed behind me.

"The on-call doctor is here," she said. "To issue a death certificate." Her hand slipped into her pocket and she kept it there, holding on to whatever she'd lifted from Giuseppe's bedroom floor when we'd discovered him.

"What can I do?" I asked.

"I need to go to the office for some . . . paperwork. Can you make sure the doctor has everything he needs?"

Gloria—I didn't think of her as death in that moment—hurried down the hall and I wedged Giuseppe's letter into my pocket before entering his room.

The doctor, a young man in a shirt and tie, was packing up his Gladstone bag with gloves on. He consulted his notes. "You're Victor?"

"Yes, sir."

"The nurse tells me you're the one who found him."

I swallowed. Gloria had moved Giuseppe to his bed, undressed him and put him into his pyjamas. The bedcovers were pulled up and she'd arranged it so that he looked as though he'd been there all evening.

"Yes," I said. Giuseppe looked like he was having a pleasant dream.

"What time was that?" the doctor asked.

"I don't—about thirty minutes ago? Maybe forty."

"Would you say it was closer to thirty or forty?"

"Forty," I said, and glanced at the wall clock. "Nine o'clock.

Give or take. I'm sorry, I haven't seen a deceased body before."

He looked at me. "You're a bit young, aren't you?"

"And what are you?" I asked, attempting a smile. "Twenty-five?"

"Twenty-eight. But this isn't a competition." He wrote something in his notes. "He was lying like this when you found him?"

"I didn't move him," I said with confidence.

"Do you know if Joseph attempted to press the emergency call button for assistance?"

"He preferred Giuseppe," I said. "And no, I don't think so. He'll have passed in his sleep, right?"

"It's possible, but I'll need more information. Was he eating and drinking normally in the last few days? Any recent falls or injuries? I need to see the daily record."

"He just lost his brother. This was his bed; they shared a room. I don't think he ate much of anything, what with the grief and all. I'm not aware of any falls."

"Has his next of kin been informed?"

"He has none," I said. "Not any more."

The young doctor flattened his lips. "That's a shame. It's always hard to see somebody go without family." He picked up his bag. "I'll need to review his medical records before issuing the death certificate."

He glanced at Giuseppe and scribbled something on a form, his pen moving with ease, as though he'd done this a thousand times before. No hesitation, no sentiment—just another name on a list, another box to tick.

"All right," he said, tearing the page from his notepad. "I'll submit this, and the undertaker will be here shortly to take care of the rest. It'll be quick. Efficient."

His words hung in the air like a smudge, devoid of meaning. Quick. Efficient. Giuseppe had been alive—and now he was just a task, a form to fill out, something to be moved.

When Gloria appeared behind me with a folder in her hands, she said, "Mr Grainger's file, Doctor."

My throat was tight as the doctor handed the paper to Gloria without a glance at me, and he took the folder.

"Thank you," I said, though I wasn't sure what I was thanking him for. The doctor gave a curt nod, and his footsteps beat a hollow rhythm as he left.

I stared at the bed where Giuseppe lay. He was gone. And soon, the bed would be empty, another resident would move in, and Giuseppe's memory would hide in the walls like all the others that were here before him. I could hear their screams.

Death was just a process. When you go, a doctor ticks a box, somebody puts you in the ground, and life moves on as if you'd never been there. The world doesn't stop. It doesn't mourn. It just continues.

Without you.

Gloria said, "Are you all right?"

I turned from her. "I will be."

She touched my shoulder, a cold hand that burned ice inside me. And then she ushered me into the hall and closed Giuseppe's door behind us. It clicked shut as if it would never open again.

I went back to James' room and he stared at me. His breath was laboured even with the mask on, and I closed his door and lay on the bed beside him. James put a weak arm around me and said, through the mask, "I'll be up there with the others soon, kicking a ball around in the clouds."

"I know," I said. I brought my hand up and linked his fingers with mine. There was no strength in him. And there was very little left in me.

"What will you do when I'm gone?" he asked.

I told him the truth. "I'll die."

chapter 34

1999

I put down the needle-nose pliers and rolled a creak out of my neck. Mr Nguyen shuffled across the shop floor above me and I looked at the muddy window at the top of the basement wall. The sun was coming up.

When the old man came down the narrow stairs, I heard the rattle of his tray before I saw him, and then he backed through the door and said, "Good morning." He sounded grumpier than usual, but mostly that was just his accent. Once you got past his grouchy exterior, he was quite pleasant. He put the tray on the counter beside me and poured green tea from a small pot. He'd brought a second cup—he always did—and I picked it up, still empty, and made a show of sipping from it. It was our daily ritual. Since I started working as his assistant in the belly of the Golden Lotus Taxidermy Shop, Mr Nguyen would bring tea and I would pretend to drink it.

"I'm not a tea lover," I'd told him.

"You drink coffee like all of America," he'd said with a snarl.

"I'm not a coffee lover either."

"This is why you are paler than a ghost," he said.

But to please him, I sipped from an empty cup, smacked my lips, and said, "*Cám ơn.*" He was teaching me Vietnamese and I offered him a few words of Irish, but he gave up learning when I told him it was a dying language.

"English is hard enough," he'd said.

He closed his eyes for his first sip of tea, savouring it, and then he put his ceramic cup on the tray and looked over my shoulder. I'd been fitting the skin of a Persian cat over a manikin frame. I fell into taxidermy shortly after arriving in New York City eight months ago when I saw a help-wanted sign in Mr Nguyen's shop window. At first, I thought I could dine on all the roadkill I wanted, but drinking from dead animals is not a pleasant experience. Don't try that at home.

But I soon realised I had what Huy Nguyen called the patience of the Buddha. Using reference photos from his clients, I would mould clay around the manikins with such determined precision, building out the shape of the client's pet, that when he presented the cherished cat, dog or gerbil back to the owner, he said, "So many tears. Never before do they cry so much." He was pleased. Taxidermy is one profession where you want your client to cry when you hand over the finished work. Huy had a cupboard full of tissue boxes that always needed to be replenished.

"I'll finish it tonight," I said, turning the cat so that he could see it from all sides. The blue-white hair had been glossed so it shone, and I was almost finished with the face. I'd had to use moulded plastic to replace some of the damaged whiskers on Jewel's left side ("Always know the name of the pet," Huy would say. "It keeps her alive."), and her eyes had been a special order, green flecked with pale orange.

"Her expression is," Huy said, trying to find the words, "too perfect." He picked up the collection of photographs. "See, here? And here. Slight difference. Never the same." He held one of the photos beside Jewel's face and said again, "Never the same."

I nodded. I'd get it right—I had all the time in the world. And once I'd fixed Jewel's expression, I'd finish with the airbrush around the eyes, nose and mouth, adding "just a hint of shadow," as Huy would say. "The dead don't live in shadows. Not fully."

I knew what he meant.

I took a final sip from my empty cup, placed it with delicate respect on Huy's tea tray, and then I bowed and called him *thầy*—teacher.

He said, "Take the weekend off. A storm is coming. Shop closed."

"Good night," I said.

"Good morning," he called after me as I went up the stairs.

I had a small room above the shop. It wasn't much, just a bed, a small table and a dresser with a drawer that didn't close. But for $400, deducted from my wage, I wasn't complaining. You wouldn't get a shoebox in New York City for less than a thousand in 1999, so I was grateful. And because the room was upstairs from my basement workplace, it meant I didn't have to risk venturing outside in the sunlight.

As the sun cut long shadows between the buildings, I pulled down the blackout blinds on my single window that overlooked a narrow alley, dragging the room into darkness, and I lay on the bed whose springs creaked as loud as Mr Nguyen's bones.

Blinking at the ceiling, I heard the music from Huy's record player sweeping up the staircase and slipping under my door, a mix of bamboo flutes and a Vietnamese zither, and its discordance was relaxing in a way that I didn't think possible.

My eyes pulled themselves shut without any help, and before I fell asleep, I heard the old man's feet on the dusty floor of the shop. He was dancing with his wife. She'd passed away twenty years ago, he'd told me, but every morning he would clutch a framed picture to his chest and twirl around the floor between the foxes and the owls, dancing with the only woman he ever loved. When he was finished, he would put the photograph back on his altar beside a statue of the Medicine Buddha, and he'd light candles and burn incense that not only scented the air for his meditation, but also masked the sweet stink of death that crept up from the basement.

I listened to the shambling of his feet, and the faint sound of his distant singing, and it reminded me of home, of James. I wished I had an altar for James' images.

I still remembered the last time I saw him, that hopeful look on his face when he stood in the doorway of the old boathouse, asking if I'd see him again the following night. That hope hurt my heart. I could never be what he needed, could never walk in the light that was his life. James had a spark inside him that brightened his path. Me? All I had was darkness and a hunger I couldn't satisfy.

Mr Nguyen saw it. He said, "Your mind is a mess."

I'd laughed. "Whose isn't?" I said, but I knew his wasn't. I sat my wire cutters on the workbench and flexed the stiffness out of my fingers before asking, "How do you do it? Be so still."

"Come," he said, and we went upstairs from the basement. He handed me a cushion and we sat on the polished floor, cross-legged in front of his altar.

"I'm not religious," I told him.

"No need," he said. "Just breathe."

I breathed.

"Focus," he said.

"On what?"

"On breath."

He taught me how to let my thoughts come, observe them as if they were cars on a highway, and let them go. There was no need to dwell.

"Dwelling on the past is like grasping for smoke. You cannot hold it."

But I didn't want to let go of the past. "My friends are there," I said.

"Friends are not in the past. Friends are in the heart."

I nodded. "And the future?" I asked.

Huy smiled. His feet were up on his thighs and his hands were folded in his lap. There wasn't a chance I could fold myself into that shape. He said, "The future isn't yours. All you have is this moment, this breath. You own nothing else."

We sat in silence, the weight of his words settling into the wooden floor around me, and the darkness inside me was softer, as if the heaviness was lifting. At least for that breath.

"Just breathe," he said. "That is where peace is."

And in that peace, I told him my truth. I showed him my teeth and I stood by the shop's door, pulling aside the blinds and holding my arm to the light. He watched as my skin blistered and bubbled and smoke curled from it to the ceiling, and he wrapped a damp bandage around it as I told him about Amaral and James and Michael and all the pain I was in, the clawing darkness that spread throughout my body and mind.

And when I was done, weak with guilt at burdening him with my life, tears streaking my pale cheeks, Mr Nguyen said, "I saw in your eyes that you were old. We should meditate. The answer is always in your breath."

I wiped my face with the heels of my hands and said, "You're not afraid of me?"

He smiled, easing his aged bones onto his cushion on the floor. "There are many things a man can be scared of, Victor Callahan, but you are not one."

For the next year, he'd work on his animals during the day, I'd work on mine at night, and in the morning, we'd meditate together before I went to bed. I asked him to tell me stories of his youth in Vietnam, and I'd tell him about my travels as I searched for my creator.

"Victor," he said, shaking his thin head. "Do not mistake those who shape your life for something greater than they are. This Amaral is not your creator, merely a catalyst in the ongoing story of you. He is a cloud, but he is not the sky."

"But he made me," I said, clenching my fists. "He turned me into this."

"Life is a series of causes and conditions. Amaral is only one condition that influenced your journey. He does not define you. Do not give him power over you that he has no right to." He tapped my leg, forcing me to pull my foot back into the lotus position. "Breathe," he said.

So I did.

And because he knew me, I no longer felt the desire to move on after a few years. Even as his shoulders slumped and his body grew frail, Mr Nguyen didn't care that I was a perpetual seventeen-year-old.

When he went to bed—like many old men—earlier in the evening, and rose before dawn, we'd meditate and share tea, and he never questioned my empty cup or my full heart. We'd sing Vietnamese songs together as my love of the language grew, and he taught me some traditional dance steps that, despite his frailty, he could still perform with ease.

I'd taken over much of the running of his shop by 2009, balancing the books, printing posters that I'd staple to trees and electricity poles throughout the Lower East Side during the night, and he'd shuffle around the shopfloor with an ornate walking cane, waving at the people who passed by outside and sitting in the sun during the day as I slept.

In 2010, I replaced his ageing dial-up modem with broadband and created a website called GoldenLotusTaxidermy.com. And while I was browsing the net, I looked up James O'Carroll's name. When an image of him filled the screen, standing next to a tall woman who was holding an enormous cheque, I couldn't help myself from grinning. He looked the same. Older, greyer, and portlier, but he was unmistakably James. He had the same bright look in his eyes and his smile was crooked, cocked on one side like he was keeping a secret.

The caption read, *78-year-old retired founder and former CEO of Ablemore, Mr James O'Carroll, presents £14,000 prize at charity auction to Susie Brindle of Lids for Kids IE.*

CEO. He always said he'd run a company one day.

I checked out their website, an agricultural tech company that specialised in developing advanced technologies in precision farming. Whatever that meant. But I stared at his smiling face as he looked through the lens, directly at me. Although he was retired, his photograph was still on the Team page as the company's founder.

I looked up his personal information on the Golden Pages website and found his home number. He was living in Limerick City, not far from the village where we fell in love.

My hand was shaking as I dialled the number, and a few seconds later, James' voice entered my heart like a song. "Hello?"

I couldn't speak.

"Hello? This is James. Is somebody there?"

I couldn't breathe.

"Hello?" he said again. I covered my mouth with a hand and felt thick tears on my cheeks. The timbre of his voice was deeper, and there was a shake in it, but in its tone, I heard him tell me a thousand times that he loved me. That he needed me. "Who's there?" he asked, and I cleared my throat. But I couldn't speak. And in the silence, he whispered, "Victor?"

I put the phone against my forehead, away from my ear, but I still heard the expectation in the silence.

"Victor?" he said again. And then, "Michael?"

I hung up and I couldn't stop the tremble in my body.

I sat at the foot of Mr Nguyen's bed that morning when he was too weak to stand, and I cried against his comforter. He touched the back of my head with gentle fingers and soothed me with a Vietnamese song that was hoarse in his throat. James was everything I wanted and everything I could never have.

Huy said, "The past troubles you again."

"I can't help it," I told him. "You get to dance with your wife even after she is gone. But I have nothing."

His breath rattled in his throat and I knew he was holding it steady, focusing his energies on it. He said, "I am weak, Victor. But even I have the strength to see the truth. Soon I will be gone."

"Everyone leaves me," I said.

He laughed, a quiet sound that swept between us like a sieve. "No one who has touched your heart ever leaves." He pointed across the room at a photograph of his wife on the wall. "Bring it to me," he said. When he held it, he brushed his finger over her young face. "In my heart, she will always be twenty-three. Though she was sixty when she went, I will remember her in her glorious youth." He kissed the photo and held it to his chest, and with his eyes closed, he said, "What is it that you want?"

I didn't think about it. I said, "I want to live. With James. And failing that, I want to die."

"Wanting and needing," Huy said. "You should also let it go."

"I can't," I whispered. "I have no heart without him."

"Then you know what you must do," he said.

I didn't. Or did I? Huy's voice drifted into another song, and although I couldn't understand many of the lyrics, I knew it was a love song. He held the photo of his wife to his heart and the words he sang sailed across the room and fell out of the window like seeds of life that would never die.

I pulled the comforter over him and closed the door behind me when his voice had failed him. And for the next three months, I nursed him. I made pho with rice noodles and beef, and fed it to him, and I listened to the breath in his chest as he weakened.

"Sell the shop," he said one day, when I had propped him against his pillows and carried a statue of the Buddha into his room so he could meditate.

"No," I said. "I will keep it alive for you."

His smile was thin and trembling. "How? You cannot work in the daylight and even if you could, a year from now, or two years, people will talk. This boy who never ages. Whose skin is as fresh as his animals, frozen in time."

"Mail order," I told him. "We don't need a shop. It's all online these days."

"Taxidermy," Huy said, touching the back of my hand with thin fingers, "is just another condition in which your life chooses direction. What is the one thing you can trust?"

"The breath," I said.

"So trust the breath. And go where you need to go."

I pressed my head to his hand and promised I would do what he asked.

Two weeks later, I scattered his ashes in the garden behind the shop. And then I set in motion a plan I didn't know I had until it began.

It took almost fifteen years to enact. I first sold Mr Nguyen's shop to a man who reminded me a little of Huy, and then I left New York and retreated in the Himalayan Mountains to meditate, where I needed no food, no water. And I prepared to face my life again. I'd stopped looking for Amaral. Huy was right, vengeance is not ours. And the more I dwelled in fear, the more power I was giving away. I kept that feeling in my heart where I let it smother all anxiety.

And when I finally stepped foot on Irish soil again, I knew this is what I needed.

I was home. And James was waiting.

chapter 35

the present

I closed my eyes and focused on my breath, the way an old friend had once taught me. I drowned out the wheeze of James' oxygen machine and the thrum of the electricity in the walls. When I was young, in the fifties, the walls weren't so noisy. Lately, they were the backdrop of my persistent life.

I held my hands loosely in my lap, sitting upright in the chair beside James' bed, and I focused on a spot on the wall near the window. I inhaled, aware of my in-breath, and I exhaled, conscious of the out-breath.

It was time. James was leaving me, and I couldn't stop it.

My thoughts wandered, and I was unable to settle them. It had been a while since I meditated, and now I didn't know how to pull my attention away from James. I watched his chest rise, fall, rise again, and it became my new meditation. I focused on him, on his breathing, inhaling when he did, letting the air out through my nose in time with him.

All my thoughts skittered inside my head—Amaral, Michael, Julien, Mr Nguyen, James. People enter your life and some of them stay long after they've gone, long after you've tried to kick them out.

A chill curled around my legs and I felt the hairs at my ankles stand to attention. Death was close.

James' breathing was getting shallower.

And I covered my face with my hands as I imagined a life with him, unhindered by Amaral and time. I was as old as he was, wrinkled on the inside. And I wanted to believe that, if Amaral hadn't ruined my life, James and I would have ended up together. The way it was supposed to be.

I remembered the first time I saw him, on the street corner, asking me for a cigarette. And I laughed. We were so cool back then. Now we knew better.

Or maybe we didn't. What is cool, anyway?

I opened my eyes when James said, "Where do you go?"

I looked up. He'd managed to pull the mask away from his face and his hooded eyes sparkled with too many questions. "What do you mean?" I asked.

His voice was soft, raspy. "Where do you go when your body is here but your mind isn't?"

I shrugged. "Everywhere. Are you sore?"

He shifted his back, dropping a shoulder and twisting his neck. "Not sore. Scared."

I leaned forward and took his hand, forcing myself not to ease his pain and hurting because I couldn't. "I'm here," I said. "Why are you scared?"

He breathed into the mask before releasing it again. And

when he looked at me with deep eyes and his crooked smile, he said, "What if there is no God? Or worse—what if there is?"

"Some questions don't have answers, James. Sometimes, the only thing you can do is live. And breathe. Whatever happens later, we have no control over. It doesn't matter. What matters is what we do with our lives while we're here."

"What have I done?" he asked.

I squeezed his hand. "You've lived. And loved. Isn't that enough? And there's the money you raised for children's charities. Fourteen thousand, wasn't it?"

He laughed. "And the rest."

His eyes were cloudy and I saw the tremble in his jaw. He eased his fingers between mine and I knew it hurt his arthritis. He said, "I wish you never left. I waited for you, every night for the longest time. But you never came."

"I'm here now," I said.

He nodded. "Will you tell me? Where you've been? What you've done?"

"Close your eyes," I said, "and listen." And I told him about my time in Dublin and London, the movies I watched in Berlin. I told him about Julien in Paris and how he loved Laurent but never lived to fulfil his dreams. I told him about Mr Nguyen and his meditations, his morning dance with a photograph of Mrs Nguyen. And I told him about the years I spent in a secluded cave in the Himalayan Mountains, at first with a frail chicken and later on my own, unmoving, just meditating, like Siddhartha himself. And I told him that, through it all, he was the only thing on my mind. He was all I needed.

When I was done, he'd fallen asleep. I drew the mask over his nose and mouth and then stepped out of his room, closing the door behind me. I touched Giuseppe's door, whispering a phrase that Mr Nguyen taught me in Vietnamese—All life is impermanent; though the fox may be dead three years, he still returns to the mountain.

Even after death, we long for our homeland, our roots.

I slipped out of Lakeshore Manor before Gloria could stop me, and I ran to the coast. I jumped over the wall where we used to sit and I tumbled down the side of the dunes. The tide was in, the water icy, and I knelt among the seaweed and settled my breath in the chill.

I took some stones, and then I went to the apple orchard.

Death was there, sitting on top of the wall.

"What do you want?" I said.

"What are you doing?" she asked.

"Nothing."

She came down from the wall after me, and she stood beside the dark earth where Michael was buried.

"Do you know what's here?" I asked, dropping to my knees.

"Memories," Death said.

"More than that," I said. "My life is here."

She shook her head. "Have you learned nothing?"

"Leave me alone."

"You've made up your mind, haven't you?"

I didn't answer her. I placed my hands on the cold ground, curling my fingers into the dried leaves and damp earth. And when I looked up, she was gone.

"Yeah," I said. "Go away. There is no soul here for you to take. Not any more." I looked at the ground. "There hasn't been for a long time."

I dug my hand into the earth, deep, feeling the chill of worms and tree roots. And I found what I came for. His hand was fleshless, thin bones that lay flat, thick with dirt and moist with seventy years of decaying apples.

I took the stones from my pocket and I placed one in his hand. "For Danny," I said. "Take him and hold him." And then I put another on his thin palm. "For Giuseppe. Laugh with him."

I had two more stones in my hand. I kissed one, gave it to Michael, and said, "For James. He'll be with you soon."

The final stone, I clung to for an hour. It didn't warm in my hand, it couldn't for I had no heat, and then I offered it to Michael.

"I don't deserve it," I said. "But if you'll take it, I give you my sorrow. The four of you made me. I was nothing before you guys and will be nothing after."

I released the stone into his hand, and then I covered it with soil. And I pressed my forehead to the ground and said goodbye. I didn't know what was coming, despite my Christian upbringing and Mr Nguyen's Buddhist influence.

But I'd already said it: Some questions don't have answers. Some don't need them.

I jumped over the wall, looking to see if Death was nearby, but I was alone. I walked home, changed my clothes and packed some things into a bag, and then I ran back to Lakeshore Manor. And when I got there, James was asleep.

Like a normal man at three in the morning.

His breath came slow and shallow, and his heart was slower. Shallower.

I wasn't sure I had the strength to lift him, but behind me, in the doorway, Gloria came to warn me. "He's at the end."

"I know."

"If you move him, he'll die."

"If I don't, he'll die," I said.

She didn't come into the room. And as I peeled back the blankets and pushed my hands under him, one beneath his legs, the other behind his back, she said, "If I don't take him, another will."

"I know," I snapped. She'd told me before. I turned to her, cradling his head against my shoulder. I'm surprised he didn't wake. I softened my expression and said, "Tell me there's no hope. Tell me there's nothing I can do to save him."

"It's the end," she said. "Maybe he's not the one that needs to be saved."

She stepped aside as I passed her, carrying James into the corridor. I said, "Goodbye, Gloria."

"You can't carry him," she said.

I looked at his sleeping face and his eyes flickered. "Yes," I said. "I can."

I went downstairs and backed through the door. And when I walked across the gravel driveway and through the gate, I knew she was in the doorway, watching me go.

"Victor?" James asked, his voice weak and tired.

"I'm here," I told him, and I held him tighter.

I carried him through the cold wind to the beach, and I lifted him over the stone wall. I unpacked a blanket from my bag, spreading it on the sand behind a boulder, facing the ocean, and I helped him to the ground, leaning his back against the stone.

I took a flask from the bag and unscrewed the lid, sitting beside him.

"Tea?" he asked, his voice weak and quiet.

"Whiskey."

He laughed. "You know where my heart is." When I looked at him, he eased his hand across the blanket to touch mine. "It's with you," he said. "It always was." I helped him sip from the flask and his breath rattled as he swallowed. "What time is it?"

"Four a.m.," I said. "Are you cold?" I took my coat off and draped it over him and he snuggled into it.

"No," he said. "Aren't you?"

I wrapped my arms around myself and said, "I'll live." I laughed. And then I cried. Because for the first time in over seventy years, I actually did feel alive. And scared.

I built a sandcastle with my hands, for Giuseppe, and I found a seashell that I mounted on top like a flag.

Wispy clouds skittered across the dark sky and James offered me part of the coat against the chill. I felt his warmth beside me. Above us, the stars were bright and the moon was waxing.

"It's beautiful," he said. And then: "This is the life." When I kissed his cheek, he turned to me and raised his hands. He placed his frail, cold fingers against my eyes. "Do you love me?"

And I smiled. "I love you."

His fingers fluttered away from me and his voice was weak. "Love is blind."

He couldn't keep his head up.

"Are you okay?" I asked.

His nod was barely perceptible. "I'm dying," he said. "But I'm okay with that. It's—I don't know—peaceful."

"You're comfortable?" I asked.

James pressed his temple against my shoulder and I felt his fingers curl around my arm. He said, "You should go home. Before it's too late."

"I'm fine here," I said.

"I won't see the dawn."

I kissed his forehead. "I'll watch it for you."

"The sun—it'll come up behind us, not in front."

"I know," I told him. "This way, it will last. It's been a long time since I saw the sunrise. And I miss the ocean."

"That damn shipwreck," he said.

I nodded. "The past is gone. All we have is now. This breath."

James said, "Those songs your Vietnamese friend taught you. Will you sing one?"

"I don't have the voice."

"Yes, you do."

"You tease me," I said.

And James laughed, soft and hoarse. "Don't be cute. Sing to me."

So I sang. I couldn't remember all the words, but I sang what I knew, a tale about love, a young man in search of his destiny and his lover. It was Mr Nguyen's favourite song, the one he danced to with his wife.

I took James' hand in mine and I let him lean into me, listening to his breath as I sang.

James said, "Love wins."

"It always does," I told him.

And then he exhaled. His head sagged against me. I knew it was over.

I kissed his head, and I didn't stop the tears as they came. But for once, I was happy. I sighed. My throat was tight and my heart was sore. But I smiled. "This is the life," I whispered. "The one I needed."

I gripped his hand tighter. Above me, the sky was turning grey. There was snow in the air, but it wasn't falling yet. I looked out to the ocean, and Gloria was walking along the shore, the water spraying around her feet. She waved to me.

And I waved back.

I kissed James' temple again and I watched the sky brighten.

If to love is to be human, I knew that's what I was. Nothing else mattered.

The sun broke through the clouds, the waves sparkling like glitter in the morning air. And as the shadows of night fell away, I closed my eyes.

I felt the sun warm me.

"I'm coming," I said.

And I smiled.

"Life and death appeared to me ideal bounds, which I should first break through, and pour a torrent of light into our dark world."
— *Mary Shelly*